# Dark as Knight

---

*A Billionaire Romance*

## Chicago Billionaires

## Alexis Winter

# Thank You!

A wonderful thank you to my amazing readers for continuing to support my dream of bringing sexy, naughty, delicious little morsels of fun in the form of romance novels.

A special thank you to my amazing editor Michele Davine who I would be COMPLETELY lost without!

Thank you to my fantastic cover designer Sarah Kil who always brings my visions to life in the most outstanding ways.

And lastly, to my ARC team and beta readers, you are wonderful and I couldn't do this without you.

XoXo,
Alexis Winter

To the man with the filthy mouth

*You know who you are...*

# If Peter stands at the Pearly Gates, then billionaire Atlas Knight stands at the gates of Hell...and I just married him.

*Hard to say no to five million dollars, even if it means selling your soul to the devil.*

His proposition was simple: one year of marriage, after which, we both walk away.

The deal of a lifetime offered to me by the mysterious, yet sexy stranger that's been coming into my coffee shop the last several months.

After all, how hard can it be to live a life of pure luxury for a year on the arm of a man that looks like a walking fantasy?

There's only one rule—no physical relationship.

A rule I'm convinced he's dying to break no matter how many times he reminds me through gritted teeth and veiled threats of punishment.

I thought a broken heart was the worst that could happen when all this was over, but I had no idea the truth that lurked around the corner, waiting to destroy us.

**A lion keeping a sheep for a pet is dangerous...
especially when she has no idea.**

# Chapter 1

## *Stella*

I close my eyes, pulling in a long, deep breath. A burst of orange behind my eyelids signals the spotlight hitting me. I've timed it perfectly, my eyes flying open the second the light hits me and I open my mouth to sing.

"You're no good for me." The words roll from my tongue just as they have a hundred times before. The sultry tone comes natural to me; having a bit of a lower register as a woman comes in handy as a lounge singer at Freddy's Jazz Bar.

I let the music consume me, the slow thump of Terrance's upright bass keeping time with Julio's muted trumpet as Clyde tickles the ivories. I smile over at him as the song picks up, his head bopping along with his fingers as he smiles back at me.

"Ladies and gentlemen, the beautiful Miss Stella Porter," Clyde's smooth voice says into his microphone, a few claps echoing through the room. I smile, giving a small bow before launching into my second song. My eyes scan the room but I already know what I'll find—the same four men that are always here sitting in their regular spots. My fingertips gently slide up the microphone stand, my body swaying with the music.

*Oh, Mr. Ozanski brought a date tonight. Must be the woman he was telling me about last week.*

The older woman next to him leans against his shoulder, her head listing to one side as she enjoys the music. The smile on his face that looks like he slept with a hanger in his mouth tells me that he's in heaven right now.

My eyes continue to scan the room. Mr. Percy is sipping his old fashioned that he nurses every single Thursday night. Jack Aiden is probably on his fourth whiskey of the night already, sitting in the front seat, his glassy eyes staring up at me like they always do.

And then my eyes spot him. The mysterious man who sits perfectly out of my view, obstructed by the bright light staring back at me. His silhouette barely visible, my eyes drop down to the only thing they can make out—a pair of expensive-looking shoes.

This is my happy place. It's a hole-in-the-wall, but for the last two years, it's been my escape. The place I can lose myself for a night and forget that come tomorrow morning, I'll be back at my full-time job. Shift manager at a coffee shop isn't a bad gig but it's not exactly my dream of being a full-time singer. The problem, this establishment isn't exactly upscale or inviting so living off tips from the "regulars" isn't going to cut it and the owner, Freddy, has a penchant for inappropriate advances that have become so overt I'm questioning how much longer I can continue to work here.

The song ends and Clyde walks up onstage to kiss my cheek and hand me a rose, the same thing he does every single night I sing. I glance past the light, lifting my hand to shield my eyes as I try and catch a glimpse of the mysterious stranger who's been attending my performances for the last few months, but it's no use; he's already gone.

"You look beautiful tonight." His whiskers scratch my cheek, the smell of stale smoke on his lips.

"Thank you." I hug him a little tighter. Clyde took me under his wing the night I auditioned to sing at Freddy's. I don't know if he could sense my loneliness at the time, but the two of us became friends almost instantly. Since then, he's become like a grandfather to me. "How's Violet doing?"

"Oh, she's perfect." He smiles, reaching into his pocket to pull out his phone and show me the latest round of photos of his first great-grandbaby. "She is my pride and joy," he coos, looking at the phone screen. You can see the love he has for her in the way he stares at the photos. "You know she just started tummy time this week."

"She is just so darling." My hand rests softly against my chest as I flip through the photos. Her cherubic cheeks practically make her eyes nonexistent in some of them, her toothless smile taking over her face.

"Your time's a'comin pretty soon." He bumps my elbow. "You're not gettin' any younger, Miss Porter."

"Soon?" I laugh, tossing my arm around his shoulders as we walk off the stage together. "I just turned twenty-four. As far as I'm concerned, I'm not even thinking about babies for another ten years."

"Ten years! I might not be around that long, sweetheart."

"Oh please, you're a spring chicken. You're the youngest seventy-one-year-old I know." I reach down and pull off my high heels, tossing them onto the floor of the run-down break room. I plop down onto the pale-blue couch that's littered with stains, a thought I push from my head as I massage my foot.

"You just wait; you'll meet Mr. Wonderful someday and all of that will change." He pats my knee, his eyes growing a touch glassy. "And I can't wait to see that day. You deserve to be happy and loved, young lady."

My hand settles over his and I give it a squeeze, unsure what to say because I've never allowed myself to have that daydream, and even though I've never said it out loud, Clyde knows. I've shared bits and pieces of my life with him, but he's never pressured me to even if he was curious.

*"The past is the past, Stella. You don't live there anymore and it*

*doesn't define you—and neither does how you were raised. What matters is who you are now."*

I didn't have the heart to tell him at the time that I wasn't raised by anyone, unless you count my parents bringing me home from the hospital only to have Child Protective Services take me away less than six months later.

Survival was the only thing on my mind when I was passed from home to home, with some distant relatives, some complete strangers. I felt like a broken heirloom that was relegated to the fringes of these people's lives, passed down over the years until finally someone realized that I was no longer just an inanimate object they could ignore; I was now a burden. So at sixteen, I had enough. I packed the few items I had into a garbage bag and ran away from my small town in Indiana to Chicago—never looking back.

"Hey, can I ask you something?" He cocks his head at me. "Have you seen that guy who's been coming in the last several months? He always sits near the spotlight in the back."

He furrows his brow. "I have. Nice man, quiet."

"Who is he?"

He shrugs. "Don't know much about him, just said hello in passing. Rich men like that don't usually come to Freddy's, at least not anymore."

"How do you know he's rich?"

"The suit he wore was bespoke, tailored for him. My daddy was a tailor for forty-three years, only a few places left in Chicago that make a suit that fine."

*I guess my assumption about his shoes was spot-on.*

"Why do you ask? Got a crush on the gentleman?" His scratchy laugh makes me giggle as well.

"No, I've never even seen his face." I playfully push against Clyde but my smile falters the second Freddy rounds the corner into the break room, his signature smarmy grin in place already.

"Evening. You two seem awfully chummy tonight."

"Evening, Mr. Freddy," Clyde nods toward him before placing his hands on his knees and slowly standing up from the couch. "We're just having a good time is all." He pats Freddy on the shoulder twice before exiting the room, tossing me a wink over his shoulder before disappearing.

"Stella." His grin widens, making my skin crawl as he takes a step toward the couch. I stand up abruptly, afraid he's going to sit next to me, but he holds out his hand to stop me. "Please, have a seat," he says, gesturing toward the couch. I sink back down slowly just as he reaches over and closes the door behind him.

My throat constricts, my chest tightening in anxiety as he closes the distance between us, taking a seat next to me.

"Yes, Mr. White?" I keep my voice steady, not wanting him to sense my discomfort. Freddy is exactly the kind of guy you'd expect to own a dive bar—greasy, pudgy, and balding, with the audacity of a man who looks like Jason Momoa. If my creep-o-meter didn't give him away, his brazen gawking at my breasts every time he's within a hundred feet of me did. "What can I do for you?"

"That's a loaded question." His smile turns sinister, showing his crooked yellow teeth. I don't respond and his smile falters as he clears his throat. "Look, kid, we both know you're the star attraction for this place and now that my dearest granny finally kicked it, I can get moving on my plans to turn this place into a fancy establishment and start making some real money."

My stomach churns at his callousness. "Meaning?"

"Meaning out with the old and in with the new. Tonight is Clyde's last night, all of them actually. We need some young sexy blood in this place."

"His last night?" I shoot toward the edge of the couch, then to my feet. "You fired him?"

"Yeah, the entire band. Look it's not personal, it's business. They're old and tired. Nobody wants to look at a bunch of decrepit old men all night. We need some fresh young meat in here."

The way he keeps referring to it as *blood* and *meat* makes my stomach churn even more. "We're not commodities, Freddy. This place is Clyde's life. He's played here for two decades and you're just going to take that away from him?"

"I don't know why you've got your panties all up in a bunch; you're not fired." He hoists himself up from the couch, tugging his pants back up under his belly. He points his fat finger in my face. "And you, of all people, should be fucking grateful because I'm about to make you a very rich girl."

"I'm not a girl." I grit the words between my teeth, my fingers balling into fists at my sides. "I'm a grown-ass woman, Freddy."

His eyes drop down my body slowly. "Yes, you are." He leers. "And you should start dressing more like it." He turns toward the door. "I want you here four nights a week and start dressing sluttier. Show your tits more. It's time we bring in the big fish." He sticks his tongue out, wriggling it at me before laughing maniacally as he walks down the dark hallway.

Tears prick my eyes as my chest burns. I picture Clyde's weathered face, his bright smile and the way his eyes light up when he plays. I can't let this happen, but I don't know what to do to stop it.

———

"Are you sure you're okay?" Matilda, my coworker who quickly became a best friend after only a few weeks of working here, looks over at me as she steams some milk.

"Yeah." I smile at her reassuringly. "I'm fine." I've said the same phrase five times this morning, not only trying to convince her but myself as well. "Just a long night at Freddy's."

"Oh, speaking of, I was actually planning on coming by next week. It's been forever since I've heard you sing and my little sis, Chloe, who you met last Christmas, is staying with me for the weekend and she's dying to see you. I told her we should do a girls' night to celebrate her twenty-first birthday."

"That sounds great." I try to be enthusiastic but the gravity of last night weighs on me. "How is Chloe doing? About to graduate, I assume?"

"Yup, she has one more semester left, then she plans to move up to Chicago with me. Since I'll be starting my clinical rotations soon and no longer able to work part-time, it'll be so nice to have someone else help with the bills."

I nod, grabbing a large bag of coffee beans and pouring them into the grinder as the morning rush continues. Pushing another not so fun thought from my head that my closest friend and favorite coworker is about to be quitting.

"I'll be right with you," I say with a touch of frustration in my voice when I hear a customer tap the bell on the counter. I grab another massive bag of beans that's probably over half my weight and drag it over to the other grinder. "I thought closing shift was supposed to handle these," I mutter.

"I got it," Matilda says as she scurries up to the counter from the espresso machine. "Good morning, what can I get for you today, sir?"

I stand back up too quickly, dizziness making me unsteady. I grab the edge of the counter and close my eyes for a second when I hear a deliciously deep familiar voice.

"Coffee, black," he says sharply.

My hands dart up frantically, wiping away the thin sheen of sweat from my upper lip and shoving my wild hairs that have fallen from my braid back into place. I turn around, keeping my eyes cast down so I don't meet his gaze. My stomach coils tightly, just like it does every Friday when he comes in.

"Good morning." I don't have to look at him to know he's speaking to me; I can feel his gaze on me. Every Friday, it's the same thing... I pretend to be busy while he watches me until eventually he catches my eyesight and my face flushes and my stomach flip-flops.

"Good morning." I smile, the words sounding rushed and way more chipper than I intend. I grab a towel and busy myself with cleaning off the counter before calling out the last two orders that are still sitting at the pickup area.

I don't know a single thing about this mysterious man, not even his name... I take that back; I know his coffee order. After seeing him every single Friday for the last nine months or so, I can still barely bring myself to make eye contact with him.

"So, how's your Friday going?" Matilda asks the man as I pour his coffee. "Got any fun date plans tonight?"

My face flames at Matilda's overt attempts to find out if this man is single. Last Friday she asked him if he was taking his wife out for dinner. Somewhere along the way, Matilda decided this man has a thing for me and she's determined to find out why he hasn't asked me out.

"Date plans?" he says slowly, repeating the words back to her like he doesn't know what they mean. His eyes burrow into me as I try to remain focused on not spilling his scalding coffee. I finish, turning to grab a lid, and my eyes finally meet his just as he replies to her question. "Afraid not."

The lid snaps into place and Matilda grabs it from me with a coffee sleeve already in her hand. She slides it onto the cup and plasters a huge grin on her face.

"Coffee, black," she says, handing it to him. "Well, date or not, TGIF."

"TGIF," he says, lifting the coffee toward us before turning to head toward the door.

"Hi, welcome in. What can I get you today?" I step up to the register after he's left, an instant wave of relief washing over me.

"So, no wife," Matilda whispers as she steps around me to start making a latte for the woman at my register.

"That'll be six fifteen." The woman taps her card and steps away from the counter.

"And no girlfriend."

"He didn't say he didn't have a girlfriend," I correct.

"He said he didn't have plans. '*Afraid not*,'" she repeats his answer back to me. "That means he wishes he did, so obviously single."

"What about a boyfriend?"

"What is with you? This man is out of this world sexy and he's clearly attracted to you." She props her hand on her hip, her question certainly not a rhetorical one.

"I'm just saying it's not out of the question."

"It's not, but trust me, he's into you."

"Into me? Matilda, he comes here and orders coffee from us once a week. I think you *might* be reading into things in this situation."

She gives me that look. "You know damn well that he doesn't just come here for coffee. Please. The way he looks at you." She fans herself and I roll my eyes. "What? You seriously wouldn't go out with him?"

"No, I'm not saying that." I try to hide my exasperation but it's too late, the weight of what Freddy told me last night weighing on me. This silly conversation with Matilda just feels so unimportant to me in this moment I feel like I'm going to cry. I'm so overwhelmed at the thought of how I'm going to make working there four nights a week work when I don't get home till after one in the morning and have to open the coffee shop at six.

"What's going on?"

"Nothing, it's just—"

"Grande toffee latte," Matilda calls out, placing the cup on the counter and turning back to face me.

"I think I'm done singing at Freddy's." My shoulders drop, my chin quivering.

"What? Why?" She glances over her shoulder to double-check there are no customers in line before grabbing my arm and pulling me toward the back. "What happened?" Her arms cross over her chest, her chin jutting out like she's ready to fight someone for me.

"He's firing Clyde and the entire band." I shake my head, choking back tears, but it's no use. A giant one rolls right down my cheek to the floor. To most people, this would just be a simple inconvenience or maybe a small bump in the road, but Matilda knows what this singing job means to me, what Clyde and Terrance and Julio mean to me. "They're my fa—family."

"Oh, sweetie." She pulls me into an embrace, her long arms wrapping around my short frame so tightly. "I'm so sorry. Why now?"

"Because Freddy is a piece of shit. His grandma died and left him some money so he wants younger talent which I get, but this is a jazz bar and these guys are legends. This is their life."

"And *your* life," she says, grabbing my shoulders. "Listen to me. You tell that asshole that unless he brings back Clyde and the rest of the band, you're not singing. Or go to a better club." She gives me that look, the same one she's been giving me for over a year whenever I talk about Freddy's. "I know you don't want to entertain the thought, but you can still see Clyde and sing at another club, a better, safer one that isn't run by a fucking goon."

"I know." I squeeze her hands, not wanting to try to explain again to her that it's not just about a better club or more money; it's about singing with these guys who have become my friends. And it's about my long-term plan to own Freddy's. I don't have a clue how, when I barely make enough to pay my bills now, but someday, I'm going to buy Freddy's and restore it to what it used to be.

"I'm sorry if that was harsh," she apologizes. "I just worry about you there."

"I know and you're right, though. I'm just going to tell Freddy that unless he brings back the band, I'm not singing." I toss my hands in the air with a huge smile, feeling a little silly I didn't say that the second he told me he was firing them.

"Good. There's that beautiful smile." She playfully pinches my cheek. "Now, I have some other good news to tell you."

"Oh yeah? Good, I need it."

"Trust me, you *really* need this." Her lips curl into a suspicious grin.

"What?"

"I gave him your number—wrote it on the sleeve when you were filling the cup."

"What?" I say again, laughing in confusion as her comment doesn't register. "You gave my number to som—" Then I realize who she's referring to.

"Mr. TGIF."

# Chapter 2

## *Atlas*

"Sir, as I mentioned in our last conversation regarding your father's trust, the deadline is less than five months away."

My eyes stay focused on the phone number staring back at me as I slowly twist the cup from side to side over and over again.

*Her bright-blue eyes stare back at me, her black hair piled on her head as a few loose tendrils tickle her neck. My fingers itch to reach out and brush them away from her delicate throat. They twitch, resting on my thigh, an image of them wrapped around her throat as I slide my tongue between her plump lips.*

"Did you need me to throw that out, sir?"

"Hmm?" I glance over at Oliver, my house manager, completely unaware how long he's been standing there. "Sorry, no." I shake my head.

"As I was saying, the trust, sir."

"The trust." I nod my head, chewing my bottom lip for a second as my pulse begins to return to normal.

"Have you thought any further about asking Miss Tate?"

"No," I say firmly, not wanting to have this conversation with him again. "As I mentioned last time, Oliver, Miss Tate and I are no longer together. End of discussion."

Oliver nods curtly. "Dinner will be ready at seven p.m. per the regular schedule. If you need anything else from me in the meantime, sir, I will be in the library." He turns on his heel and walks toward the door of my home office.

"I'm working on it. I have a plan." My words stop him and he turns to face me, smiling softly while giving another nod.

"I hope so, sir."

Oliver has worked for my family for four generations, starting out as my father's driver when he was barely eighteen years old to now running the entire house which means managing the chef and cooks and the garden crew, as well as driving me around at his insistence even though we have a driver, Mac, who works full-time for the house. He's always been like a second father to me, but when he oversteps, I will remind him that I don't need him meddling in my affairs. The same way I let my father know when he was still alive.

The door shuts with an almost silent click. I reach into my middle desk drawer and produce the trust that Oliver was referring to. Almost as soon as I begin to read over it for the hundredth time, I toss it back onto my desk in frustration.

"Bastard," I mutter, standing to walk over to the bar cart in the far corner of the room. I pour a generous three fingers of scotch, taking half of it down in one gulp before refilling the glass.

My father, Byron Knight, one of the last truly self-made billionaires this world has known, loved nothing more than to make everyone else feel stupid. It was the only thing in life that truly made him happy, making others feel less than. He was fucked in the head. But what really pisses me off is that he knew exactly what he was doing when he had this trust written. When he died, he left me all of his physical assets, money, investments, you name it. The only thing he didn't outright leave me was the only thing he knew I wanted or cared about—Knight Enterprises.

I have spent every fucking second of my adult life, most of my teenage life, and even some of my true adolescence dedicated to this company. I've made more money than I'll ever spend. I own houses and cars I'll never drive or sleep a single night in. But what I don't own... a majority stake in the company that has my goddamn name on it. Being CEO of my father's company isn't enough. I deserve those majority shares and I've done more than enough to deserve the fucking power.

And that is where she comes into play—Stella Porter.

The night I first saw her, I had drunkenly stumbled into a jazz bar on the opposite side of town from where Eleanor Tate, my live-in girlfriend was currently cleaning out her side of our closet. The same closet I had custom made for her a year earlier. The same closet I had stood in just a few hours ago when she looked me in the eye and told me she wasn't in love with me anymore.

Stella captivated me. Her long, black hair was pulled away from her face, her full hips encased in a burgundy velvet dress. Her pouty lips were painted bright red, begging to be bitten. Everything about her was mesmerizing. I sat wondering how someone as beautiful and talented as she was, wasn't headlining a club in the heart of downtown or a show in Vegas.

I swirl the remaining ounce of scotch in my glass before bringing it to my lips and finishing it. I savor the burn, the sweet afternotes hitting the back of my throat. For the last nine months, I've spent every spare second researching a loophole in my father's trust but it's pointless. I have until my fortieth birthday to marry or all of his shares will be released back onto the market.

*"I'm tired of asking you, son, so I'm going to start demanding an answer. When are you going to settle down with Eleanor?"*

*"We are settled down, Dad. She moved in a month ago. I'd say that's pretty damn settled." I finish the remainder of the brandy in my glass and place it back onto my father's marble bartop.*

*"You know what I mean, Atlas. I'm tired of having this argument with you. You know damn well that I worked my ass off to make this*

*company what it is and I'll be damned if you don't keep it in the family. As an only child, you owe it to your mother and me."*

*"Then be dammed," I reply, adjusting my cuff link absentmind-edly. His face grows redder than I thought possible, a hint of purple staining his cheeks. If he were a cartoon character, steam would be blowing out of his ears.*

*"This is exactly what I told your mother would happen to you if she coddled you like she did." He sneers at me, his bottom lip curling as he points a crooked finger at me. "I told her she'd ruin you."*

*"Are we done here?" I stand, buttoning my coat. My father stares at me, his eyes glassy as he sits hunched over in his chair. He doesn't look like the same powerful man I saw eviscerate people time and time again growing up. The same man who could silence a room of thou-sands just by standing. The same man who could financially ruin his opponents before nine a.m. on a Monday. But life hasn't been kind to him these last few years and if you ask anyone who knows the name Byron Knight, they'll tell you the same thing: it's karma.*

*"Dad, I'm in love with Eleanor. I'm happy with her. I'm not going to promise you I'll marry her because I'm not there yet. It could come to that, it could not, but if you plan to take this to your grave, that's on you." And with that, I turn and walk out of his house.*

At the time, I didn't understand why he was so hell-bent on me marrying someone. It wasn't until I met with his lawyer after his death that I found out he had added an addendum to his trust the day we had that conversation.

Which leaves me with only one option as far as I'm concerned. Ask a complete stranger to marry me... with compensation, of course. A simple contract outlining that they will be required to stay married to me for one year, live together, zero requirements or desires for any sort of sexual relationship. The cold and callous look in Eleanor's eyes when she walked out of my life was exactly the reminder I needed to stay focused on the only thing that matters, taking over Knight Enter-prises. Never again will a woman hold that kind of power over me.

I can't keep the smirk off my face at the thought that my father died thinking he'd won. If there's one thing my father did teach me, it's that control is the ultimate form of power and to be completely heartless in the pursuit of it.

Between another glass of scotch and staring at my computer screen, my attempts at distraction are fruitless. The only thought on my mind since she wrote her number on that coffee sleeve is Stella.

*Who the fuck are you kidding? The only thought that's been on your brain since you first saw her... is her or some variation of fucking her.*

So I do what I always do when I can't focus my thoughts; I call my driver. While I know she only sings on Thursday nights, I find myself telling Mac to take me to Freddy's. It's the only place, besides her job at the coffee shop, where I know she goes. The only place that weirdly feels close to her.

*Shit. Fuck.*

Thoughts like that are the ones that get you in trouble. Thoughts like that will have you falling in love and getting your heart ripped out while losing sight of what's important. I have to stay focused. She is my only option right now for a contract and based on what I've witnessed of her life, she isn't exactly in a position to turn down a million dollars and taking life off for the next year.

So, the fact that I've imagined fucking only her in every way possible while I stroke my cock these last months won't even be an issue when she says yes. I won't let it be an issue because as far as she will be concerned, I'll want nothing to do with her.

A few moments after Mac stops outside Freddy's, I open my mouth to tell him to head back home when I see a cab stop a few feet away and a woman emerges. It's Stella, her long black hair flowing in the wind behind her as she runs across the street and ducks into the bar.

I reach for the car handle. *What am I doing? Am I approaching her tonight with the offer or am I thinking with my cock?*

This isn't a situation where I want to feel unprepared. I need to have the upper hand. I slowly release the handle, sitting back in my seat. "Head back home, Mac. I don't feel like being social tonight, after all."

# Chapter 3

## *Stella*

The door swings open; the ever-present stench of stale smoke and nicotine permeating the thirty-year-old carpet in the entryway wafts upward.

There's a lot more to this place than meets the eye, remnants of its days of glory still present with the stunning crystal chandeliers that have turned dingy and gray, and the copper detailing on the bar having oxidized more than a decade ago. Even a deep cleaning would give it a facelift, but according to Julio, Freddy has snorted more money than he's ever put into this place.

"Hey, Dennis, is Freddy in?" I don't bother stopping by the bar; I just ask the question in passing as I head straight to the back office.

"Oh, hey, Stell, what are you doing here?"

He doesn't answer my question and I don't answer his either. I just grab the door handle when I'm within reach and fling open Freddy's office door.

"What the fuck?" He stands up, brushing a powdery substance from his nose. "What the hell are you doing here?" His tone softens a touch when he sees that it's me, his eyes doing their usual perusal of my body like I'm a piece of meat.

"I'm here to talk about your demands—the extra performances and a new band." I pull a rusty chair away from the wall and drag it till it's facing him across from his desk.

"What is there to talk about, sweetheart? I'm the boss, remember?" A string of saliva pulls between his lips as they widen into a grin, my stomach knotting at the sight.

"And I'm the talent," I say confidently. "We both know that you need me here and I won't perform unless you bring back Clyde and his band." I cross my arms over my chest, regretting it instantly when his eyes drop. I release my arms, placing them awkwardly in my lap.

"Babydoll," he grunts, hoisting himself up out of his chair, "you might be *the talent*, as you put it, but you don't bring in a crowd." He walks behind me, my eyes following him until he's out my peripheral. I jump when I feel his sweaty hands come to rest on my shoulders. He presses me down into the chair as he leans forward, his rank breath coming out in small puffs against my cheek. "You're easily replaceable just like those old bastards so don't push your luck with me."

I lunge up out of my chair, brushing his hands off me in one motion before turning around to look at Freddy. "Fine, I'll do the four performances a week and I'll—" I swallow down the vomit that threatens to rise at what I'm about to say. "I'll wear sluttier clothes." He smiles grotesquely. "If," I say, holding out my hand, "and only if, you bring back the band." His smile falters but I can tell he's considering my offer.

"Fine." He nods. "You win. I'll bring them back, but you better be here this Saturday night to perform and your tits better be out."

"Done. Thank you." The smile I offer is fake. "And one more favor?" He lifts a brow. "Can you let me tell Clyde about the new plans?"

He grunts, clearly still agitated at the fact that I got my way. His eyes narrow and he points his finger in my face. "Yes, but no more favors or I'm going to start demanding some of my own."

I don't respond. I just give a nod of understanding before exiting his office and running back out of the bar. My shoulders sag in relief and I let out a long sigh. A smile breaks across my face as I walk the two short blocks to the train station.

Through the entire ride back to my apartment and my routine of making myself a cup of lavender chamomile tea while drawing a bath, my mind races with how I can bring in more money to save up.

*Maybe the extra three nights a week will mean more tips.* I visibly frown in the mirror as I brush my hair.

"Be realistic," I tell myself as I pull my hair back in a slicked-back bun to keep it from getting wet in the bath. The water is perfect, and I slide my foot beneath it after dipping my big toe in to test it. The warmth engulfs me and I close my eyes to try and will myself to relax. I've been using my bath time to remind myself to remain positive about ever having enough money to buy Freddy's, but some nights it just feels impossible. After several minutes, my eyes fly back open and I stare up at the flaking paint on my ceiling. "Yeah," I say to myself, "you're gonna need a miracle."

———

"Did he call?"

"Who?" I glance over at Matilda.

"You know who."

"Oh." I roll my eyes. "No, of course he didn't. Did you actually think he would?" I grab the tray of muffins she's handing me and slide them onto the bakery cart.

"Yes," she says emphatically. "Why wouldn't he?"

I shake my head half in exasperation, half in humor at the fact that I'm seriously having this conversation with her. "Mati, I say this as no slight to myself," I clarify, knowing full well how much she hates my self-deprecating jokes. "But he's literally the kind of guy who looks like he walked off a mega yacht that he owns and was filming a cologne commercial on surrounded by half-naked models.

He's not going to call the coffee shop girl who can't even make eye contact with him. This isn't a Hallmark movie."

She scowls. "For all you know, he's knitting with his grandma right now and he saves kittens on the weekends. He's looking for love but in all the wrong places because he just hasn't met the right woman yet." She clutches at her heart, her eyes brimming with fake tears like she's practicing for an audition.

"You're right." I chuckle. "But I'm not going to bank on it. That being said, if a man who looked like him ever did ask me out, I'm breaking my *not on the first date* rule."

"I mean, duh." She fans herself and we both burst into laughter, all thoughts about Freddy's gone for a few minutes.

"Hey, I need your help with something." I hold back, questioning if I should mention it but the truth is, I really do need her help.

"Yeah, sure. Anything." She wipes her hands on her apron and leans against the bakery cart. "What's up?"

"I, uh, I had that talk with Freddy and he did agree to bring the band back."

"Oh my God!" Her hands shoot upward. "That's great news."

"It is, but I had to compromise." Her excitement fades. "I agreed to the four nights a week which will mean more in tips so that's good, but I also told him I'd dress sluttier," I say, using air quotes.

"Eww, was that at his request?" I nod. "Gross fucking piece of shit. What do you need help with, burying his body hopefully?" She smiles at her own comment.

"I need something slutty."

"At least you got that part right," she says.

"What do you mean?"

"Coming to me to find something slutty, you know I've got good taste." She winks. "We'll go after our shift."

"Perfect. I'll go over to Clyde's apartment after we're done so I can tell him the good news. I called him after Freddy fired him and he was still so positive about it all, but I could hear it in his voice, he was heartbroken."

The next four hours fly by. I toss my apron in the dirty bin and say goodbye to my coworkers as Matilda and I walk toward the exit.

"I know the perfect place to find you a dress that's slutty, yes, but in a very sophisticated, classy way."

"Is there such a thing?" I give her a skeptical look and she pretends to gasp.

"Rude, don't question my abi—" Her hand darts out and stops me in my tracks as we exit the coffee shop.

"What?" I look up at her, my eyes then following her gaze to across the street where an expensive-looking black sedan is parked. It's not the car that has her mouth hanging open; it's the fact that Mr. TGIF is leaning against it, staring at me.

"*Oh my God,*" she says over and over in a hushed tone. He pushes off the car, closing the distance between us as he crosses the street.

"Good afternoon." His deep voice sounds even sexier when it's directed solely at me. His eyes are hidden behind tortoise Wayfarer Classics; a single lock of his dirty-blond hair that's usually perfectly styled has fallen over one corner of his sunglasses. His navy suit fits like a glove, like it was made for him. I recall my conversation with Clyde about his father who was a tailor. *Now I realize why they cost so much.* The man is definitely wearing the suit in this situation, not the other way around. His broad chest looks accentuated, his thighs filling out the pants perfectly.

"Say something," Matilda whispers, nudging me. "You look insane."

"Afternoon," I repeat back to him hurriedly, completely unaware how long I stood lost in thought.

"Did I catch you at an okay time? I had hoped to discuss something with you."

"Yes," Matilda answers for me, shoving me toward him before I can protest. "She was just saying she had no plans."

I look back at her, my eyes wide. *What the hell?*

"Great. Would you mind coming with me?" He holds out his hand, gesturing toward his car.

*This is crazy, he's a complete stranger. An extremely hot and very built-looking stranger but still...* I feel another shove against my lower back from Matilda.

"Well, I'll see you tomorrow morning." She waves at me and I turn to face her so that he can't see my face. I flash her my *what the hell is going on* look, hoping she sticks around, but it's not working. "Have a great night, you two." She emphasizes the word *night* even though it's just after one p.m.

"Shall we?" I smile, resting my hand in the crook of his elbow as he leads me toward his car. He opens the back door and motions for me to slide in. After closing the door and walking around to the other side, he gets in and the driver pulls into traffic.

"Oh." I look in the opposite direction. "I actually live back that way." I thumb over my shoulder.

"We're not going to your place, Stella." He slowly pulls his eyes from looking straight ahead to looking right at me. It feels like the breath has been sucked from my lungs being this close to him. He takes up space, his legs spread wide and stretched out in the back seat of the car. His woodsy cologne permeates the small space that I'm now very acutely aware of. "We're going to mine."

Instead of coming to my senses like a normal person and asking him to drop me off so I can grab a cab home, I reassure myself that a man who looks like him, drives a car like this, and wears suits that expensive wouldn't risk it all for some silly little nobody... *Then again, these are exactly the kind of rich people that get away with stuff like that.*

"How'd you know my name?"

He lifts his hand, a smirk forming at one corner of his mouth as he slowly leans toward me and touches my name tag.

"Oh." My cheeks flush with embarrassment. "Right."

"It was also written on the coffee sleeve along with your number." He's turned his gaze back forward, one of his massive hands resting on his thigh. A gold ring encrusted with rubies sits on his pinky finger, a Rolex just a few inches up on his wrist. This is exactly the kind of man who should be wearing a pinky ring and weirdly, it looks good.

"I-I didn't write that," I say in a half-hushed tone.

"I know." I continue looking at him, but his eyes stay forward, fine lines crinkling at the corners. "That's why I didn't call. If *you* had wanted me to call you"—he looks over at me again—"you'd have given me your number, wouldn't you?"

I nod, unsure what exactly I'm agreeing to but something about this man, his presence has me so off-kilter, so giddy, and yet scared that I feel completely unlike myself.

We sit the rest of the ride in silence. He remains focused on his phone while my hands nearly tear through my purse strap as I nervously knot it over and over again in my lap. I watch out the window as we drive farther north, just outside the city, until the car slows in front of a large gate that opens up automatically. The driveway curves through trees, rounding a corner and coming to a clearing where a massive, almost gothic-looking Victorian mansion sits far back on a lush green lawn that is very clearly professionally manicured.

"This is your house?" I try to sound nonchalant but the size of my eyes as I look around give me away. I lean toward the window, craning my neck to take in the magnitude of the estate.

"It is." He's already opening his door and getting out the second the car pulls into a massive garage. He walks around to my door, opening it and holding out his hand to me. I reach forward, my fingers delicately gracing his before yanking my hand back.

"Wait." I look up at him nervously. "I don't even know your name."

"Atlas Knight." He extends his hand out toward me again.

I take it. "Stella Porter." I smile and he shakes my hand before helping me out of the car. His other arm is behind me, his hand coming to rest at the small of my back as he ushers me toward a door that I assume leads to the house. I'm suddenly very self-aware that I'm in my work uniform. My jeans are still peppered with flour, a few coffee stains on my pale-blue polo, and I'm sure my makeup is half-melted off along with my hair that's fallen down.

"This way." Atlas gestures as we walk through a long hallway with vaulted ceilings. Wooden beams stretch the entire length of the ceiling. We pass a kitchen that looks like it could be featured in *Architecture Digest*, complete with a massive La Cornue oven. We round another corner and walk down another hallway until we reach a massive wooden door that he pushes open. "My home office."

*Office? Weird place to discuss a date.* I take in the room, trying not to gawk or seem overly impressed when it feels like I could spend hours exploring in this place.

"Please, have a seat." He gestures to two large leather chairs that are placed exactly opposite his desk. He stands next to his chair, unbuttoning his suit coat and taking a seat. I follow his lead, plopping down almost unceremoniously.

"So, Mr. Knight, what did you want to discuss with me?" I try to flutter my eyelids, crossing one leg over the other as I tilt my head.

Do I sound flirty? *I want to sound flirty. Hell, I want to toss everything off his desk and crawl across it like I've seen in movies. Grab him by the tie and tug it until his lips are—*

"Straight to business, I like that. How old are you, Miss Porter?"

"Twenty-four," I say. "Why? How old are you?"

Completely ignoring my question, his eyes narrow on me, like he's trying to figure me out or perhaps he's second-guessing asking me here. Maybe he thought I was older than I am. But then he joins his hands together in front of him, placing them on the desk as he leans slightly forward.

"I need to get married, Miss Porter, and I want you to be my wife."

# Chapter 4

## *Atlas*

Her lips part, a smile taking over her face as she lifts her hand to stifle her laugh. She thinks I'm joking, something I expected to happen. "And here I was worried you were going to murder me or something."

I remain stoic, my expression conveying that despite the insanity of this revelation, I am, in fact, not joking.

"Wait." Her smile fades, her eyes widening as she juts her chin slightly forward. "You're serious." It's not a question, but more of a statement.

"Completely."

"You don't even know me."

"I know enough," I reply. I understand that I do have the upper hand in this situation, not only because of money and status, but because I've been watching Stella since that first night I saw her at Freddy's. I continued going back every Thursday night, sitting perfectly behind the spotlight so she doesn't recognize that I'm the same man who orders the same black coffee from her every Friday morning.

"Who even are you?"

"I told you, Atlas Knight."

"But *who* are you?" she says again as she stands and gestures around my office. "This house alone is like American royalty or something, you realize that, right?"

"I'm a businessman who came from money and has made even more money is all."

"Is all?" she questions as she walks over to one of the massive windows to the left of my desk. She lifts the gold tassel tie back on the velvet drapes that frame the window.

I stand from my desk, stepping around it and sliding my hands into my pockets. "Like my father before me, I am the CEO of Knight Enterprises, only he actually founded the company." The tassel falls from her hand.

"Holy shit. Knight Enterprises, as in the name stamped on the back and bottom of every product on the shelf?" I nod. "So you're a multibillionaire, not just a businessman?"

"Something like that." I shrug.

"I feel like an idiot; I had no idea. I guess I thought you looked a little familiar, but I just thought that you were maybe a model or one of those sexy thirst trap influencers who do outfit videos, but no, you're the man who recently bought the Chicago Blackhawks."

"Sexy influencers?"

"You know, the guys who show different outfits and do transitions where they jump"—she proceeds to hop in place, her breasts swaying with her movement—"and then they're in another outfit."

"And they're sexy?" I stifle a chuckle as a blush creeps up her neck, but I don't linger on the subject. "Shall we continue our discussion?"

"I'm sorry." She shakes her head and walks back toward me, her delicious hips swaying with the movement. "I'm still having trouble wrapping my head around your—"

"Proposal?" I interject.

"Yes." She says the word slowly, realizing that I did, in fact, just propose to her. "I feel a little embarrassed. I thought you were asking me..." She looks down at her feet, her cheeks redder than ever.

"On a date?" I finish. Her head whips upward and her eyes light up, and my stomach drops at the rapid change to disappointment when I answer her. "No, I am not asking you on a date. I guess jumping straight to proposing might seem romantic, but I assure you this marriage arrangement, if you will, would be purely transactional, a business agreement," I say, internally reminding myself that is exactly what this is, nothing more.

"Business agreement?" Her expression transforms as she struggles to understand what I'm saying. "I don't—" Her face scrunches. "Can we start with why you *need* to get married?"

I walk back around my desk and reach for the contract, sliding it across toward her. "Due to an unfortunate clause in my father's trust he left to me, I have to be married to inherit it when it matures on my fortieth birthday. Which is the reason why I need to get married. There is no way around it, no loophole, no legality that I can get around, unfortunately, so I've decided the next best option is to be completely transparent with someone that too would benefit from my predicament."

"Benefit how?"

"Payment, of course." I reach into my desk drawer and pull out a pen to place next to the contract for her. I lean back in my chair as she picks up the document and begins to look it over. "Obviously, I'd expect you to take that and have a lawyer read it over before signing it, but the terms would be that we would need to be legally married within ten days of you signing that document, after which you would move into my residence where you'll live, with your own room, of course. All your expenses would be paid for during that time and you will be allowed to live as you please, just no partners during that time as this needs to be seen as legitimate. After one year, you will be given a no-contest divorce and you'll be able to keep any and all assets acquired during the marriage."

She lifts her eyes from the document. "What's in the trust?"

I hesitate, not a question I was expecting, but there's no point in lying. I need her to say yes. "The majority shares of the company I've dedicated my life to."

"And why is his one requirement that you be married for a year?"

I run my hand over my jaw, thinking through how to explain things in the most concise way. "Basically, my father didn't feel I deserved the company unless I had an heir to pass it along to. He thought that by tricking me into marriage, I'd end up falling in love and having kids. What he didn't expect was for me to beat him at his own game and just find someone who would agree to a contractual marriage with all terms outlined, thus mitigating any chances of love, children, or staying together." She stares at me, unblinking, most likely shocked at my bluntness about how fucked up my family is. "My father had a sick sense of humor." I smile, attempting to soften the fuckery.

She nods, offering a nervous laugh before going back to the contract.

"I'm sure I am only adding to the growing list of questions you have but I'm happy to answer them for you. As for our *relationship*, like I said, it would be purely transactional. There will be events I will need you to attend as my wife for work, but you will not be required, expected, or desired to do any... *wifely* duties."

"Wifely duties?" Her hand drops into her lap and at first I think she's playing coy but she has a genuine furrow of confusion to her brow.

"Sex, Miss Porter. This contract has no requirements for sex, as that would obviously be illegal, but beyond that, sex or any sort of sexual relationship between us is neither required, expected, nor wanted on my end."

"Oh." Her face drops and I almost think she's going to cry, but then her expression turns a touch angry. "So, you thought you could bribe me into marrying you because what—you think I have a crush on you or something?"

"No, not at all. In fact, I think if you did have a crush on me, you would have given me your number, but your friend did because she wants you to like me." She focuses her scowl on me. "I thought that we could both benefit from a problem that I have. Obviously, I would get the majority shares of the company and you would receive a payment of at least one million dollars, along with the other benefits I mentioned earlier."

"A million dollars?" Her mouth hangs open. Now I have her attention. "Lead with that."

"At a minimum, should you want to negotiate, I'm more than willing. I have no interest in lying to you about any of the details of this contract, Miss Porter. All I want is to fulfill this requirement of my father's trust in the most simple and smooth way possible. No complications."

"And marrying for love is a complication?"

"Indeed." I smile. "It's not an option at this point in time and frankly, I don't have the time or desire to embroil myself with someone romantically."

"Or sexually," she reiterates my point from earlier.

"Also a complication. And since it seems neither of us want to fuck each other, I'd call it a win-win situation."

She flinches at my brash word choice. "Wow, what an elaborate way to let me know you have zero interest in me physically or romantically." She laughs.

"My apologies. That wasn't my intention. I guess I'm not very good at proposing."

"Why me?" I'm surprised it took her this long to ask.

"Why not you?" She gives me a *seriously* look. "Honestly, you are one of the only women I see on a consistent basis who doesn't work for me in some capacity. And in sticking with honesty," I say, in part to ease my own conscience on the fact that I am bald-faced lying to her right now, "you're a young woman who works in a coffee shop. I assume you need money. I'm sorry if that assumption makes me sound like an elitist pig."

Lying because I chose her after stalking her for months.

Lying because I, in fact, know she needs money because if she doesn't accept my proposal, I'll make sure she has no other option but to.

"Right." She runs her top teeth over her bottom lip like she's thinking it through. In one motion, she stands and places the contract back on my desk. "While I can see that I would be a good person to approach with this kind of scenario, being young, somewhat naïve, and yes, you're right, pretty much broke, I have more dignity than selling myself for a million dollars, Mr. Knight. So no, thank you." She turns on her foot and heads toward the door but stops. "Actually, I have no idea where I'm going and I need a ride home."

I sit in actual surprise for a few seconds. I guess I assumed that someone in her position would jump at the opportunity to walk away with that kind of money.

"Stella." I clear my throat, narrowing my eyes on her to convey my seriousness. "This isn't a trap and I will give you my word that there is no hidden agenda here, no plan to force you into bed or—"

"It's not that," she interrupts me. "Hell"—she shrugs—"I probably would have gone to bed with you today had you offered. And yes, I realize you have no interest in me like that; you made that abundantly clear earlier." She flinches like she didn't mean to admit that out loud. "I mean, it's—I would have been more open to a one-night stand or a fling with you than this. I might not have fairy-tale dreams about love and marriage, but I know that if I ever do decide to get married, it will be for love. I'm not that jaded yet."

I stare back at her. "Five million," I say confidently, expecting her to run back and grab the pen from my desk but she shakes her head.

"It feels icky, Mr. Knight, like I'm selling myself, and that is a pretty low ask of someone just because they're poorer than you."

"I'll give you a ride home." I want to hang my head and apologize to her, but the reality is, my selfish need for her to eventually agree outweighs my sympathy. Instead, I turn around and head toward the garage.

We walk back through the halls of my house in silence, only the sounds of our shoes echoing off the marble floor. She walks a few feet in front of me and I adjust my gaze to watch her ass move beneath her jeans. Maybe it's her outright rejection of me or the fact that now that she said no, I could allow myself to fuck her. I have the strongest urge to grab her, pull her to me, and take her mouth.

*Would she push me away or would she grab my shirt and pull me toward her like she can't get enough? The way I imagine I would be if I were to let myself touch her. Frenzied. My hands tangled in her dark curls, the sound of her moans against my tongue as my hands slide over her hips to grab her perky ass.*

My cock strains against my slacks, my hand reaching down to adjust myself before she notices. Her admission about a one-night stand pops back into my head when the idea hits me that maybe I should seduce her; maybe this will be the way to convince her. I reach my hand forward, softly pressing my fingers against her waist as I guide her down the other hall toward the garage.

She tenses, turning her head slightly to glance at me in her peripheral. "Allow me." I step even closer to her, my chest bumping against her arm as I reach around her to open the door to the garage.

We walk down the steps toward the Bentley we were driving earlier. Only this time, I open the front passenger side for her to get in.

"Thank you."

"My pleasure." I say the words low, hushed near her ear as I usher her into the car. I see a slight shiver run over her body. She keeps her eyes forward, her hands tightly clasped in her lap as I pull the car from the garage. "Where do you live?"

"I live over near b—actually"—she taps around on her phone before turning it to face me, an address typed into her maps app—"could you take me here? It's my friend's house."

"Boyfriend?" Something I failed to ask before propositioning her with marriage. Maybe he's the reason.

"No." She shakes her head. "Just a friend." She turns to look back out the window, remaining in silence the rest of the ride until I pull up outside of her friend's apartment.

"Look, I'm sorry if I've made you uncomfortable or offended you. I thought being very straightforward about my intentions would make things less weird, but I get the sense I was wrong?"

She glances my way, a slight smile forming. "No, it's... okay. I mean, it's certainly a very strange request and honestly probably one of those things I'll remember for the rest of my life, but it's okay. I know you didn't mean for it to be demeaning."

"Am I still allowed to come into the coffee shop or will that be awkward for you?" I flash my most charming smile, reaching out to run my finger over the back of her hand. I hear a sharp intake of breath and once again, I'm fighting to hold myself back from kissing her. But this, this isn't real and this can't happen. I can't get distracted by lust if she does end up agreeing to this deal. The last thing I need is to fuck things up by bringing sex into this deal.

"No, it won't be awkward. Maybe we can actually be friends now."

"Friends," I repeat the word back to her, dragging my thumb slowly over the back of her hand one more time before releasing my seat belt and stepping out of the car to open her door.

"You don't need to walk me—" she says as she steps out of the car and stands up.

"Would you have said yes?" I interrupt, my body so close it has her pinned against the car. "If I had asked you on a date instead, would you have said yes?"

She looks up at me without hesitation. "Yes. But you wouldn't have asked because—"

"Don't say it again." I place my finger against her pillowy lips, her little smirk slowly fading into a heavy-lidded lustful gaze. I should pull my hand away, but I don't. Her lips slowly part until the tip of my finger rests between them. I feel the wet tip of her tongue graze my finger as she slowly bites down on my flesh. I stare at her for a few seconds, questioning what the hell I'm doing and where this is going.

Maybe it's just a fucked-up, selfish desire to know that she wants me too. I blink, breaking the spell and pulling my finger from her lips.

Seducing her isn't the answer when I know damn well I won't be able to say no to this woman. I need my head clear. I need her to come crawling to me because she has no other option. I need her to need me.

"Have a good afternoon, Miss Porter. Thanks again for your time." I step around her and head back toward the driver's side. "And do me a favor, keep this between us." I don't look at her before sliding back behind the wheel of my Bentley, also not bothering to look in the mirror at her either as I drive away.

Something about her pulls at me like an invisible string; something inside me wants her in ways I've never wanted someone. An almost bloodthirsty craving for her that I'm scared to deny. I feel out of control just being near her *but not enough that I'll throw it all away just to fuck her*, I remind myself. Because at the end of the day, that's all it would be for me—fucking.

I'm not a man who wants or needs love. I was once not too long ago and look where that got me. There's only one thing I want and I need her to help me get it. Before I head to Freddy's to do the one thing I know will guarantee her crawling back to me, I stop back at home first, grabbing several stacks of cash from my safe.

When I pull up outside the bar, I place the cash in a black duffel bag before walking inside.

"Freddy in?" I ask the man behind the bar. He nods toward a dingy hallway. "Thanks." I nod back, making my way down the long, dark hallway till I reach an office with a bent, half smudged off sign that once said *Management*. I don't bother knocking; instead, I swing the door open and walk inside, startling the asshole half-asleep in his chair.

"Fire her."

"Who the fuck?" He tries to right himself, reaching for a drawer where I assume he hides a weapon. I reach over the desk, holding the drawer closed just before he grabs the handle.

"I wouldn't do that if I were you."

"Who the fuck are you and what do you want?"

"Who I am doesn't matter, what I want does. Fire Stella. No questions asked." I bring the bag up from my side and place it on his desk.

He looks from me to the bag, slowly reaching his hand out to unzip it and look inside.

"It's one hundred thousand. Count if you want but it's all there. Fire her and I won't come back looking for that. Don't fire her and I'll make sure the person I send to retrieve it won't be as nice as me."

I know this is a dangerous game I'm playing, a lion keeping a sheep as a pet, but I can't undo what I've already set in motion. So my only option is not to allow myself even a single taste. Because that's all it will take to bring me down.

# Chapter 5

## *Stella*

"Clyde, it's Stella. Open up." I knock on his door, a little louder this time as I bounce from foot to foot with excitement. "I have great neeeeews!"

"Calm down now, girl, I'm an old man. Takes me twice as long to get to the door than you." He waves me inside, laughing when I tell him he's still just a young man. "It's good to see you, sweetheart. How are you holding up over there these days?"

"Well..." I can't keep the secret inside any longer. "I got you your job back!" I throw my hands in the air in excitement. "Julio and Terrance too." Clyde's face is a mix of excitement and confusion. "I-I should start by apologizing first." I reach for Clyde's hands. "I had no idea Freddy was going to fire you guys. He came in my room afterward and told me what he'd done."

"Hey now"—he squeezes my hands—"you didn't do anything wrong. Why are you apologizing?"

"I just felt so bad, like I should have fought harder for you guys. It wasn't until I was talking to my friend Matilda and she told me to tell Freddy that the only way I'd perform was if you guys came back. I even agreed to his four performances a week and he agreed to rehire you guys." I can't hide the disappointment on my face when Clyde isn't as excited as I am.

"Stella." He pulls me closer, his face growing serious. "Did Freddy make you agree to anything else in order for us to come back?"

"I—" My brows shoot upward. "Oh, no, no, I promise, Clyde. I... There's no way I ever would or could agree to anything with Freddy." I can't hide the disgust on my face and the shudder that runs through my body.

"Phew." He claps his hands together. "Well then, that is damn good news." Now he's excited, his smile growing wider by the second. "I might not be able to keep up with four shows a week for too long."

"What do you mean?"

"Oh, I'm not getting any younger. Gotta start slowin' down sometime." He winks at me, reaching over to squeeze my knee. "But don't worry, my son Dexter is moving back to Chicago in a few months. He's been living down in Memphis for a few years doing music."

"You want him to join the band? Will Freddy be okay with that?"

"Not join, take over for me."

"Clyde."

"Not right yet, Stella. It's okay. But soon."

My shoulders sag, the excitement melting away into sadness when reality sets in. Clyde's been old since I've known him; it's not like I thought he'd play forever but I wanted to buy the club while he still had a few years left... let him experience the place restored to its former glory.

"I want to buy the club." I blurt the words out, verbalizing them for the first time. "Like seriously buy it, restore it to what it was back when you started playing there. We could see it turned back into a local neighborhood hot spot with quality, affordable drinks and some amazing live entertainment." Clyde's eyes sparkle but I can tell he's holding back. "It would be a great way to showcase local Chicago-area talent too."

"That sounds mighty lovely, Stella, it really does but..."

"I know it's going to be expensive," I say before he can. "And a lot of work."

He nods, smiling. "Well, I know if anyone is going to accomplish their dreams, it's you." He narrows his gaze. "It is *your* dream, isn't it?"

"It is." The afternoon sun has begun to set, bright-orange ribbons shining through Clyde's kitchen window. "You know, when I was little, I never felt welcome or like anywhere was home. The only time I felt truly happy was lost in a song. Either I was singing it, writing it, listening to it... whatever was going on around me, if I had music, I could allow myself to imagine I was anywhere but where I was. But when I met you and the guys at Freddy's, I felt welcomed and accepted. For the first time in my life, I could just be me. I could sing and get lost in the music and I didn't have to worry if I was disrupting someone by being too loud or taking up too much space." I let my words trail off as I look out the window. "I know it's a hole-in-the-wall right now but—"

"I believe in you." I smile at Clyde, reaching over to take his hand again. "You light up when you sing and you've been given a talent that everyone deserves to hear." He tugs my hand, pulling me forward until our foreheads touch.

———

After leaving Clyde's apartment, I check my watch.

"Shit." I don't have time to find a dress for tonight. I have to be dressed and ready for my first song by eight p.m. If Matilda wasn't a solid foot taller than me, I'd run over to her place and see if I could borrow something. Instead, I'll just have to make do with what I have. Maybe there's a long-lost party dress shoved in the back somewhere.

On the walk back home, I pull out my phone, dialing Matilda to fill her in on my interaction with Atlas earlier. I chew my bottom lip, thinking through what exactly I'm going to tell her, the offer of one million dollars rolling around in my head over and over again.

"I can't," I say to myself, shaking my head. I hit dial and after only one ring, Matilda answers breathlessly.

"Oh my God, tell me everything!" she pants.

"What are you doing?"

"I'm on a spin bike at the gym but this can't wait. Spill everything."

"Well, go ahead and relax because it's nothing too exciting."

"What? What do you mean?"

I hear the excitement drain from Matilda's voice instantly and I feel guilty. Mainly because I'm about to lie to her but also because the request Atlas made to me is about as exciting as it gets and I wish I could tell her about it.

"Well, I just mean that I—he asked me out." My voice sounds unnaturally high.

"Holy shit! Wait, why'd you say it wasn't exciting?"

"Oh, well, I didn't say yes." The phone goes silent. "Mati?"

"Yeah, I'm here. I'm just really trying to understand this, Stella. What the actual hell?"

"I told him I'd think about it but that I was pretty busy. I thought maybe play hard to get?" I pull that last part out of my ass; it seems like advice she'd give me and clearly it works because I can hear her clapping.

"Well done." She laughs. "You are going to have that man eating out of your hand by the time you say yes!" she squeals. "You are going to say yes, aren't you?"

Everything would be so much easier if I said yes. I could afford the down payment for the club, have money for renovations, and maybe even give the band a raise. When I had said no the first time, he upped the offer to five million, a number I can't even wrap my head around at the moment.

"Yes," I say, "of course. What's the worst that can happen, ya know?" I shrug, a pit forming in my stomach. I know I'm not going to say yes to him but the fact that all I'd have to do to fix all my problems is to say yes is a thought I can't escape.

"Right? Maybe you'll walk away with a fancy condo or one of those ten-thousand-dollar purses."

"I don't want or need either of those things."

"I knooooow. It's just fun to fantasize sometimes, Stell. Imagine what it's like to feel how the other half live."

"I know." I reach into my pocket to grab my keys. "And when I move into my mansion, I'll make sure I invite you over to raid my closet." I giggle.

"Invite me over? Pshhh," she scoffs. "I'm moving into my own wing."

"You know, once you graduate nursing school, you won't be able to use that as an excuse any longer. I'll be the one trying to set you up with someone."

"Trust me, I'll be begging you by that point. And on that note, I've finished my workout and I have exactly eighteen minutes to shower, eat something, and run nine blocks to my class."

"Good luck!"

I shut my apartment door behind me, glancing around at the almost cavelike studio they're allowed to rent out for an astronomical amount while considering it a one-bedroom since technically there's a room the size of a closet with a sliver of a window.

"I would also no longer have to share my living quarters with a mouse family." I sigh, hanging my purse on one of my entryway hooks. My fridge groans, the hissing sound it's been making lately growing even louder. I make a mental note to call the super for the fourth time.

I walk to the pantry cabinet, too afraid to open the fridge. I root around in my box of snacks, finding a half-broken granola bar and a pack of fruit snacks.

"A dress." I walk to my closet, turning on the light and letting my eyes peruse the closet, popping a fruit snack in my mouth. They're probably past their expiration but considering they're just a mix of chemicals, I figure they can't be too far gone. I finish the snacks, groaning when I realize I have nothing even close to being remotely slutty.

I toss the wrappers in my trash can before walking back over to the closet. I reach back as far as I can, tugging the clothes forward till I reveal the satin edge of a dress I completely forgot I owned. My fingertips reach the edge of the material just enough I tug it off the hanger and pull it out so I can see it. The silk of the material shimmers, and large red roses wind their way up the dress to the swooped neckline and black velvet straps. It's stunning and I've been too afraid to wear it since the second I bought it from a resale shop nearly five years ago.

*"It's vintage."*

*"Oh yeah?" I smile at the associate, the fifty dollars I have in my pocket reminding me that I cannot afford the seventy-five-dollar dress I've been staring at for two minutes.*

*"The lady who brought it in said it was her great grandma's. Apparently, she was a jazz singer at The Green Mill back when Al Capone used to hang out there and it was a real speakeasy." The girl shrugs. "You never know if people are telling the truth about their secondhand items, but it still makes for a fun story a lot of the time."*

*"Sure does." I stare down at the dress, an image coming to mind of myself wearing it, clutching the mic in my hands as I close my eyes and sing at The Green Mill.*

*"You should try it on." She nods toward the curtain hanging limply on a wire in one corner of the shop.*

*I debate it for a second but shake my head. "Nah, I don't even have enough for it anyway." Besides, I tell myself, I don't have curves in the right places for a dress like that, one that was clearly designed to accentuate an hourglass figure.*

*"How much do you have?"*

*"Hmm?" I look back up at the associate, my hand still resting on the dress hanger. "Oh, fifty." I smile and look back down at the dress one last time. "Maybe in the—"*

*"Take it," she says.*

"What?"

"It's yours for fifty. You've been staring at the dress for fifteen minutes and you can't take your hands off it. Clearly, you're meant to have that dress."

"I couldn't," I say, my hand holding it even tighter. But I did. I took the dress home, imagining the perfect situation in which I'd wear this dress, saving it only for that occasion... one that never came.

I place the dress on my bed, grabbing the hem of my t-shirt and pulling it overhead, tossing it aside. I undo my shorts, kicking them to the side and reaching for the dress. In five years of owning it, I've yet to try it on. At least I've filled out a little more since I bought it. Now that I'm not an awkwardly thin twenty-year-old, maybe it will fit better. I hold my breath, sliding the cool material up my thighs and over my hips, then I pull the straps over my shoulders, reaching around to pull the zipper up gently.

"Oh, wow." I can't deny how perfectly the dress fits my body or how much it accentuates the curve of my hip out from my waist. The velvet straps continue down beneath the breast, giving them a lift so I'm half spilling out of the scoop neck design. "Holy shit," I gasp when my eyes reach my cleavage. The material ends just below my knee, and I run my hands over my hips, up to settle on my waist. I can't take my eyes off myself; I'm completely unrecognizable. I pull my hair out from my bun, my curls tumbling over my shoulders. I flip my head over, fluffing my hair up and grabbing a red lipstick from my bathroom. I slick on the bold color, sliding my feet into a pair of vintage-looking pumps I found at Goodwill for six dollars.

"Ladies and gentlemen, Miss Stella Porter." I wave in the mirror, laughing at myself.

For the first time in a while, I feel giddy with excitement about going to Freddy's tonight. I promise myself that when I get home tonight, I'm going to sit down and figure out how much I can save by taking on more shifts at the coffee shop and the extra shifts at Freddy's. If I have any time left over after sleeping, I'll see about picking up a third job with a local food delivery company.

I turn on some music, letting my body sway with the rhythm of Ne-Yo's voice as I sing along. I dance into the bathroom, focusing on my makeup and hair while I warm up my vocals. Finally, all thoughts of Atlas Knight disappear.

————

THE SECOND I OPEN MY MOUTH TO SING, ALL INSECURITIES about my body being on display in this dress, everyone's eyes on me, completely dissipate. I can feel the energy of the crowd tonight. It certainly helps that there are a few more people here, but it also feels different. I smile over at Clyde, his eyes bright as his fingers bounce across the piano keys. Maybe the time off is what the guys needed to come back refreshed. It feels like magic.

I glance toward the spotlight, the familiar silhouette coming into focus a few seconds later. This time, instead of looking away, I let my eyes stay focused on the mysterious stranger. He has to know that I can't see him and I'm starting to think that's exactly what he wants. I just can't imagine why. I close my eyes, letting my hands slide over my body as I sing the words right to him. I imagine myself as his scorned lover, the woman whose heart he broke.

The song tells a forbidden love story about a woman who falls for a man with lips that call to her, a man who appeared in her life at the perfect time—a man whose heart is as dark as night.

# Chapter 6

## *Atlas*

She sings the words as if she's singing them directly to me.

I sit up straighter, half convinced that she can see me, that she knows exactly who I am and she's caught on to everything. I reach for my glass, taking a long sip of whiskey and reminding myself that it's not possible and I'm merely overthinking things.

"Coming to make sure I hold up my end of the deal?" The unwelcome heavy breathing of Freddy interrupts my thoughts as he sidles up next to me. "You've got nothing to worry about; she's getting fired tonight."

I don't tell him that's exactly what I'm doing here. I was actually surprised to see Stella walk out onstage but the second my eyes landed on her, I couldn't look away. "Any particular reason you decided to wait until after her performance?" I keep my eyes focused on her.

"I think you're answering that question for me." He laughs, hitting me with his arm playfully. "I took one look at her in that dress and thought it was worth it." He laughs even harder, his nicotine breath coming out in a heavy puff.

"I'd like to enjoy the rest of her performance in peace, Freddy." I hand him my now empty glass as if he's a waiter. "And I promise you, you'll never see me darken the doors of this place again."

He doesn't leave right away. He stands there for several seconds, I'm guessing contemplating if it's worth it to lose a hundred grand by running his mouth right now or worse, slamming that whiskey glass into my head. Instead, he turns, waddling away and leaving me to enjoy the final few songs. I close my eyes, sinking back into the worn leather chair, imagining removing that dress from Stella's body with my teeth.

I know I'm fucked. I've convinced myself that I'm allowed these little leeways. That she hasn't technically accepted my offer so fantasizing about her isn't something I can't come back from. I've allowed myself to believe that only fantasizing about pleasuring her is fine, that it's not a line I can't uncross.

I order another whiskey, then another, downing them in record time as I check the clock. Her set is ending in twenty minutes and I'm almost seeing double. I stare at her, wanting the image of her in that dress burned into my mind. A sudden urge to march down the stairs and pull her from the stage overtakes me. I grip the armrests until my knuckles turn white, the wood creaking beneath my hands as I clench my jaw at the thought of other men seeing her like this. How can a woman I've never touched, never held, never kissed have this kind of control over me? The thought of other men wanting her, touching her, fantasizing about her churns my stomach so I stand. I sway, steadying myself on the chair before half stumbling down the back stairway to my waiting car.

"Straight home," I mumble to Mac before closing my eyes and letting my head fall back against the headrest.

I don't know what time it is when I hear a pounding at my front door. My eyes fly open, the sound of my record player still turning even though it's hit the end of the songs. I blink a few times, trying to recall the journey from my car to my office. I run my hands through my hair, reaching for my water and taking a drink before standing up to check if I actually heard what I thought I heard.

I'm halfway down the main stairs when I hear it again. "Fuck," I groan, the pounding reverberating through my still whiskey-laden brain. I glance at my watch, it's half past midnight. Oliver would already be in bed. I reach for the door, pulling it open to see Stella, her high heels in one hand, her purse in the other. I stare in confusion, then surprise when my brain registers that she is, in fact, standing on my doorstep.

"Stella?" Her name sounds gruff and raspy, my whiskey-soaked voice deeper than usual.

"Rough night?" She gives me a curious look, noticing my slept-in suit pants and shirt that I didn't change out of.

"You could say that."

"Can I come in?" Her head is cocked slightly, an unreadable expression on her face.

"Sure." I step aside, motioning for her to come inside and then closing the door behind us. "What, uh, what brings you by?" I run my hands over my face, trying to sober up before turning around to face her.

"Why me?"

I pause for a second, curious why this is coming up... then I remember, she was supposed to get fired tonight, hence why I tried to drink myself into an early grave apparently. "I told you," I say with a charming smile, "why not you?"

"Yeah," she says confidently, her arms crossed casually over her chest. "I don't buy that."

I freeze, studying her expression. *Does she know it was me? Watching her from behind the spotlight all these months. Getting her fired.* I step closer to her, now having to look down to meet her gaze. "What's that mean, Miss Porter?"

"It sounds like the answer you rehearsed, the answer you thought I'd believe or that would convince me to say yes to your *proposition*." She emphasizes the last word.

"What do you want me to say? I told you why I made you the offer; you let me know it was rude and insensitive which I see now, and I thought you could use a little extra money. Simple as that." I shrug, maybe to make it seem more believable or to cast an aura of innocence on my part.

"And let's not forget that other little reason," she says in a lower, more sultry voice, her hand coming out to rest gently against my chest, "because I'm a woman you don't want to fu—"

"That's enough, Miss Porter." I cover her hand with mine, wrapping my fingers around hers. "Is that why you came? For your pound of flesh now that you've rejected my offer?" I step closer, my chest pressing softly against hers. I look down her body, letting my eyes settle on her cleavage that's spilling out of her dress. Clearly the whiskey is still raging through me because I decide to call her bluff. I look back into her eyes. She's not relenting, but then I see it, a tiny crack in her façade, and I decide to push her. "Tell me, Stella." I lean into her, my lips hovering over hers. "Would you let me?"

Her throat constricts as she swallows down her nervousness, her arms slowly coming to rest at her sides again before answering. "Let you what?"

I chuckle, lifting my hand to rest against her hip. I don't have to say for her to know. I resist the urge to reach my hand around her, grabbing a handful of her ass. Instead, I slowly slide it up her body, over her stomach. Just before I reach her breast, I remove my hand, settling it softly at the base of her throat so that I can tilt her chin upward to look at me.

*What the fuck are you doing?*

The words bang against my head over and over in rhythm with my heartbeat. I tell myself to stop but I don't want to. Her tongue darts out to wet her lips, her eyes fluttering, and I fully expect her to say yes, or maybe even please. My cock stiffens at the imagery of her begging me to fuck her from her knees. I feel my own eyes grow heavy as I sway toward her. I'm seconds away from telling her in graphic detail just exactly *what* I mean.

"I-I-I'll marry you."

My eyes fly open and I stare at her, unsure if I'm happy she just said that. "Why?" That isn't what I expected to say but it's the first thought that came to my mind.

"I need the money." She says it in one rushed word, her shoulders sagging after like she's been holding it in.

I step back from her, a wave of relief washing over me as the words finally hit me. "You will? You'll do it?"

She nods. "Yes. But for five million." She flinches and I'm sure she's expecting me to counter, but I don't.

"Done." I thrust my hand toward her, but she steps toward me, throwing her arms around my neck.

"Thank you," she says through an almost muffled cry. "Thank you."

When she finally releases me, we both take a seat on the main stairs. "What made you change your mind?" I ask, fishing for an answer when I already know it. But to my surprise, she doesn't say anything about the club or losing her job.

"I dunno, common sense maybe?" She laughs. "I guess I realized how stupid it was to walk away from an opportunity like this. It's not like people like me are offered millions of dollars very often and it's probably my only chance at ever actually achieving that kind of wealth."

"That is a pretty valid reason. Although..." I hesitate, questioning if I should express a question of doubt.

"Yes?"

"Well, you seemed pretty adamant that it went against your morality and who you are as a person. I'd hate for you to resent me the entire time and grow to hate your life."

She shrugs. "Who can afford to have morals these days?" She jokes, laughing. "The reality is, I just have to put myself aside for a year so that I can fulfill some future dreams. I can do that."

"Good." I smile and look over at her. She's still barefoot, her shoes on the floor next to her along with her purse. She rests her elbow on her knee, her chin propped on the heel of her hand. "What has you all dressed up tonight?" I nod toward her dress.

"Oh." She looks down at herself. "Yeah, I guess it's a far cry from my usual coffee-stained blue polo and jeans." She smiles again and I'm waiting on her to tell me about the club, but again, she avoids it. "A date. A date that wasn't successful obviously."

"And what makes a date unsuccessful?" I pry, not sure where I'm wanting this conversation to go. A curious feeling settles in my stomach at the thought of her on a date. Not jealousy, but discomfort perhaps.

"I guess the fact I'm sitting in your house right now and not his?"

"His loss is my gain." I wink and she laughs, but I want to know what it's hiding. Maybe there's more to Stella Porter than I realize, more than my last several months of research didn't reveal. "You sure you're ready for it to be your last date for the next year?"

She sighs. "Wow, guess I hadn't thought about that part of it yet. We won't go on any dates?" she asks, somewhat hopeful.

"I'm sure we will, work-related and whatnot. I just meant legitimate dates. Ones that might end more... successfully." I look over at her as a heavy silence settles between us that's slowly turning into tension again.

"So, soon-to-be hubby"—she gives me a coy grin, bumping my shoulder—"now what?"

I shake my head. "Not that," I say in a low, almost growl. I don't know if *that's* what she was insinuating, but it's exactly where my brain and cock are right now. I actually feel my face flush and I turn away, hoping she doesn't notice.

"Looks like that's where your mind is." She giggles and when I just shake my head, she bumps me again. "Even though we are definitely not each other's type and you have zero desire for a sexual relationship." She partially repeats back to me what I'd told her when I offered her this position. At the time, I was hoping it was true for her; it would make it easier on me if I knew she had no attraction to me. I, however, was a lost cause the second I saw her. Any man with half his eyesight would be slack-jawed at the sight of Stella Porter. Mysterious dark-green eyes and even darker hair with a perfect little heart-shaped pout and full hips and thighs.

"We both know that was bullshit." I roll my eyes and she laughs.

"I'm just surprised you actually admitted it." She's teasing me, flirting, and it feels good. So I do it back.

"I wouldn't say I *admitted* anything—technically." There's a flutter in my lower belly, a curiosity that, if I'm not careful, could turn into a longing before I even realize it.

*You're playing with fire.*

"Fine, Mr. Atlas Knight, do you swear under oath that you knowingly lied to me about being attracted to me and told me you didn't want a physical relationship with me so that I'd say yes?"

"I plead the fifth," I say, humoring her, hoping it puts an end to the conversation I shouldn't have started.

"You're no fun." She pouts, reaching for my wrist. "What time is it?" I observe her as she holds on to my arm, reading the time on my watch.

I tell myself I don't know why I do it, but I do it to try and scare her. To make her see that I don't want a physical relationship. What I fantasize about with her is far more raw and primal.

"No," I say, staring back at her. "I didn't lie to you about not wanting a physical relationship with you so that you'd say yes."

"Ah." She laughs. "So we're back to denial. Got it. It's getting late."

"I said that to convince myself, not to convince you. Because I know that if I'm able to convince myself that I don't want to tear that dress from your body and fold you in half while I'm buried fully inside you for eight hours straight... it'll make this marriage a helluva lot fucking easier."

She blinks a few times and while I know I shouldn't have said it, I think it might have had the desired effect because when she replies, it's not at all what I'm expecting.

"So, should I sign the contract now or...?"

I shake my head, standing and reaching a hand out toward her to help her off the stair. "Let's have dinner here tomorrow night. We'll discuss everything in more detail. I'll have Mac, my other driver, pick you up at your apartment at six."

"Sounds good." She smiles up at me as our fingers stay tangled together once she stands. It's like we're waiting for the other person to say something. "Would it be weird if I stayed in your guest room tonight?"

I open my mouth to answer her when a thought occurs to me. "How did you get past the gate earlier?"

She shrugs. "It was open."

"Interesting." I make a mental note to ask Oliver about that tomorrow, very unlike him.

"So." She claps her hands at her sides. "Can I stay or...?"

"In that dress?" I say, looking over at her, "not a chance in fucking hell."

"Well, you're in luck," she says, reaching behind her back, "because I don't have anything to sleep in so the dress won't be an issue." It's only now as she begins to struggle, I realize her fingers are searching for the pull of her zipper. I take a quick step toward her, grabbing her hand and tugging her against me, stilling her movements.

I stare at her again, a hunger in my eyes I know is obvious. Her lips are parted, her laugh from just seconds ago now silent as her eyes drop down to watch my teeth run over my bottom lip. "While I realize that you get some thrill from teasing me about what I said before, I suggest you get it out of your system now or I will make damn sure it's out of your system before you sign that contract."

"Or what?" She narrows her eyes at me and I realize this is going to be much harder than I realized.

"Or the deal is off. My way"—I wink at her—"no highway option with this opportunity."

———

I stare out my office window, waiting for Oliver to pick up on the other end of the phone.

"Good morning, sir," Oliver says. "Did you forget something?" Considering I've only been out of the house the last two hours, it's a genuine concern.

"I didn't. I wanted to tell you not to worry about things with my trust and marriage. I've got a plan in place."

"Oh?"

"Yeah, a woman named Stella Porter will be joining us for dinner. I was hoping you'd have Mac swing by and pick her up at her place at six."

"As you wish, sir. And should he bring anything with him? Flowers? Wine?"

"No," I say curtly, not wanting him or her to get the wrong idea. "It's a business deal, Oliver, not a date. I guess daddy dearest never planned for me to just offer a woman a marriage contract to bypass his stupid clause. By the way, did you leave the gate open last night?"

"No, sir. I believe Mac went out after me. I'll check with him."

"Thanks."

I'm sure he's confused when I hang up, but I plan to explain things to him later. Right now, I focus on convincing myself that Stella is far better off marrying me than working at that hole-in-the-wall club. And after our deal is over, she'll be set for life if she invests wisely. I have no doubt a woman like her already has a plan.

I laugh to myself, imagining my dad's face scrunched in anger at the thought that I was able to game the system. But just as quickly, the sweet taste of victory turns bitter. A small pit forms in my stomach, a scowl furrowing my brow. I had thought I'd be marrying Eleanor until she made the decision for me when she left me. I glance at my phone at the thought of her, half expecting to see a missed call from her or a text but there's nothing. When she stormed out of my house that night for the last time, I made a promise to her and myself.

*"I won't chase you, El. If you don't love me, then there's no point."*

*"I know that, Atlas. That's one of the reasons I'm leaving. Nothing, not even me, will ever be as important to you as your job."*

*I stare at her, my brain telling me to say 'you know that isn't true,' but it is. Even if I wanted to argue with my own damn heart about it, I've shown more attention to Knight Enterprises than I ever have to Eleanor. Her icy-blue eyes narrow and she purses her lips.*

*"And that's all the confirmation I needed. Goodbye, Atlas." She slings her purse over her arm, turning on her heel as I reach for her.*

*"El, wait," I say, but it's no use. She brushes past me like I don't even exist and marches downstairs to her waiting car.*

I've been tempted a number of times to reach out to her but the embarrassment of crawling back to someone who made it abundantly clear they didn't love me has kept it at bay. My phone vibrates in my hand, pulling me back to the present.

"Atlas Knight," I say into the receiver, carrying on with my day and pushing any remaining feelings for Eleanor Tate to the basement of my mind.

Refusing to admit to myself that I counted down the minutes till I left work, I slide into the back seat of my car, a nervous energy vibrating through me. Elvis flows gently through the speakers. "Turn up the music, Oliver, if you don't mind?" He obliges, "Suspicious Minds" filling the car as he pulls into traffic.

I make sure I give myself enough time to freshen up for dinner. I straighten my tie, buttoning my suit jacket, and running a comb through my mildly untamed hair. I debate on if I should shave again, running my hand over the layer of stubble on my jaw, but I decide against it. I pause, giving myself yet another once-over in the mirror. There's something in the air around me—tension, perhaps? Or maybe it's just my nerves. Either way, I shrug it off and make my way downstairs.

"Evening, Regina. Something smells amazing." I lean over a simmering dish on the stove, Regina poking my side.

"No putting your fingers where they don't belong." She scolds, picking up a utensil and stirring the sauce in the pan. Regina has been my private chef for the last four years. Eleanor actually hired her.

"Yeah, I've been trying to remind myself of that," I mutter under my breath, not expecting her to hear it.

"Ohhh, someone catch your eye, Mr. Knight?" She smirks.

"Perhaps."

"And that's a problem because...?"

She looks at me and I feel a weird tug in my gut, almost like a reminder that Eleanor became quite close to Regina over the years and I should watch what I say. I push it aside, reminding myself that Regina is a professional and I do trust her but at the same time, the less people who know my marriage isn't real, the better.

"I guess I'm just nervous is all. I don't want to ruin things. Tonight is kind of a big deal for Stella and me." She pauses stirring and looks over at me when I say her name. "I know, it's pretty quick after Eleanor moved out."

"Pretty quick? It's going on a year now."

"I know. It just felt soon to me." I hear voices in the entryway and I turn my head in their direction. "Well, it sounds like she's here. Dinner smells excellent as usual, Regina." I exit the kitchen and make my way down the hallway, Stella's voice greeting me before I even see her.

"Damn, how did I already forget how insane this house is?" I watch as she twirls in the hallway, her head back, her eyes closed, her arms outstretched. "Makes me feel like a little kid again."

I stand back and watch her for a moment, the way she naturally converses with Oliver, a smile on his face as she makes him laugh. She's genuine and carefree. Her reactions aren't calculated or designed to manipulate anyone; they're just Stella. A smile starts to pull at my lips, a warmth settling into my chest at the thought and image of her in my home.

"Good evening, Stella." At the mention of her name, she spins around, her emerald-green dress, which falls a few inches above her knee, lifting just enough it makes my cock twitch at the sight of her bare legs.

"Atlas." She smiles, walking toward me with purpose. I expect her to stop but she doesn't. She lifts her arms, wrapping them around my neck as she envelops me in a hug. My body tenses beneath her touch and she must notice it because she quickly releases me, stepping back and putting space between us. "Sorry." She blushes, scrunching up her face in embarrassment. "I don't know why I did that."

"Well, are you hungry?" I gesture toward the kitchen.

"Starving and it smells fantastic!"

After Regina serves us and explains the dish, we both dig in.

"I don't mean to be uncouth but I'm going to go ahead and just outline a few things regarding this business deal between us." She stares over at me as she chews her filet. "You knew my company the second I said it which means the rest of the world is also very well aware of who I am. I'm not sure what your experience or comfort level is with your photo being taken or your name in the gossip columns but it's a very real possibility."

"I understand."

"It also means that you'll carry my family name so there will be a level of... expectation regarding behavior." She crooks an eyebrow at me, her wineglass halfway to her lips.

"Sounds like you're trying to scare me off."

"Not at all." I toss my napkin on the table, leaning back in my chair as she savors the last of her wine. "I just want to be clear with you about everything. I'm in the news. It's not often my love life is. However, seeing as how this will be a whirlwind romance, I'm sure it'll make a few headlines."

"And that scares you because you think I won't be able to handle it?"

"I didn't say that. I think you are an extremely capable woman."

"Well..." She smiles, placing her now empty glass on the table. "Where do I sign?"

I direct her toward my home office, following behind her with my hand on her lower back as I guide her, my eyes drifting down her body to her ass that bounces slightly with each step.

"Stop looking at my ass, Atlas. I'm not your wife yet." She turns her head slightly, her peripheral catching me. The urge to pull her back against me and run my tongue up her neck burns in my chest. Instead, I let her feel that she's still in control... for the moment.

Once we enter my office, I reach into a drawer, producing the contract and a pen. I place it on my desk, letting my hand linger on it briefly. "Stella," I say softly, her eyes drifting around the room before locking on mine. "The last thing I will say about this is, you will be required to sign an NDA along with this contract."

"NDA?" Her head tilts to the side.

"Nondisclosure agreement, meaning you cannot tell *anyone* about this arrangement between us. It has to seem legit."

"Oh." Her face falters a bit.

"Which means that Matilda needs to believe that this is real, that you and I are in love." She lets out a shaky breath. "Want to think it over further?"

She chews her lip, crossing her arms over her chest, then uncrossing them. I think for a second she's going to say she can't do it but she almost half lunges at the desk, grabbing the pen and signing her name to both the contract and the NDA.

"I guess there's no going back now." She tosses the pen back down like it burned her and laughs nervously.

"I guess not." I pick up the papers, placing them back in my desk drawer. "My lawyer will send you a notarized copy of the documents and as far as the payment and your room, I'll ha—"

"Can we just stop for a second?" she interrupts, taking both of my hands in hers and stepping toward me. "And take this in? I just signed a contract to be your wife." Her eyes are big and round as she says the word wife, making me laugh. "I feel like we should dance or something." She shrugs nervously.

I drop her hands slowly, walking over to my record player and carefully selecting one of my favorites, "My One and Only Thrill" by Melody Gardot. One that I happen to know is a favorite of Stella's to sing at Freddy's. She was singing one of her songs the first night I saw her.

"You know Melody Gardot? I love her lyrics; it's so amazing the way she tells a story."

"I agree, she's fantastic."

"Relax," I whisper, my fingers lacing with hers as I slowly sway our bodies to the music. "It's a celebration, right?" I turn my face to look at her, our lips so close. Her smoky voice fills the room and I wrap my arm around Stella's waist, pulling her warm body against mine. A soft puff of air hits my cheek when she makes contact with my chest.

"Yes, a celebration." She smiles, her eyes dropping down to my lips, then darting back up. "You just got yourself a pretty kick-ass wife." She tosses her head back and giggles. "Or soon-to-be wife I should say. Not yours yet." She winks and playfully jabs a finger against my chest. I still our movements. I tighten my grasp of her waist, pulling her closer against me as a surge of possessiveness rushes through me.

"You signed the contract, Stella." My hand slides up her arm and into her hair as I grit the words out slowly, making sure she knows damn well whom she belongs to because this isn't a game to me.

"You. Are. Mine."

# Chapter 7

## *Stella*

"Look." Matilda stops wiping down the counter to turn and look at me, one hand resting on her hip. "I know I said I'd give you time or space or whatever about this date with Atlas, but I am *dying* to know the status of things between you two. Did you say yes yet?"

I smile nervously, a giant knot of guilt forming in my stomach at the thought of lying to my best friend for the next year of my life.

"I did say yes." I barely finish the sentence before her mouth is hanging open. I rush the next part, hoping to tell her not to make a scene or freak out, but the look on her face tells me there's no point. "And I had dinner at his house so technically we've already had a date, but please do—"

"Oh my God!" She tosses the rag in the air and walks away from it. "How am I just now finding out?" Before I can answer, she's peppering me with more questions. "How was it? Is he big? What's his house look like? Oh my God, tell me everything!"

The knot of guilt only tightens. I swallow hard.

"Okay, one thing at a time." I lean against the counter, the afternoon lull setting in which means very few, if any, customers. "I got thinking about it and thinking about what you said, and I just figured, I might as well go for it, ya know? I was at Freddy's and I—" My words catch in my throat when I realize I haven't told Matilda about getting fired.

"And?" she says, staring at me in confusion.

"Sorry." I laugh, hoping it's not obvious I'm internally panicking and only adding to my growing list of things I'm hiding from Matilda. "Anyway, I couldn't stop thinking about him, so I decided to tell him yes, and next thing I know, I'm at his place for dinner last night."

"Last night?" she squeals. "So how was it?" She gives me a cheeky grin, lowering her voice.

"*It* didn't happen." She frowns and I hold my hand out. "But I'm seeing him again tonight and I do really, really like him." When Atlas dropped me off at my apartment last night, we exchanged phone numbers and he said he'd be texting me today to let me know the plan for tonight.

"Awww, you're smitten."

"Maybe." I shrug. I don't have to do much to sell that I'm crushing hard on Atlas; it's harder to remind myself that this should be an act, not my actual heart on the line.

"What's he like?"

"Intimidating." I laugh but it's the truth. "But also very sweet." I recall the way he went along with my request to dance after I signed the contract last night. "And so intoxicatingly handsome and smells so damn good."

I close my eyes, remembering the way it felt to feel his body against mine, to feel his lips at my ear. I fell asleep last night to the fantasy that he wanted to celebrate a different way...

"Girl, I think you might be in love already."

I open my eyes and realize I've slipped into a daydream of Atlas taking me on his office desk. "Nooo." I shake my head. "Or maybe." I shrug, realizing I have about nine days before I'm supposed to be getting married so I don't have time to pretend to play hard to get. I just have to go for it. "Either way, it just feels... right." I sigh.

"Oh..." Matilda covers her face with her hands briefly. "I think I'm going to cry." She reaches her arms out and grabs me. "I'm just so happy for you."

"I'm not married yet." I laugh as she hugs me tighter.

"I know but there's something about this one; he's different." She pulls back to look at me, her face growing serious. "I mean it, Stella. I feel like he could be your forever."

I smile at her, fighting back tears of my own because I know that there is no such thing as forever when it comes to Atlas Knight. The only thing he'll be in my life forever is a memory.

"Hey, you're seeing him tonight? I thought you were singing—I was going to bring my sis by this week to see you, but unfortunately she had to cancel."

"Oh yeah. I meant I'm going to see him before the club and then probably after."

"After—yeah, girl." She hip checks me, walking up to the counter to help a customer. "Hey there, welcome in. What can I get for you?"

My stomach feels like it's curdling. *If Matilda knew why I was lying to her, she'd understand. She wouldn't hate me or judge me.* Tears prick my eyes again when I start to really grasp the gravity of the situation I've gotten myself into.

"It's for the best. You're fine, Stella," I say aloud as I fan myself. I slip into the back, taking in several deep breaths. My head falls against the wall. I wish so bad I had a mom or a sister I could run to for advice. Hell, if I had family, I most likely wouldn't even be in this situation.

I reach into my pocket to check my messages when I see one from Atlas.

**Atlas:** *I'll stop by your place after work—sixish?*

My heart flutters... it actually *flutters* when I see his name on my phone. I grunt and stomp my foot like a child, frustrated with myself that I'm letting this stupid crush complicate things. The only thing that can come of that is a shattered heart. I type out a simple response, letting him know that works fine, before sliding my phone back into my pocket and finishing up the last two hours of my shift.

"Have fun tonight." Matilda waves at me as she walks in the opposite direction down the sidewalk. "And let me know what night you want me and my sis to come see you sing!"

"Will do, see ya!" I shout back.

I hurriedly walk to the train station, making it just in time to catch it. I watch out the windows, my foot anxiously bouncing. I have no idea what I'm going to tell Matilda as to why I'm not at Freddy's anymore. She knows me too well; she knows I wouldn't just calmly walk away. She knows I'd fight and I did, but it was no use; his mind was made up. It was like someone else was pulling the strings and Freddy was just the messenger, but I know that's not true. He'd never let anyone tell him how to run his business, even if it was good advice.

*If I could just tell her that me not singing there is merely temporary because I'm getting the money to buy the club, everything would be fine.*

I chew the inside of my cheek till it's almost raw, mulling the thought over and over again in my head as I walk up the four flights to my unit. I battle between convincing myself that Matilda is trustworthy enough that I could tell her and trust she wouldn't tell anyone and reminding myself that would mean breaking an NDA that I know is most likely ironclad and would result in me walking away empty-handed. I kick myself for not even reading it before signing it.

The hours seem to drag by, my stomach a mix of excitement and guilt. I took my time showering, hoping it would ease my anxiety, but it was useless. I flop back on my bed, looking over at the clock. It's five thirty.

*You have time.*

I sit up, pulling open my bedside drawer to look at my vibrator. I shut it just as quickly as if it were going to bite me. I laugh at how ridiculous I'm being and open the drawer again, reaching for the toy. I practically rip my towel from my body and lie back, thoughts of

Atlas crawling up my body, snaking his tongue between my breasts before wrapping his lips around my nipple and sucking.

I slide the toy between my thighs. They fall open slightly and I gasp the second the vibrating tip hits my clit.

"Ohhh," I groan loudly, my back arching as I imagine his thick, strong hands pinning me to the bed as he whispers filthy things into my ears with his raspy voice. His piercing blue eyes stare into mine as my mouth falls open and I cry out my release. I'm trembling, shaking as I keep the vibrator in place when I hear a knock coming from my front door.

"Oh my God!" I jump up from the bed, the vibrator flying across the room to God knows where. It's still on, the gentle hum of the toy taunting me from somewhere in the room. I drop to my knees trying to find it but it's no use. It must have rolled under my bed behind something. The knock sounds again and I scramble to my feet, throwing on a pair of sweats and an oversized t-shirt before sprinting down the hallway to my front door. My breathing is rapid, so I take in a few long, slow breaths that come out in shaky puffs. I open the door, hoping the huge grin on my face distracts from the state of the rest of me.

"Wasn't sure you were going to answer." Atlas smirks, his hands in the pockets of his dark-gray dress pants. He's not wearing a tie today, just a simple white Oxford. His dirty-blond hair flops over his forehead and I want to reach out and run my fingers through it.

"Sorry, I was—in the shower!" I say the thought as if it just came to me because it did. "I was in the shower," I repeat more calmly, "so I didn't hear you. I just grabbed some clothes and threw them on." I look down at my stained, ripped, and stretched out t-shirt that I kept from a previous boyfriend I think and baggy faded sweatpants. "Clearly not my best." I laugh.

"Works for me." His eyes settle on my chest, my nipples poking against the already thin fabric that I'm sure is partially see-through, a naughty grin on his face. "Are you sure you're okay? You seem... flustered."

"Yeah, totally." I absolutely hate trying to act nonchalant; I can never pull it off no matter how hard I try. My wet hair clings to my neck. "I just thought you said six so I was surprised to see you early is all." I smile, closing the door behind him, now far too aware of my body being naked beneath these clothes.

"Sorry about that. I snuck out of work. Figured I'd get in early with you before heading to my next meeting."

"Another meeting? This late?"

"Dinner meeting. Work never stops I'm afraid."

"Glass of wine?" I ask, turning toward the kitchen to occupy myself.

"Please."

I pour us both a glass and we sit at my small island.

"Our goal in the next sixty minutes is to come up with our dating story, how we met, when we knew, along with details about our backgrounds."

"Okay." I take a sip of my wine and think about how we really did meet. "Why not just start from the truth? You came into the coffee shop I worked at and over time we struck up a friendship, and then you asked for my number."

"Oh, I asked, huh?" He arches a brow and it makes me laugh. "I guess we're rewriting history here, I see."

"You wanted it to be believable, didn't you?" I tease him.

"You've got a lot of snark tonight, Miss Porter." He reaches across the open cushion and pokes my ribs, making me jump. "Maybe you need a lesson in paying attention?"

"Fine." I sit up and roll my eyes at his stern tone. "So for our first date we had dinner at your house and it was love at first sight. We were inseparable ever since, both of us just head over heels, so we decided why wait and go through all of the traditions of an engagement and wedding when we both can't wait a second longer to belong to each other forever. So, we elope."

He blinks several times. "You just came up with that right now?"

I shrug, taking a larger gulp of my wine this time. The truth is, I did come up with it just now out of desperation. The thought of sitting here with him for longer than a few minutes coming up with a beautiful love story that's completely fake is a touch nauseating when you want it to be real.

"Well, it works so let's stick with it. Now, as far as timeline. I mentioned that the contract stipulated we would be married within ten days of signing it; however, I'm willing to change that timeframe to a month."

I let out a sigh of relief. That had been one thing about this that had me even more stressed out than I was. Trying to convince Matilda that I'm that in love and eloping in ten days was feeling impossible.

"Good, that was weighing on me a bit."

"As for the wedding, if you'd like a ceremony perhaps just us on a beach or—"

I shake my head. "Eloping at the courthouse is perfect." He looks at me questioningly, probably surprised that I didn't jump at the chance to have a gorgeous beach wedding in Aruba or something. But this isn't a wedding I want to hold place in my memory. This is purely a wedding of convenience that will merely be a blip on my radar in the not-so-distant future. When I get married for real, for true love, it will be a gorgeous, but small ceremony on a beautiful cliff somewhere overlooking the ocean.

"Okay, easy enough. I'll supply the rings. As for my background and family, I was born and raised into money and business, went to an Ivy League school for both graduate and undergraduate, played tennis, rowing, graduated with honors. Add in a touch of dysfunctional family and fucked-up values. Copy and paste background of any billionaire. It's boring and all easily accessible on the internet. As for my family, I have none. I was an only child, born to an only child, and the other had a sister die in birth. Neither of my parents are alive; my father passed three years ago and my mother a decade previous."

When he finishes talking, he takes a sip of wine, then looks at me as if to say, your turn. "Oh, okay. So, like you I also have no family—

actually I do but I don't know where they are. I was taken away from my parents in infancy, lived with a grandma for a bit, then ended up in foster care." My eyes shift from his to my lap, and I start to pick at the fuzzies on my pants as I talk about my life. I feel ashamed, embarrassed of the fact that I was born into a terrible situation I had zero control over. "I, um, graduated high school and that's it. I did zero sports or extra stuff. I basically did just enough to get a diploma so I could run away... which I did when I was a minor. Lied about my age to get jobs and stuff." Maybe it's the wine or maybe it's the complete exhaustion from the emotions pumping through my body twenty-four seven these days but I can't hold back. A single giant tear drops from my eye to my lap where it lands on the back of my hand.

"Hey." Atlas reaches his hand out, wiping the tear from the back of mine before taking it in his. "Look at me."

I lift my chin, smiling. "Sorry." I roll my eyes at myself. "Must be my period."

"Don't do that, Stella. Don't take on a burden that isn't yours." He reaches his other hand out, cupping my chin. "How you were raised or what you were born into wasn't your choice. I'm sorry you've had to suffer because of others."

I stare at him, wanting so bad for him to pull me into his lap and tell me everything I've ever wanted to hear. To hold me and tell me it's going to be okay, but he doesn't. Instead, he places my hand back into my lap and sits back in his seat, focusing his attention back on our story.

"Are there any skeletons in your closet I need to know about? Anything that a reporter could dig up?"

"Like? I've never been arrested or to jail or anything if that's what you're worried about."

"Well, yes, that but also any other marriages? Children? Evictions?"

I shake my head, trying not to take his questions personally. "No, there's nothing that will come out about me that you don't already know. I mean, I'm sure there's a ton of court records because I was in the system but nothing because I broke the law or got in trouble. I've never been married, never had children."

"Good. Now as for when you'll move in—"

"Wait," I interrupt, "don't I get to know if you have any skeletons in your closet?"

He flashes a smile but it doesn't seem genuine; it seems like he's annoyed. "Like you, I too have never been married, no kids, no criminal record, and no evictions."

"No crazy exes I need to worry about?" I half joke, trying to bring back a little levity to the situation but his eyes go dark.

"No," he says briskly. "Now, back to what I was saying." And just like that, his face completely changes, back to his charming if not flirty smile. "As for when you'll move in. We can keep it to officially after the wedding. However, before then, you should plan to stay the night for the sake of appearances."

"Right." I finish my wine, wishing I had more when my brain instantly imagines us tangled up in the sheets. I can feel the flush of the wine already so adding to it a layer of embarrassment won't be as noticeable.

*Shit! Get it together.*

"I'll show you your room and give you a tour tomorrow night."

"I'm coming over tomorrow night?"

"Yes."

"Okay."

"One other thing." He interlaces his fingers, leaning forward with his elbows on his knees. "We are going to need to build trust between us; that means honesty, even if it's uncomfortable. I've outlined some expectations regarding it in more detail in the contract."

"I understand."

He finishes his wine, placing his glass on the coffee table and checking his watch. "I need to head to my meeting." He stands, reaching out to take my glass and puts both of them in the kitchen sink. "Thank you for that by the way. Mind if I use your restroom really quick?"

"For sure." I point toward the hallway. "It's the door on the left." I run my hands through my air-dried hair which I'm sure is a frizzy mess by now. I'm focused on trying to tame it in the reflection of myself in the TV when I hear a laugh along with a buzzing sound that's growing louder.

*Oh my God, this isn't happening. This is a nightmare.*

I pinch myself to try and wake up when Atlas emerges with my vibrator in his hand. He switches it off, the buzzing finally going away. I don't know what to say so I yell at him.

"What were you doing in my room!" His smile is practically from ear to ear.

"I'm sorry, you told me door on the left so I went in and it wasn't the bathroom."

"I said right!"

"You said left." His voice grows a touch stern.

"Why the hell would I say the wrong direction in my own home?" I gesture widely with my arm. I'm well aware I'm in the wrong, but the embarrassment of the situation and the wine on my empty stomach has me digging in my heels, making a complete idiot of myself.

"The second I opened the door, I heard the buzzing and looked to my right to see a vibrating pink cock on your floor."

Mortified doesn't begin to describe how I feel but it quickly turns to anger. "Well, you didn't have to pick it up. You should have just shut the door." I jut out my hand. "Give it to me."

"I was merely saving you battery power." I lunge for it but he lifts it out of my reach. He looks at it. "Not unless you tell me when the last time you used it was."

"You're disgusting," I snarl at him. His smile fades as he lowers the vibrator and takes a step toward me.

"When?" He steps even closer, his head tilted down to look at me. "If we're going to be husband and wife, we shouldn't keep secrets, Stella."

"You're not entitled to know about my sex life when I'm not

sleeping with you." I give him my best *kiss my ass* facial expression and it only makes him angry again.

"I am absolutely entitled to know about your sex life because you are going to be my wife." He reaches for my chin but I dodge his hand. His eyes narrow, his jaw clenching as he snakes his hand behind my neck and tugs me toward him. "You agreed to the expectations in the contract and what we spoke about earlier regarding honesty and trust—maybe this can be your first exercise in being an obedient wife. Just because this pink cock is fucking you instead of me doesn't mean that you get to hide anything from me."

"And my masturbation habits fall under that umbrella?" I offer sarcastically. "Should I keep a log for you?"

"That can be a requirement. I'd like to know my wife is being satisfied regularly."

"And I didn't agree to obey you; that will not be in our vows." I point my finger toward him.

His grip on my neck softens, his thumb beginning to rub back and forth against my skin. The way my body starts to respond under his touch is pissing me off, but I can't deny the underlying tension between us that seems to be growing thicker by the second.

"Oh, but you did agree to obey me." His smile is almost sinister. "You really might want to read over that contract you signed, sweetheart. It's going to make this year much easier if you do."

"Fine," I say, looking up at him. "Earlier, right before you got here." He's confused so I elaborate. "I actually came right as you were knocking." His thumb stills. I watch the regret pass over his face slowly when he realizes that two can play at this game. "And when you walk out that door, I'm going to do it again." I smile, snatching the toy from his hand. "Looks like I won the battle." I step back, putting space between us so he can't grab it back from me.

"Maybe." He rubs his jaw for a second and chuckles like he can't believe I bested him. "But I won the war. Trust me." He winks at me, stepping around me to head toward the front door. "And Stella, when you come over tomorrow"—his head is turned just enough I can see his profile—"plan on staying the night."

The second the door closes, my hands shoot upward into the air in celebration. "Stop it," I remind myself, pulling them right back down. "It's just for appearances." I repeat Atlas' words back to myself, still a little giddy from the flirty but very confusing exchange we just had. My phone rings. I lean over to grab it, seeing Clyde's name on the screen, my stomach instantly dropping.

I stare at the screen, my thumb hovering over the answer button but instead, I hit ignore... again. This is the fourth call from him that I've ignored. The knot of guilt in my stomach feels like it's taking over. I don't know what to tell him. I convinced him and the guys to come back, promising I'd be there, then I got fired. I feel like a failure but even more, I don't want to have to also lie to Clyde about everything.

I curl up on my couch, guilt and sadness eating at me. The one thing I'm looking forward to in all this is living with Atlas. It feels like the loneliness of my apartment is getting to me. I close my eyes, feeling tired enough from the glass of wine to take a nap or maybe it's everything else I have going on. I inhale, reminding myself that all of this is for a reason. Once I have the money and can buy the club, everyone will understand.

———

"AND THIS"—ATLAS TURNS THE HANDLE ON THE LARGE mahogany door—"will be your room." I follow him into the room, my eyes shooting upward at the vaulted ceilings. It's dark, the walls painted a deep maroon. It's stunning but almost coffin-like.

"Oh." I look to my right and see a massive four-poster king-sized bed but it's through another doorway. "That's a second room?" I point as I walk toward it.

"This first part is more of a sitting room, and then the second room is the bedroom with an en suite."

He stands in the middle of the room watching me as I take it all in. He looks incredible, his perfectly disheveled hair that almost looks styled that way hangs slightly over one blue eye. He's wearing all black today, his beard at least two days old.

"What do you think?"

"It's beautiful." The windows are massive, the light streaming in illuminating the room.

"Feel free to do whatever you want to it. I'm happy to hire painters; you can paint it any color you want. If you want new furniture, that can be ordered."

"What about my own furniture?" I turn to look back at him. "Where will that end up?"

"In storage on the property here."

I nod, stepping farther into the room. I walk around the bed, running my hand over the stunning stark white bedspread that looks like a cloud. When I reach the bathroom, I flick on the light. A giant mirror in an ornate gold frame is centered over a double vanity. I look to the right, a walk-in shower you could fit a car into on one side, a custom claw-foot tub that looks deeper and wider than normal on the other.

"You could fit a football team in here." My voice echoes a little off the marble of the shower wall.

"Please don't." I turn, half-startled, to see Atlas leaning his shoulder casually against the doorway. "I'd hate to have to dream up a punishment that large." There's an edge to his voice and slight glint to his eye. It's the same look he had last night at my house. It's almost like he's wearing a disguise but every once in a while, his true self peeks out.

"No plans." I rub my hand up and down my arm, goosebumps pricking my skin at the way he's looking at me. "It will only ever be just me and Ken."

"Who the fuck is Ken?" His voice booms around me.

"My vibrator." I scowl, half covering my ears. "His name is Ken. Relax."

"Why Ken?"

"Because he's plastic like Ken." He stares at me blankly. "Like Ken from Barbie and Ken."

"Ah." He smirks. "That's clever actually."

"Thanks." I smirk back. "I thought so too."

"So yeah, again this is your room. You are free to do with it whatever you please. As for the payment, the money in the full amount will be wired to a trust in your name that you will be given full access to with zero strings attached the second it's one year and one day after our wedding."

"Only one day after?"

"Yes. Why not?"

"It's a pretty small window. What if there's some hang-up or whatever with you gaining access to the shares of your company from that trust?"

He steps toward me, that rare side of him peeking through again. "Why? Did you say something to Matilda?"

"What? No." I shake my head back and forth rapidly. "I swear." I hold up my hand for some weird reason. "I didn't mean like that. I just didn't know how quickly things like that work, if you'd be given the shares at the same time."

His expression softens. "Sorry, I understand what you're saying and no, there shouldn't be any issues. It's simply a matter of paperwork. Now as for your life, it will be completely financed by me. You will have a brand-new car, whatever kind you want." He waves his hand casually like he's just offered me a snack size of my favorite candy. "Trips, food, clothes, all expenses will be covered as well as an allowance that is not part of the five million lump sum."

"An allowance?" I don't even pretend to hide the smile on my face. "Like spending money?"

"Yes." He reaches out and brushes my hair away from my face. "As my wife, you will not work. I will provide for you." My heart flutters and my stomach does that drop thing. It's these moments, these tender, flirty moments that confuse me with him. I know he wants us to be in the habit of making this seem genuine, but it's confusing. I want to ask if any of it's real, if him denying himself being with me is truly because he doesn't want a relationship or if it's because of it turning into something real. "You are my responsibility."

"Four romantic words every woman wants to hear." I giggle and it makes him laugh too. We're standing close again. Somehow our bodies have managed to move, although I don't remember either of us taking any steps. It's like gravity wants to pull us together. His eyes stare into mine. I feel my lips part and I want so badly for him to just give in. I can see it in the quickening of his pulse at the base of his throat. He wants to.

"And lastly, after this, I promise to leave you to your evening." The moment is gone, disappearing as fast as a warm breath on a cold night. "As I've mentioned previously, there will be no sexual relationship between us."

"Okay." I shrug, nodding my head.

"You also cannot have any physical or sexual relationships with any other men or go on any dates."

"Yeah, I understand." I say, a touch annoyed at the amount of times he's going to drill this into my head.

"Good." He stands there briefly, then turns. "On that note, I'll—"

"What's the difference between a physical or sexual relationship?" I ask, confused at the way he worded it. Is he saying I can't even hug a male friend?

He turns back to me. "A physical relationship meaning you and I will have to have some sort of physical relationship in public; all couples do, but you and I won't fuck."

I flinch at the bluntness of his candor. The way he talks about fucking me or us fucking isn't something I'm used to being said so casually. It's exciting and feels a touch naughty, but every time I hear him say it, it's like a lightning bolt straight to my clit. I imagine him saying it to me while he's thrusting inside me, his voice thick with desire as he tells me all he's thought about today was fucking me.

"Right, totally, I get it," I say nonsensically, completely flustered.

A few beads of sweat break out across my upper lip and I wipe at it nervously.

"With that, I'm going to head back to my office to get some more work done. If you need anything, just text me."

I wave at him like a complete idiot, dropping my hand down as soon as he exits the room. I face the mirror, leaning forward as I place my palms flat atop the cold marble. I breathe, leveling my eyes at myself in the mirror.

"You have a year of living with him; you have to get it together."

His comment about how he and I would have a physical relationship takes over my brain. *What does that mean? Hold hands? Hugging? Kissing? Oh my God, will he kiss me?*

I feel like a silly teenager, lying in my bed on a Thursday night, looking at my crush's social media profile and imagining that he'd ask me to the prom. I laugh, shaking my head at how ridiculous and dramatic I'm being.

"It's a crush, a stupid crush that you'll get over," I say. Besides, he's a man; he's bound to screw up bad enough to piss me off and make me annoyed with him at least once a week so that will help.

I spend the next hour on my phone, looking at ways to brighten up this room. I take my time scrolling through social media, letting myself spend more time on it than normal since I literally have nothing to do. I can't call Matilda; she'll wonder why I'm not spending time with Atlas since she knows I'm at his house. I flip back to YouTube, watching several videos about how to build a business, how to run and own a business, and a few on my favorite jazz artists.

It's nearing nine, so I reach for the remote next to the bed and flip on the TV. There's not only cable and satellite but every possible streaming service you could imagine. There's even access to movies that are in theaters, not yet released.

I jump out of bed, stretch, and decide to go find Atlas. I walk down the long hallway, getting turned around twice before finding the stairs. I hear his voice as I walk down the hallway toward his office; it's quiet like he's half whispering. When I reach his door, it's propped open, and I knock. I hear him say something and then a quick goodbye.

"Come in."

I open the door, stepping inside. "Hey."

"Hey." He smiles. He's leaned back in his chair, a second button undone on his Oxford. He looks like he's been running his hands through his hair. "Do you need something?"

"No, I just wanted to see what you were up to."

"Working." He gestures toward his desk. "Same old."

"I noticed on the TV in my room that you have access to movies that haven't even been released yet."

"Yeah." He laughs. "A friend runs the studio."

"The entire movie studio?" My eyes bulge.

"Yes," he says so casually, as if we all have such a friend.

"Anyway, I wanted to see if you wanted to have a movie night. I could make some popcorn and we could watch one of those new movies." I sit down in one of the chairs across from him.

He gives a sympathetic smile and I already know what he's going to say before he even says it.

"I can't tonight. I have a deal that needs my full attention, I'm afraid."

"Okay." I jump up from the chair. "Have fun with work." I give him a playful smile as I exit his office, hiding the disappointment that is burning in my chest.

I walk slowly back upstairs to my room, jumping into bed and selecting a movie for myself. Within twenty minutes, I'm already nodding off, falling asleep alone, watching TV just like I do at my apartment.

# Chapter 8

## *Atlas*

"That event I need you to attend with me is tomorrow so you will need to get a dress for it. I'll call Neiman Marcus or Saks, whichever you prefer, and have them set you up with a knowledgeable sales associate."

I don't lift my gaze from my iPad as I scroll the news. Stella pulls out a chair at the table and sits down with her coffee.

"Tomorrow? I work today, though."

"I know. Go after."

"I guess it's good I didn't have other plans," she mutters half into her cup as she lifts it to her mouth.

"Are you always going to be this difficult?" I drop the iPad on the table with a thud, making her jump. I watch as her eyes narrow and I know she's thinking through some snarky comment about how it's too short of notice but I'm not in the mood today. Last night, when she walked into my office in her tiny silk shorts and matching top that clearly showcased her lack of a bra, I wanted to pull her across my desk and bite her nipples through her shirt. I wanted to hear her cry out in pain before soothing them with my tongue. My cock pulses against my thigh in my lap, letting me know that I'm going to have to start jerking off daily if I'm going to keep my hands off her.

Instead of a snarky comment, she just shrugs, taking a long sip of her coffee. "Yeah, probably."

I try to hide the twitch of my lip but I know she saw it. She bites her own lip.

*She knows I like when she's difficult. She saw it that night in her apartment too, the way I wanted to devour her when she defied me.*

"I'll text you with the name of the woman to go to at Neiman Marcus and at what time you need to be ready for Mac to pick you up and take you there."

"I can do it myself. Mac doesn't need to take me; I'll take the subway."

"Stella." I sigh, placing my napkin on the table. "You don't take the subway anymore. You're about to be my wife so please, just do what I say. I told you, it's for your own safety."

"Okay, fine. I guess I wasn't thinking about it that way."

"Please start thinking about your safety. You have to do your part with this deal as well. If you're going to be in this world with me, you need to be aware and you need to read the contract."

"Yes, will do today," she says completely unconvincingly.

"Great. Have a good day, darling." I give a pet name a try.

"Mmmm."

"No?"

"It's good, just feels like more of an in-the-moment pet name, not an everyday one."

"How about sweetheart?"

"Generic but still a good one. When you think of me, what name comes to mind?"

Without a second thought, I answer, "Temptress." And before she can tease me or ask me to elaborate, I head out of the kitchen.

———

"Good morning, Florence." I nod toward my assistant, while my thoughts are consumed by Stella. *What is she doing? Showering? Doing her makeup?*

"Good morning, Mr. Knight. I have your messages along with..."

I'm nodding back to Florence, but I'm too lost in my daydream to even comprehend what she's saying. I like imagining Stella in my home, in my space.

"Sounds good." I nod one more time and then close the door behind me so she can't follow me inside my office. She's a terrific assistant, best one I've ever had, but my God, does that woman love to talk. I've met her husband half a dozen times over the years and I'm fairly confident I've never heard him say a word.

I sink down in my office chair, an almost hangover-like heaviness to my head. I rub my temples, closing my eyes for a brief second before Florence is reminding me about my meeting in ten minutes.

*Is she slipping on her panties? Running her hands through her silky hair?*

I grit my teeth, my fingers curling against my palm to keep myself from doing what I so desperately need—release. I know she could see it in my eyes last night when I reminded her about the rules between us. It wasn't a reminder for her; it was for me.

"Sir, I've shown your first meeting to the executive conference room." Florence's voice over the intercom in my office startles me.

"I'll be there shortly," I reply back to her. "Also, please call the personal shopping department at Neiman Marcus and set up an appointment today at three p.m."

"For yourself, sir?"

"No, name will be under Stella Porter. Have the associate pull evening gowns for her."

"Anything else, sir?"

"Tell her to keep the selections conservative." As if that will somehow keep a leash on my thoughts tomorrow night when she's in my arms at this event.

The deep breaths and inner monologue about how this is all a really fucking stupid idea and it's not too late to back out are doing little to keep my thoughts in line as I make my way to my first meeting.

After lunch, I finally get some release—my three o'clock meeting pulling my focus back where it should be.

"Mr. Knight, we are willing to negotiate any of our terms if it means working with Knight Enterprises."

I stare at the already extremely agreeable terms in front of me, reaching beneath the table to dismiss my phone that's vibrating in my pocket. I read through them another time, my phone vibrating in my pocket again. This time I pull it out, looking at the screen to see Stella's name. It stops ringing. I have two missed calls from her, a voicemail, and seconds later, a text.

**Stella:** *Call me ASAP! Emergency!*

My stomach plummets and I stand up suddenly. "Excuse me, my apologies." The room goes silent as I walk out. I hit the dial button and hold my breath as I wait for her to answer.

"Hey." Her tone is hushed and my stomach drops. I immediately imagine her in a dangerous situation. "We have a serious situation here."

"What is it? Are you okay?" I keep my voice calm, not wanting to panic her any further.

"I'm sorry if Mrs. Hoskins is a friend of yours, but the dresses she chose are all terrible." I let out a sigh of relief which is quickly replaced with annoyance. "Hello? Atlas?"

"Is this your emergency, Stella? Ugly dresses?"

"Well, yeah, I don't want to make my debut in a dress that you hate but I don't want to hurt this poor lady's feelings." Her voice is strained; she's totally serious which does make this pretty damn adorable.

"I'm in the middle of a very important meeting. Figure it out yourself."

"She told me you requested conservative dresses."

"And?"

"Why? That's why she has me in mother of the bride outfits with pearls and shoulder pads."

I laugh, picturing her in the dress she's describing. "I'm sure you're overreacting. Just pick the best one and be done with it. I'm going." This time, I actually hang up.

Back in the meeting, my phone buzzes, again with a text.

**Stella:** *Sending you some pics of the options.*

I panic, someone in the room asking me a question as I type out a rapid response. The last thing I need is photos of her, especially in a dressing room where I can't stop picturing her already, half-dressed, bent over a bench with every angle of her on display in the mirrors.

**Me:** *Please don't.*

I'm halfway through my next sentence when my phone alerts me again that I have a text. I look down, struggling to stifle my laugh when I realize she wasn't exaggerating about the dress choices. The color is awful, a lemon yellow with pearls and beads sewn all over the shoulders and chest. Another comes in, this one is bright purple with a floor-length jacket reminiscent of something a villain might wear.

**Stella:** *There's more...*

I look at the clock; this meeting has been going for almost an hour. "Gentlemen, let's wrap this up in the next five minutes. Seeing as how we haven't come to an agreement within the last hour, I doubt we will today. Let's convene again. Florence will schedule for a follow-up meeting." They nod and begin to finish up their discussion as I type out a response to her.

**Me:** *Will be there shortly.*

I see the look on Florence's face when I tell her I'll be gone for an hour and not to forward my calls. "Everything's fine," I assure her before she makes an assumption. "I just need to tend to something momentarily."

I'm practically skipping out of the car when Oliver pulls to a stop in front of the department store, my brain reminding my cock not to get distracted with every footstep.

"Personal shopping?" I ask a young woman who points me in the right direction.

"I'm not sure." I see Stella skimming through the dresses with the lady next to her. "Maybe I should try on a few others?"

"These all looked so lovely on you, dear." Stella's eyes look pleading, then she sees me and waves.

"Thank you very much, Mrs....?"

"Hoskins." She holds out her elegant, weathered hand toward me and smiles, her bright magenta lipstick a touch outside the lines.

"Thank you, Mrs. Hoskins." I lean down and plant a kiss on the back of her hand. "You have been absolutely wonderful to my girlfriend, but my afternoon freed up and I promised her I'd stop by to help her make a decision on the dress."

"Oh, that's so lovely," she swoons, clapping her hands together as she looks from me to Stella. "Don't you just love love." She floats away, humming a little song to herself.

"What?" I look over at Stella who's shaking her head as she laughs.

"You have a way with the ladies, even when they're old enough to be your grandma."

"Got you out of wearing one of those, didn't it?" I nod toward the stack of dresses. "I don't have a lot of time; let's pick out a few that you do like."

She takes the stack she chose and hangs them in the dressing room of the private suite. "Wait, you're not leaving already, are you?"

I glance over my shoulder at her. "I was going to head back to the office."

"Oh, you're not going to stay while I try them on?"

I want to tell her I can't, that I'm already barely hanging on, that if I'm sitting on the other side of that velvet curtain while she's stripping her clothes off, I just might snap. Instead, I remove my suit jacket, taking a seat on the plush sofa.

"Happy to stay." I smile back at her, her face lighting up. I don't know what it is about this moment in particular, this expression on her face, but suddenly a feeling of guilt hits me harder than it has during all of this. I push the feeling aside, focusing on my phone until the curtain timidly slides open.

"Do I have to go to this event?"

"Hmm?" I look up, her head poking out but her body hidden behind the curtain still. "Yes, why?"

"I just feel so uncomfortable."

"Will you please come out here." She tucks her head back into the dressing room, then slowly steps out. The dress she chose is black sequins. It's tight, the neckline cutting deeper than I think she expected it to. My mouth goes dry at the sight of her, her tits on full display down to the underboob. "What's wrong with it?"

She tugs at the front of it. "It's just very revealing"—she looks back at how it hugs her ass—"and very, very expensive." She gasps when she looks at the price tag. "Oh God, no."

"Stella." I grab her arms, stopping her. "Turn around." I spin her so she's standing in front of the mirror, my hands resting on her upper arms as we both look at her. "The price doesn't matter." Her mouth opens and I hold up a finger. "I understand you don't like it, but it's not an issue." My hands slide softly down her arms. "And if this dress makes you feel uncomfortable, then don't wear it. I want you to be comfortable."

"Okay." Her eyes are staring at my hand that rests against her lower belly, pressing her back against me slightly. I don't even remember placing it there. Before it escalates, I step back, taking a seat on the sofa again.

"Continue," I say, reaching for my phone, turning my attention back to my screen. She ducks back into the changing room, the sound of the zipper sliding down her back not missed by me.

"I think this might be the one." She parts the curtain a few moments later, emerging between the panels and walking straight for the large mirror. I watch her spin around, the burgundy material encasing her body in a cascading river of silk. It's understated and elegant, her body turning it into a work of art. This is the definition of the woman wearing the clothes and not the other way around. She smiles at herself in the mirror.

"Looks nice." I turn back to my phone, not wanting to allow myself to linger. I flip through the same email I've read half a dozen times now.

"Nice?" She cocks an eyebrow at me in the mirror. "That looked like more than nice." She steps down from the platform in front of the mirror, walking over to where I'm sitting. She playfully nudges my leg with hers. "Come on, you can tell me I look beautiful."

She's teasing me again and I could flirt back, keep the fun going, but I'm genuinely annoyed—not at her, but at myself for getting so fucking wrapped up in this woman. A woman who's looking at me right now as if I really am her lover. A woman who has no idea the kind of man I really am.

"It's nice, Stella." I repeat the word, glancing up at her only briefly before turning my attention back to my screen, hoping I convey just how mundane I want it to sound.

"Okay, but do you like it?"

I shrug. "If you like it, get it." Frustration is evident in my tone. I'm not trying to be a dick; I'm trying to avoid letting myself enjoy her. To avoid standing up so that my raging hard-on isn't obvious. To avoid admitting to myself that I'm going to snap.

"Seriously? Just tell me if you like it, Atlas. I don't understand the big deal?" She turns back to the mirror, her expression confused. "I thought you came here to give your input?"

I want to tell her that she looks so goddamn good I lost my train of thought, but I don't. "It looks nice, I like it but your tits looked better in the other one. There." I smile. "I gave you my input. I don't know what else you want to hear."

"Just forget it." She rolls her eyes.

I stand and grab my jacket. "As much as I would love to stay and play these little games with you, I don't have time. I'll see you at the event. Be ready to leave by five thirty. Oliver will pick you up." I walk out of the room as if I don't give a shit because that's exactly what I want her to think. I can't let her see the cracks in my armor that the thought of breaking her heart bothers me.

We're only a few days into this arrangement but already I know this is going to go one of two ways. Either I'll give in and consume her, discarding her broken heart at the end of this year or I'll be the one to fall and when she finds out what I've done, how I got her to say yes to this entire thing, she'll be the one to break my heart.

I shower and get ready in my private office bathroom. I always keep a few suits and a tuxedo in my office en suite in case of events that take place on my downtime. I head downstairs, ducking into the back of my car.

"Evening, Oliver."

"Evening, sir. On to pick up Miss Stella?"

"Yes."

I'm not surprised when she opens the door with a scowl on her face. "Oh look, my knight in shining armor," she says deadpan and it makes me laugh. Even with her brow furrowed together and her shiny pink lips in a frown, she still looks breathtaking. A nest of curls sits effortlessly atop her head, a few dangling down her neck. Her makeup is simple, her blue eyes so bright against the dark contrast of the dress they sparkle.

"I deserve that."

"You deserve to go alone tonight." She pulls the door closed behind her, reaching to slide her key into the lock but I reach around her and take them from her hand.

"Allow me." I lock the door, sliding her keys into my pocket. "After you."

"My keys?" She holds out her hand as we descend the stairs.

"You won't be needing them."

"Are you making that decision for me?"

"You look beautiful," I say, ignoring her question.

"Even with my tits not out?"

I open the door to her building, ushering her outside and into the back of the car. I don't want to concern Oliver with our issues so the ride is quiet. "Give us just a moment," I say to Oliver as he steps out of the car to open my door.

I turn to face Stella, reaching out to cup her cheek. "I'm sorry about how I handled things at the department store earlier, but tonight is important. It's our first outing together so can we agree to smile and we can talk about our issues later?"

"Fine, but I want you to know we have a lot more to talk about than just earlier. I read the contract." Her lips are set in a rigid line. "You want me to obey and submit and literally do everything you say?"

"So that's what this is about?" I straighten my cuff link. "Well, first of all, you should have read the contract before you signed it; that's on you, not me. Second, yes, that is exactly what I want you to do and what you will do."

"And if I don't?"

"Didn't we have this conversation already, Stella?" There's frustration in my voice and I do little to hide it. "If you don't cooperate, the deal is off. You get no money, end of story."

"That doesn't seem fair. I signed because I'm agreeing to marry you and I fully plan to fulfill that duty and you can just what? Cancel the contract and dump me at any point if I'm not behaving how you prefer?"

I rub my forehead. "Jesus Christ. No, that's not what I'm saying. If you want to play games and threaten me with acting out, then the deal is off; that's what I'm saying. If you can obey me and for fuck's sake not make something difficult, then this will work just fine. It's not that hard, Stella." Her mouth pops open, her eyes narrow but I grab her hand and lower my voice. "Now, put on a smile and fucking behave so we can go inside."

I slide my arm around Stella's waist once we exit the car, the material gliding beneath my fingers as I drag them around her hip to grip her as we walk inside. Her tits bounce with each step and she catches me looking.

"Something you want to say, Mr. Knight?" She keeps her gaze forward as we make our way through the lobby and into the large ballroom of The Peninsula Hotel downtown Chicago.

"Yeah, I was wrong about your tits looking better in the other dress." I pull her against me tighter as we approach someone I want her to meet.

"Good evening, Tom, Mary." I nod to the Jacobsons. Tom has been on the board at Knight Enterprises for over two decades and Mary was a close friend of my mother's. "I wanted to introduce you to my girlfriend, Stella Porter." I don't give a rat's ass about Tom or Mary's opinions of me or Stella, but they're exactly the kind of people who need to know that they're important. Tom has a lot of sway with the board and Mary is known for running her mouth in our circles. So the sooner she gets to know Stella, the better.

"So wonderful to meet you both, I've heard so many great things." Stella grabs Tom's hand with both of hers, smiling sincerely. I haven't told her a damn thing about anyone here. I look at her out of the corner of my eye. She turns to Mary and gives her a warm hug, complimenting her shoes. Instantly, they launch into small talk, Stella's energy radiating from her. She's the kind of person who immediately puts you at ease. I relax. Maybe convincing everyone this is legit won't be so hard after all. With the way she already has Tom and Mary eating out of her hand, I don't think it will take much convincing of people to understand why I married her so quickly.

"She's something else," Tom says with a chuckle as he steps away from his wife. "A spitfire." He practically leers at her and I'm about to tell him to keep his eyes on his own fucking wife when he continues. "Don't wait too long with a woman like that." He nudges me and I smile, a shit-eating, fake-as-fuck smile.

*Bingo, he put the thought in his own head.*

"Trust me, I won't." I watch as Stella laughs and smiles with a few other women who have gathered around them. Mary introduces her to them; they too are instantly smitten with her charm. It isn't just the people she's speaking with that are enamored with her. I noticed the men standing at the door stare at her, the woman at coat check complimented her, every single straight man in this room has stolen more than one lingering glance at her tonight. I watch in jealousy, flagging a waiter down and ordering a scotch.

An ache forms in my chest as I watch her. These people don't deserve to know her. Part of me wishes I could keep her locked away from people like them but then again, I'm like them. I stare down into my glass, swirling the scotch around a few times and taking another large gulp to finish it. When I look back at Stella, everyone has left but a woman is approaching her quickly. My ex, Eleanor. I almost trip over a waiter as I rush across the room. When I reach her, she's just introducing herself.

"Hi, Eleanor. It's so nice to meet you. I'm Stella, Atlas Knight's girlfriend." I practically bump into her as I grab her and pull her toward me. "Oh." She laughs, giving me a confused look. "Here he is right now. Atlas, this is—"

"Eleanor," she interrupts Stella, delicately holding her hand out toward me. "So nice to meet you, Atlas." She cocks her head to the side, a coy grin tugging at the corner of her lips. She looks a touch thinner than the last time I saw her, her eyes duller than normal too. I want to ask her if she's okay, but I simply nod and take her hand. I glance at Stella out of the corner of my eye, her focus on how Eleanor is looking at me. I debate on clearing the air right now on who Eleanor is but figure it will only add to the stress of Stella's and my situation for no reason. Eleanor and I are in the past.

"Pleasure's all mine." I turn to Stella. "Shall we?" I don't wait for her to answer and usher her toward a far corner of the room away from everyone else.

"What was that about?"

"Nothing." I shrug. "I just wanted to get away from everyone for a moment and see how you were doing."

"I'm okay. Hey, do you know her or something?"

"Who?"

"That lady, Eleanor. She came up out of nowhere before you came over and introduced herself to me like she knew who I was or something."

I step closer to Stella, letting my hand settle back on her hip, my eyes focused on her delicate neck. "Afraid not," I say dismissively, as if I'm already done with the conversation. I reach my hand toward her, my finger running softly over her collarbone, making her shiver and distracting her from Eleanor who is watching us from across the room.

"What are you doing?"

I glance up at her heavy eyes. "Admiring," I say softly, twirling one of her curls around my finger. "Since everyone else in the room gets to." I run the pad of my thumb back and forth over her hip as I keep us just in view of the room.

"What do you mean?"

I circle her slowly, inching my way around her body until my chest is at her back. "I've watched every man in here tonight stare at you." She turns her head to look back at me. "I don't blame them; you are by far the most stunning woman in the room. But I'd be wrong if I said I didn't want to remind them who you're going home with."

"To my own bedroom," she adds.

I run my fingers over her shoulder, circling my fingers and dragging them over her skin before brushing against the material of the off-the-shoulder strap. "True, but still, it would be a shame to let a perfectly good opportunity to show everyone how in love we are go to waste. Lean back," I tell her, pulling against her hip slightly. She complies. I stretch my hand out, covering her entire right side as I lean in and drag my lips softly against her neck.

"Ohhh." She doesn't realize she audibly moans; it's just above a whisper but loud enough it sends a shock straight to my dick. I know she feels my hard length twitch against her ass but she doesn't stop me from pulling her back against me even harder.

I plant a featherlight kiss on her neck, goosebumps breaking across her skin. "Perhaps we should dance?" I step back, breaking our physical contact. She stares up at me when I walk in front of her, a look of desire on her face that has me wanting to fall to my knees and devour her. I move her around the dance floor, her body against mine, her lips parted, a pink flush creeping over her breasts and up her neck. I watch the men around us, each one having to pry their gaze away from her.

"I lied," I say finally, breaking the silence.

"What do you mean?"

"About the dress." I slide my hand down the back of the dress, past her waist till I reach her ass. I grab a handful, the silk material feeling practically nonexistent between me and her warm skin. I don't know what comes over me, the realization perhaps that I can use moments like this to excuse touching her, holding her, kissing her. Or maybe it's the white-hot rage I feel when I see every man in this room eye fucking her right now. "You look fucking fantastic."

"She's staring at us again."

"What?" I release my hand, pulling back to look at Stella.

"Eleanor. She's just staring at us."

I don't dare look over my shoulder to where she's standing. Instead, I continue to dance. "I'm sure she's just admiring the dress too."

"It's you." She looks back at me. "She's staring at you."

"And yet, I only have eyes for you." I pull her attention back to me with a dramatic dip, hoping it shakes loose any remaining thoughts of Eleanor. It does the trick because the second I bend her back, a smile burst across her face.

"That's right, sir." She giggles as I pull her back up. "I'm about to be your wife, after all. You know what they say. Happy wife, happy life."

"I hesitate to ask what would make you happy," I tease, spinning her out of my arms and back in. Her eyes shift from mine to behind me again.

"I THINK IT'S TIME EVERYONE KNOWS EXACTLY WHO YOU BELONG to." Her expression grows more serious as she turns her attention back to me. She points her finger seductively in my chest, then slowly she begins to slide her hand up my chest, around my neck, and into my hair as she rises up onto her tippy-toes. Her fingers tangle with my hair as she pulls me closer, our bodies pressed against each other.

Within seconds the energy between us goes from fun and playful to heated and charged. The smile has fallen from her lips that are parted, glistening, begging to be bitten and sucked.

I can't do this. I can't taste her. I'll want more. I'll need more.

So I don't. I tilt my head to the side just enough that she ends up in a hug in my arms. I try to play it off, nuzzling her neck. "I think they got the hint when I grabbed your ass."

I've embarrassed her. It's written all over her face. I feel like a piece of shit. I should have kissed her. She just smiles and laughs at my comment, neither of us addressing it for the rest of the night.

When we arrive back home, she stretches, stifling a yawn as she grabs her overnight bag Oliver brought in from the car. "I'm going to head to bed. Good night."

"Stella." I slide my hands into my pockets, unsure what I'm going to say. I know what I want to say, that I can't stop thinking about kissing her. "Thank you for tonight. It meant a lot how engaging you were with people."

"No need to thank me." She smiles. "Just doing my job."

"Good night." I nod and head to my office where I promptly rehash tonight over and over again in my head. The way her ass felt in my hands, her breasts pressed against me, her lips so close to mine. Then I think of the almost kiss. The way she looked at me in my arms, if I had wanted to drag her into a closet, she would have let me.

By the time I've finished another glass of scotch, I've walked up the stairs and down the hallway toward Stella's room. I stand there, telling myself it's a bad idea. My heart thuds in my ears as I take the last few steps to her door. I look down, a warm glow coming from beneath the door. I rest my hand on it for a moment, curling my fingers into a fist and walking away.

# Chapter 9

## *Stella*

I watch as the shadow beneath my door stops, but less than a minute later it disappears. Something passed between us tonight. There was a moment; I know he felt it too. I reach over and turn off my bedside lamp, closing my eyes to replay our almost kiss as I fall asleep.

The next morning I stretch my arms overhead, reaching over to turn off my alarm. Normally I'm at work by six a.m. but I requested a late start at nine a.m. today since I had the event. There's a text from Matilda already.

**Matilda:** *OMG, can't wait to hear about last night! That dress you wore looked stunning, drop-dead, seriously. And Atlas? I'm on the floor.*

I scroll up to the picture I sent her last night of the two of us. He had pulled me into his arms and I snapped a quick selfie of us in a giant mirror at the hotel the event was held at. I toss my phone onto my bed, pulling my hair up into a bun before heading downstairs for coffee.

"Good morning." I head straight for the espresso machine, so focused I don't even realize I'm all alone. I press the button and turn to ask Atlas how his morning has been but he's not at the table. "Oh." I look around just as Regina walks in.

"Morning, sugar. Mr. Knight said to tell you he had to head into work early."

I make small talk with her while I pick at a bagel and enjoy my coffee. "Can I ask you something?"

"Sure." She wipes her hands on her apron and stops what she's doing to look at me.

"Is he—is it always like this?"

"Busy, you mean?"

"Yeah."

"Afraid so. If you look up workaholic in the dictionary"—she points her finger—"there'd be a picture of that man. I tell him to take it easy, but he doesn't listen to me." She shakes her head. "What's the point in all this money if you can't live a little and enjoy it is all I'm saying."

"Yeah." I rest my head in my hand, turning to look out the large bay window across from me. It gives an amazing panoramic view of the yard and gardens. "I agree. Such a shame nobody uses all this space. Feels lonely."

She gives me a questioning look. "Already? Baby girl, this is supposed to be the fun part of the relationship."

"Oh." I wave away her concern. "It's amazing." I drag the word out, reminding myself I'm supposed to be head over heels for this man. "I just meant it's lonely with just the two of us in the house. It would be cute to hear little feet running around these halls."

She's turned her back to me, reaching into the fridge for something when she pauses and turns back to look at me. "Yeah, that would be cute." I can't read her expression but it's gone just as quickly as it appeared, a smile in its place as she goes back to what she was doing.

I finish my coffee and head upstairs to get ready for work. By the time I make it in, the rush is still going. I grab my apron and throw it on, jumping behind the register to start taking orders.

"I still want to hear about last night," Matilda says in passing. "The way that man looks at you..." She fans herself with one hand, her other hand carrying a tray of dirty dishes as she ducks into the back.

I turn back to the register, just as the bell jingles again. "Welcome in," I say, not looking at the person and instead turning to Jason, one of our regulars whom Matilda has also tried setting me up with.

"Hey, Stella, you look beautiful as usual today." He smiles and pulls a few bills from his wallet.

"Hey, Jason, how are you doing? How's Aria?"

"She has recently started getting into absolutely everything so that has been both adorable and terrifying at the same time." He laughs, pulling out his phone to show me a recent video of his two-year-old daughter who is giggling and clapping. "She looks so much like her mom when she smiles." He pulls the phone back and looks at it one more time before sliding it back into his pocket. "Anyway, the usual today, maybe a large actually." He adds on, "She's also been waking me up at five a.m. sharp."

"Ouch." I shake my head at the thought of waking up that early. "Well, she is adorable so you can't be mad at her." I look up, my eyes catching Atlas standing a few feet behind Jason, staring at me.

"I've got it," Matilda says as she starts Jason's drink. She says something to him I don't catch and it makes him laugh. She's known him longer than I have; she's the one who told me about his wife passing just four months after giving birth to their first child together. They used to come here on Friday morning dates before work.

I step around her, exiting the counter area and walking toward Atlas. I smile as I approach him but his expression looks pained.

"Hey, I didn't expect to s—"

He takes two steps toward me, closing the distance between us. Before I can register it, his hands are in my hair, tilting my head as his lips come down on mine.

The kiss is soft and warm. His lips move against mine before pulling away for a second. I follow him, though, when he pulls back, leaning forward to kiss him again. This time he deepens it, his tongue finding mine, massaging it, enticing it to come out and play with his. I completely lose track of time and my ability to breathe, so much so that when he pulls back and breaks the kiss, I'm practically panting.

"That was for last night," he says. "And this"—he nips at my bottom lip—"is for flirting with another man in front of me, you fucking tease." He bites my bottom lip before sucking it into his mouth. It's almost painful but I claw at his chest, wanting more. "And now, he knows exactly who the fuck you belong to." He tightens his grip on the back of my neck, his eyes burning into mine. "Do you know who you belong to, Stella?"

"Yes," I half whisper.

"Who?" His lips hover over mine, so close I can feel the warmth of his breath against them.

"You."

He steps back without a word, his eyes ice-cold. I almost stumble but right myself as he moves around me and exits the coffee shop. I stand there, feeling drunk and dazed. I look back at the corner where Matilda and Jason stare slack-jawed at me.

"I think we all need a cigarette after that." Matilda shakes her head and hands Jason his coffee.

"I'm so sorry," I say to both of them, my hands cupping my flaming-hot cheeks.

"Don't apologize." Jason laughs. "That was pretty intense." He blushes as well and Matilda bursts into laughter.

I don't even have to pretend to be a gooey mess after that display but the little butterflies dancing in my belly as I fill Matilda in on last night are a reminder that this isn't real.

"You're living an actual fairy tale, you know that, right?"

*Actually, the exact opposite of a fairy tale... unless I missed the one where she sells herself out of financial desperation.*

"I keep pinching myself to make sure it's real." The guilt of lying to my best friend rears its ugly head again but I swallow it down. We both stare off into the distance, smiles on our faces. "So what about you and Jason?" I ask, changing the subject.

"What about us?"

"I think he's into you."

She scrunches her nose. "Ew, he's kind of like an older brother to me."

"Oh please, you giggled when you were talking to him. Giggled." I repeat the word loudly.

"I did not!" She snaps the towel in her hand at me.

"I know what I heard. You guys look cute together and being that you are friends, that could really work in your favor." She rolls her eyes and turns her attention to wiping down the espresso machine. But something in her expression tells me there's more to it. "Hey," I say, reaching my hand out to grab her elbow. "You like him, don't you?"

She pauses, looking over at me as her shoulders sag. "Maybe."

"Mat, why'd you try to set him up with me before, then?"

She shrugs, her usual outgoing self suddenly quiet. "I dunno. I wanted him to be happy and you're like his wife—petite, sweet, super bubbly."

"So you think he won't like *you*? Just because you're taller than me? Mat, you're super amazing and hilarious. You're an amazing person, like working full-time and putting yourself through school yet you still care more about others and volunteer and so many other things I can't name them kind of amazing."

Her eyes well up. "Dammit, why do you have to make me cry?"

I grab her and give her a hug. "Seriously, go for it with him. He's always nice to me but you guys, there's a spark there. Why do you think I never took you up on the offer?"

"I'm scared of losing him, of losing Aria if things don't work out or ended badly. Plus stepping in as a mother role is just—I don't know, a lot."

I stare at her, wishing I had some wise advice but I don't because I'm far too scared to go after what I want. I'd rather walk away from this contract with my dignity somewhat still intact than my heart destroyed. The bell chimes and a group of three people enter, chatting and laughing, pulling us away from our conversation and back to work.

The last hour of work flies by. Matilda and I are alone again as we change out of our aprons in the back and clock out.

"Oh, by the way, are you singing this weekend? Chloe ended up canceling on me last time but she's for sure coming this weekend. I was thinking we could come by, see you sing, then we all head out for a girls' night in the city." She bends down to change her shoes. "God, I could use a few drinks. School is kicking my ass lately."

*Shit.*

"Yeah, for sure." I can't think of anything to say to get out of it. "A girls' night sounds fun."

"I know, right? Plus, you can share with us all the juicy details about you and Atlas." She wriggles her eyebrows at me. "Can I just say that it's so cute his last name is Knight; it's perfect like he's your knight in shining armor."

"Yeah," I say with the most enthusiasm I can muster at the moment, knowing full well that even if I wanted to gush about Atlas and me, I can't because it's not even real. "I could use a girls' night." My phone buzzes in my pocket. I reach for it, seeing Atlas' name on my screen. I slide my thumb across the screen to read his text.

**Atlas:** *I'll be home late, meetings. Don't wait up. Oliver will give you a ride home.*

"Everything okay?"

I put the phone back into my pocket and tug my apron over my head. "Yeah, just tired from staying up so late. I need a nap." I yawn, hoping it masks my frustration. Another lonely night at Atlas' house, I might as well just stay at my place.

"Ugh," Matilda groans, pushing open the door to leave. "At least you have someone keeping you up late. I can't even remember back far enough when there was a man in my bed but that will all soon be in the past once I graduate. I'll finally have some time for a personal life." She gives me a quick side hug. "I gotta run to class. I have a huge test. Love you!" She takes off jogging down the block toward the train station.

"Bye!" I stand in the middle of the sidewalk for a moment, Oliver offering me a small wave from where he's standing with the car door open, waiting to give me a ride. I wave back to him, walking over to the car. "Hey, Oliver, how are you doing today?"

"Oh, I'm doing just fine, Stella. How are you?" he asks, adjusting the rearview mirror before pulling into traffic.

"Tired." I look out the window, wishing I was singing at the club tonight. I don't miss the atmosphere, the heavy stench of stale smoke and mold from the old carpet almost burning my nose. "Hey, mind if we stop by my apartment first? I'd love to grab a few things."

"Of course, Miss Stella."

When he pulls up in front of my building, he looks at me in the mirror. "Would you like some help?"

"Actually, yeah, if you don't mind?"

"Not at all."

I pack some fresh clothes, my journal, and a few other odds and ends. Then I grab some records and put them in a box, along with my record player and speakers.

"A woman after my own heart." He smiles, picking up the box.

"You like jazz?" I ask as he glances through the records.

"I do, any music really. I've got a collection of vintage vinyl myself. Happy to let you look through and borrow them anytime."

"That would be amazing." We continue our small talk as we walk back down to the car. I switch to the front passenger seat, our discussion of music continuing, morphing into other topics along the way back to the house.

"Here you are," he says, placing the box on the floor in my bedroom.

"You're so kind. I could have carried that up here."

"Bah." He waves me away, his hand going to rest against his lower back. "I may be nearing sixty but I'm still a young man at heart." He winks. "Now, whenever you want to take a look at my record collection, just come knock on my door. I live in the cottage on the back of the property."

"There's a cottage?"

"Oh yes. It was originally built as a stagecoach house way back when the house was first constructed, but it was converted into living quarters years ago."

I'm curious about Oliver, his past, and if he's spent his entire life living here and working for the Knights. I want to ask him more but he turns to leave my room, flashing me another grin and wink before exiting.

After putting my record player on the dresser and setting up my speakers, I walk down to the kitchen to see what's for dinner. There's a note on the fridge from Regina with a list of all the meals prepared and how to reheat them. I pull out a chicken dish, tossing it in the oven before setting off to explore the house.

I GLANCE AT THE DOOR TO MY ROOM AFTER MY EYES SHOOT open, a sound waking me. My room is pitch-black. I sit up and rub my eyes, squinting as I grab my phone to see the time. It's 1:38 p.m. I toss the covers back, slowly cracking open the door to the outer sitting room after tiptoeing across my bedroom.

It's Atlas. He's walking away from my room, down the hall toward his room with a bottle in his hand. His body sways from side to side and that's when I realize he's drunk. I open the door a little farther, just as the bottle slips from his hand and lands on the ground. Without thinking, I fling the door open, scurrying down the hall to grab the bottle that's spilling its contents onto the hardwood floor.

"Hello, darling." His words are slightly slurred, his eyes glassy as he smiles down at me. I right the bottle, trying to make sure he doesn't step in the puddle of whiskey at his feet. "You look good from that angle." His voice is thick and gravelly.

"Oookay." I take his arm and drape it over my shoulders, wrapping my arm around his waist as I begin to guide him toward his bedroom. "I think you might have had a little too much to drink tonight. Time to sleep it off."

"It's your fault, you know," he mutters as he runs his hand through his hair. "You women."

"Well, you men certainly don't make it easy on us," I half joke, releasing his arm from my shoulders as he slides down onto the edge of his bed.

"Why are you doing this?"

"Because you're drunk and could use some help. Plus"—I lean down and untie both of his shoes—"you woke me up."

"That's not what I meant." He reaches down and touches my chin. "This, with me." He's probably drunk enough he won't remember this tomorrow and he probably wouldn't remember if I told him the reason why, but I don't. "You're too good for this. You deserve Jason."

I'm half convinced that this is some sort of guilt trip he's having regarding paying a woman to marry him for a year and maybe it is, but this is a can of worms I don't want to open, especially not right now.

"Maybe so, but the contract is signed so let's just focus on this next year, then figure it all out from there."

"Is that all this is for you?" His eyes grow darker. "A contract?"

"I—" My heart thuds in my chest so loud I'm confident he can hear it. "Are you going to be okay?" I stand up, looking down at him but he doesn't answer. Instead, he reaches out for me, grabbing my waist with both hands and pulling me toward him.

"Sing a song for me."

"What?" I grab his hands, stilling his movements. He looks up at me. "What did you say?"

He closes his eyes, leaning his head against my belly as he squeezes me tighter. I'm unsure what to do or say or where this is going but the butterflies I've been trying to avoid are back in full force, the warmth of his fingers burning through my shirt so hot I'm sure they'll leave a mark. I lift my hands, gently running them through his hair. Finally, he says something against my stomach. It's so muffled I almost can't make it out but if I'm not mistaken, it's a warning. And instead of making me want to run, it makes me want to find out exactly who is Atlas Knight.

"You have no idea—no idea who I really am."

———

MY THOUGHTS ARE SO CONSUMED WITH WHAT ATLAS SAID TO me last night I don't even notice when he walks through the door of the coffee shop the next day until he's standing right in front of the register.

"Hi." I smile, blushing like he knows that I've been consumed with thoughts of him.

"Hi." He smiles back. "How's your morning been?"

"Okay, woke up a little tired today, though." I give him a knowing glance and his eyes shift away from mine.

"About that. I owe you an apology."

"No need." I lean in a little closer to him. "What you did after made up for it." I give him a wink, dragging my teeth over my bottom lip in a flirty manner. His eyebrows shoot upward and I burst out laughing. "Gotcha."

"Coffee, black," he says, unamused even though he's smirking.

"You got it." I step to the side, grabbing a cup. The bell jingles and Jason steps through just like he does every day. I watch as Atlas turns to look at him, then checks his watch. I place the lid on his drink and place it on the countertop. "One coffee, black."

He picks up the coffee, turning to place it on the empty table behind him. "Come here." He motions for me to follow him so I do. I step out from behind the counter to where he's standing. He steps toward me as well, our bodies coming together and just like the day before, his lips find mine.

This kiss is different though. It's more urgent, his hands almost frantically trying to find a way to hold on to me. His tongue is demanding, his lips soft and warm. I'm lost in it, my eyes in the back of my head as my toes curl in my Converse.

"I'm sorry," he growls against my lips, "for being a drunk asshole last night."

"If that's how you apologize, you can do it every night." I know I shouldn't let these little thoughts escape my brain but it makes him laugh. "Meetings last night not go well or something?"

"Something like that." His hands are still in my hair, his body pressed against mine as he looks at me. His eyes drop down to my lips again, whispering against them before kissing me again. "I could consume you."

I'm breathless by the time he breaks the second kiss, all thoughts fleeing my mind of wanting to ask him about his comments last night and if it was just a coincidence that he got here just before Jason did. I'm like a weightless cloud, floating around, until moments after he leaves, I receive the same text I did yesterday from him and my stomach sinks. Looks like it's going to be another lonely night.

**Atlas:** *I'll be home late, meetings. Don't wait up. Oliver will give you a ride home.*

After the third night of the same thing, I've had enough. Tonight, I decide to wait up. I check the clock minute after minute, hour after hour. It's nearly two a.m. when I finally hear his footsteps coming up the stairs. I stand in my doorway, waiting, as I hear him ascend the stairs, finally taking a step toward him once he reaches the landing.

"Must have been a late meeting." His head jerks to the right. I think I've startled him even though he doesn't jump.

"It was." He takes a step toward me, his suit jacket clutched in his hand. "Why are you still up?"

"Couldn't sleep." I shrug. "Never heard of a meeting running this late before."

"It didn't. I went to my office after. I needed to get a few things done and figured since I was already downtown..." I nod. "Is there something you want to say, Stella?"

"It doesn't look good, my fiancé out late night after night while I'm at home with no idea where you actually are." I didn't realize I was upset by this until now. It does feel like a double standard considering he's lectured me a few times now on my behavior in all this.

"I was at the office," he doubles down. "I can get you the security footage if it helps. And before that I was at Morton's, stayed till close."

"And the night before?"

"Same. I had work that needed done so I stayed late at the office." I stare at him, unsure if I actually believe him. He steps toward me. "Look, I'm sorry. I know that work has been exceptionally busy but the good news is, there's a fuck ton of money at the end of this contract and while we agreed on eloping, it doesn't mean there won't be a kick-ass honeymoon." He reaches out and touches my chin softly.

"Oh yeah?" I smile, giddy at the excitement of a luxury vacation that I'd never be able to afford on my own. "Where are we going?"

"It's a surprise."

"Will we fly first class?" I can't hide the excitement at the thought of my own private bed on a plane.

"No, darling." He smiles. "We'll fly on my private jet."

I shake my head. "I seriously keep forgetting just how rich you are. I think my brain has trouble computing that." He laughs and then the moment dissipates between us, but the tension, that thick, underlying feeling of something so much more brewing between us hangs in the air. I can't help myself, I reach my hand out toward him, my fingers fidgeting with a button on his shirt. "Don't you ever get lonely?"

"Yes." My eyes dart to his. I'm surprised he admitted it.

"Then why not choose not to be lonely?" I step closer to him, my fingers sliding from the button to flat against his abs. I can feel his muscles tense beneath my touch, his hand darting out to grab my hand, stilling my movements.

"Because if I choose to not be lonely, Stella..." His hand releases mine, the other dropping his jacket on the floor. He cups my face. "I will fuck up your entire world." His voice is low, his breath warm as his eyes bore into mine. He stays like this for several seconds like he's fighting something. He leans in closer, his lips brushing against mine. "You are far too good for a man like me." Then he steps back and picks up his jacket.

"Maybe that's exactly what I need." My own voice is strained. "To learn a lesson."

He smirks, shaking any wrinkles out of the jacket. "Trust me, Miss Porter, I can think of about half a dozen lessons I'd love to teach you right now, the hard way." His hand is back against my cheek. "I know it's lonely and it will be at times because this isn't real, but this is what you signed up for." My eyes blink rapidly, like an involuntary response of blinking back a stray tear.

*This isn't real.* I say that to myself over and over again, hoping it takes root instead of these feelings.

"Just think of the money, Stella." He smiles, then steps away toward his bedroom. "Good night."

# Chapter 10

## *Atlas*

The restraint I'm showing by walking away is taking every ounce of willpower I have. My legs feel like lead weights. I'm seconds away from turning around when I manage to shut the door behind me.

"Fuck." I toss my jacket on my bed, running my hands through my hair as my cock begs for attention. I reach for my belt, undoing it along with my zipper. I shove my hand beneath the waistband of my underwear, fisting my cock.

"Ohhhh, fuck yes." I lean against the door, my head making an audible thump as I close my eyes and allow myself to get lost in the fantasy of fucking her. I squeeze my shaft, my strokes growing feverish as my orgasm builds. My neck is strained, so I push off the door, turning around to lean one hand against it as I jerk my cock. The door creaks beneath my force and if anyone was on the other side, they'd know damn well what's happening in here right now.

I'm panting, my legs burning as I pump my hand up my length one last time. My release spills on the floor, my breath coming out in near shouts as stars burst behind my eyelids. My shoulders sag, and I rest my forehead against the back of my arm as I try to catch my breath, knowing full well there's a good chance Stella heard me just now... and I hope she did.

————

I STAND IN THE FAR CORNER OF MY OFFICE, STARING OUT THE large plate glass window. The last time I had a ring in my pocket was because I had figured I was going to marry Eleanor. Obviously, a stupid assumption on my part. But this time it's different; it's a safe risk because it's not based on love.

I pull the ring from my pocket, rolling it around between my fingers. It's the same one that I had designed for Eleanor. Call it bad luck or maybe just poor taste, but like I said, it's not a real wedding so I can't imagine that Stella would actually care. Not to mention she'll never find out. She'll be too distracted by how large and glittery the diamond is, I'm sure.

I picture Eleanor's face as I hold the ring. The image of seeing her the other night at the event flashes through my brain. I know I wasn't imagining things when I thought she looked tired and thinner. What I didn't expect was for her to call me the next day and confirm my suspicions, also letting me know that she was, at current, very unhappy and contemplating whether or not she had made a huge mistake in leaving me.

As much as I wanted to pull her into my arms and hug her and let her know that everything was going to be okay and that I was sorry she left me too and that I missed her dearly, I didn't. Because I can't take the risk that she'll walk away from me again before we would get married.

I assured her she simply was having a hard time adjusting to seeing me with someone else and that I was head over heels in love and truly happy for the first time. Her eyes filled with tears and I watched her heart break in front of me before she walked out of my office without another word.

So I did what any man would do who was battling his feelings of still missing love lost and possibly falling for someone he can never have. I drank myself almost to death, stumbling home only to have Stella help me to bed. I was so close to telling her everything that night. I wanted to pull her to me and feel her lips against mine as I buried myself inside her, forgetting everything that was going on around me.

An image of Stella, laughing as she conversed with Jason, pops into my head. I was angry at the jealousy I felt when I watched her. Or maybe I was angry at myself for feeling jealous when I have absolutely no right. A hollow feeling settles in my chest when I think about Stella and Jason. I can't help but wonder if that's a relationship she will pursue once our fake marriage is over. My stomach sours at the thought and I shove the ring back into my pocket. There's only one way that I can make myself feel better about this situation. I glance at my watch and reach over to hit the intercom.

"Hold the rest of my calls and meetings for the day, I'm running out."

I grab my jacket and head out of my office, not bothering to tell Florence where I'll be heading. It's nearly three thirty. Stella should be home by now. I don't bother telling Mac I need a ride. Instead, I hail a cab and head toward Stella's apartment.

Her face is bright with a wide smile as she flings the door open. "Hey, I wasn't expecting you to stop by. What are you doing here?"

"I changed my mind." I can feel my brows draw together, the expression on my face probably conveying an emergency situation because suddenly her face drops.

"Changed your mind? About us?"

"What? No." Her face softens, relief washing over her. "I meant I changed my mind about putting off the wedding. I want to elope today." I pull the ring out of my pocket, reaching for her hand.

She does that thing again where she laughs but I don't, and she quickly realizes I'm serious. "What? You want to elope today? Why, what's going on?" She jerks her hand back.

"Nothing's wrong. I just decided that there's no point in waiting.

Besides, I thought you would be happy because the sooner we get married, the sooner the year is over and you can move on with your life and get paid." I give her my best, reaching for her hand and sliding the diamond down her finger.

"Oh, okay." She looks a little concerned as she watches my movements, but again, she doesn't seem to notice the diamond or at least she doesn't comment on it. "Can we do that right now? Is the courthouse open?"

"They're open till five. I double-checked, but that won't be an issue. You're also supposed to get your marriage license at least three days beforehand which we didn't do, but trust me, they'll take care of it."

"Let me guess. It has something to do with being Atlas Knight?" She gives me that cute little grin and cocks her hip to one side. "Wow, so are we really about to go get married right now?"

"Unless you're telling me no. Are you telling me no, darling?"

"Would you even allow me to tell you no?" Her tone and demeanor are flirty again. This time she holds out her hand and looks at it.

"Only if it was allowed in the contract." She rolls her eyes and offers a halfhearted laugh. "Do you have a specific dress or outfit that you wanted to wear?" I'm realizing now that simply showing up to a woman's apartment in the middle of the day and demanding she be wedding ready even if it is just an elopement at the courthouse is a bit of a stretch.

She looks down at what she's wearing. She has showered since work. Her face is free of makeup, her half-damp hair hanging loosely around her face. She's wearing a pale-pink top tucked into a cute pair of white shorts.

"No, no special outfit planned." She gnaws on her bottom lip, looking down at herself once more than back to me. "I feel a bit underdressed, though, compared to you."

I look down at my suit. I remove my jacket, tossing it to the side, then reach to undo the buttons of my white Oxford. She watches me, her eyes following every movement of my fingers. When I've unbuttoned the final one, I pull the shirt over my shoulders and down my arms, tossing it to the side next to my jacket.

"Better?"

She shrugs one shoulder. "Yeah, you somehow still look way over-dressed compared to me. I'm starting to think you just look rich." She laughs.

I take a step toward her and mindlessly reach out to run my fingers through her hair like it's a natural thing between us. "You look beautiful, as always."

"So, should we go, then?" She shoves her hands nervously into the pockets of her shorts, sliding her feet into the sandals by the front door. She seems jittery on the trip to the courthouse, her leg nervously bouncing. I reach my hand out and rest it on her knee, hoping it gives her the reassurance she needs.

"I don't have a ring for you," she says suddenly, looking over at me.

I reach into my pocket. "I took care of the rings." I hold out my hand, revealing matching gold bands.

"Oh good, thank you." She looks relieved for a second, then the worried look of consternation settles back onto her face.

"Are you sure you want to do this, Stella?" I don't know why I ask it. She's signed the contract, the contract that outlines clearly that if there's any breach of contract, I will pursue her with full legal action. But looking at her right now, all thoughts of why I need to do this go out the window.

"And if I said no?"

I stare at her, then shift my gaze out the window. The devil on my shoulder, my constant companion, the one I let make most of my decisions, is warring with my often-neglected angel. I can't explain it, what this woman has over me—then again, maybe it's just lust and I'm thinking with my cock, but without another thought, I look her right in the eyes.

"I would tell you to tear up the contract and walk away." I don't need to look up into the rearview mirror to know that Oliver is looking at me. I'm sure if he could, he would tell me this is dangerous.

"You would?"

"Yes, but the offer is extremely time limited, so you need to make a decision."

She stares at me wide-eyed, her thumbs twisting around each other. "Yes, yes, I want to do it. I want to marry you."

Every muscle in my body is clenched but the second I hear that I relax. I reach for her hand. "Then let's go make you my wife."

"Make it sound more like I'm a piece of property if possible," she hisses at me as I pull her from the car and onto the sidewalk.

"You are my property, signed and notarized, baby." I reach around and grab a handful of her ass, guiding her toward the entrance of the courthouse.

"And do you, Mr. Atlas Maxwell Knight, take Miss Stella Gwendolyn Porter to be your lawfully wedded wife?"

"I do."

After some surprised exchanges with a few efficient courthouse workers, we were able to secure a last-minute wedding in front of a judge.

"And do you, Miss Stella Gwendolyn Porter, take Mr. Atlas Maxwell Knight to be your lawfully wedded husband?"

"I do." Her cheeks flush a little, a small smile on her face as she stares at me nervously.

"By the authority vested in me by the State of Illinois and with consent of Atlas and Stella, I now pronounce you married. Congratulations." The judge's tone is flat, not even a hint of a smile as he stamps the paper and hands it to his recorder on his left. "Next."

Stella looks at me, then to her right as another couple files into the room. I pull her to me for a quick kiss before ushering her out of the room and toward the hallway.

"Wow, that has to be the fastest wedding I've ever been to." She laughs. "Actually"—she cocks her head—"that's the only wedding I've ever been to."

I stop in my tracks. "What?"

"Huh?" She looks to her left but I'm not there. She spins around to look back at me. "What happened?"

"You've never been to a wedding before?" She shakes her head, shrugging like it's not a big deal. My heart sinks. I feel even more like a piece of shit than I did before. It's bad enough I'm ruining her own first wedding, but I didn't realize I was ruining the entire experience of a wedding for her too.

I walk up next to her, reaching down to take her hand and lead her back outside to the waiting car. Oliver holds the door open, a smile on his face.

"Congratulations." He nods toward us.

"Thanks, Oliver." I squeeze his upper arm and slide into the back seat beside Stella.

"I can't believe I'm married." She stares at her hand, wiggling her fingers so the sunlight catches the diamond. "It is a beautiful ring; what made you choose this design?"

She looks over at me and that feeling comes back, the one that makes me feel like the piece of shit I am. "No reason. I just thought it was interesting," I lie. I had it designed based around three very specific ring choices that Eleanor had let me know she approved of. It's not a very romantic ring in my opinion; it's more severe and abstract with harsh lines and a giant fucking stone. The ring is one hundred percent Eleanor. Cold, with sharp edges, and a rock for a damn heart.

But it's not Stella, not at all. She's delicate and warm; her energy is almost magnetic. She looks out the window, then back to her hand. I can tell she's trying not to focus on it just like me. I twirl my ring around my own finger. The foreignness of it will likely wear off with time but part of me hopes it doesn't because every time I notice it, I think of Stella.

I can feel the anger in my chest returning, burning as it gnaws its way through me. I hate that I'm taking away this monumental moment in her life but I'm also too selfish not to. I also hate that starting today, the countdown to losing her is officially on.

I stay buried in my phone until we reach her apartment building. I step out of the car and walk around to her door to open it.

"Oh, am I staying at my place tonight?"

"No, but you need to get your passport." I follow behind her as we climb the stairs, my hand lingering on her lower back, dangerously close to her ass. I've let myself sneak in these touches, even lingering longer when my hand does slip down to her ass cheek. It's dangerous, her letting me get away with it, but I can't seem to stop myself.

"My passport? Where are we going?" She smiles, tripping slightly but catching herself on the stair in front of her. My hand darts out, shooting around her waist. "The Maldives." She gasps. "You need to text your boss and see if they can find someone to cover you for the next week." I hold her against me as she stands back up, her head tilting slightly to the left to look at me. In a split second the energy grows charged.

I want her.

I need her.

My hand slides upward, resting against the base of her throat as I lean in a centimeter closer. But then she turns her face away, leaning forward to climb the last two steps.

I stand there for a second, then I take the last two steps in one. "Stella." My voice is deep and heavy with need as I grab her around the waist, spinning her toward me. I tilt her head in my hands as my lips caress hers. I'm lost in her, my tongue lapping against hers over and over again as I begin walking us backward till her back hits the wall.

The kiss is wicked. I show no mercy as I take her mouth. Her hands claw at me, digging into my flesh through my shirt as her pants and moans only make my cock harder. I adjust my hips, my cock firmly between her thighs as I tilt my pelvis slightly forward. My tongue slides deeper into her mouth as the head of my cock presses firmly against her clit.

"Ahhh." She trembles against me, her body almost melting into mine. Then I step back. She stares at me, her body half-limp against the wall, one arm still outstretched against my chest, her lips puffy and red.

"Thank you for marrying me." I lean in again, this time kissing her gently. I have to pull myself away or I won't be able to stop at all. "Now that we've had our wedding kiss, I need you to go inside, lock the door, and find your passport."

"Lock the door?" She laughs. "Who are you worried is breaking in?" She reaches into her purse and pulls out her keys. I take them from her, unlocking her door and opening it. I push her through the door, then reach for the handle, my other hand grabbing my still half-rigid cock as I wink at her. "Me, sweetheart."

# Chapter 11

## *Stella*

I giggle, turning the deadbolt over, then peering through the peephole. He runs his hands through his hair, pacing back and forth in the hallway. I turn around, letting out a silent scream as I dance in place.

"Oh shit. Mati! What the hell am I going to tell her?"

I run down the hall to my bedroom, dropping to the floor to pull out the shoebox I shove important information into. I riffle through a few documents, grabbing my passport when I see it buried at the bottom. I double-check the expiration date, holding my breath. "Oh, thank God." I shove the box back under my bed and stand up, letting out a steadying breath before I walk back toward the front door.

Then it hits me. I grab my phone and type out a quick text to Mati.

**Me:** *Hey. I'm about to text Jerry to let him know I won't be in tomorrow and see if Marsha can cover my shift because... I'm going to the Maldives with Atlas tomorrow on a surprise vacation!*

Relief washes over me as I slide my phone back into my pocket. Now I have a solid excuse for not being at the club this weekend when Chloe is in town. But... I want to hang out with them, and I wish I was singing at the club this weekend. That feeling of excitement that's been bubbling the last few hours thinking about this fantasy life is slowly being eaten away by guilt.

I stand in my hallway, paralyzed by this conflicting feeling. Then I close my eyes and remind myself that I'm doing what I have to do to survive. I take in several breaths, letting the last one out slowly before opening the door.

"Good news, I found my passport and it's not expired." I hold it up and he smiles. "Bad news"—his smile falters—"you said we're leaving tomorrow and I have zero luggage." I gesture around me at nothing.

"There's actually good news about your luggage. It will all arrive in the Maldives ahead of us so no need to worry about that."

"No, I mean I didn't pack anything."

"Now, Mrs. Knight..." I can't help it. I burst into a smile when he says it, a million little butterflies breaking out into a dance in my belly. "Do you honestly think that I would let you show up to your honeymoon with nothing to wear?" He cups my cheek, realizing what he just said. "Then again," he says, his voice dropping, "most men would probably insist on you wearing nothing if they married you."

It's moments like this that confuse me. The tender way he's touching me, the look in his eyes as he scans my face, his eyes settling on my lips like they often do. I inhale a sharp breath, my pulse quickening as I clutch my passport in my hand. It isn't just lust; it feels like more—so much more.

My phone buzzes, making me jump and causing Atlas to drop his hand and step back from me.

"Let's go have a celebratory dinner." He reaches his hand out toward me, taking mine and leading me down the stairs and out to our waiting car.

Once inside, I reach for my phone, giving my boss a call to let him know about my sudden absence next week. He groans, telling me that I'll have to make it up when I get back which I readily agree to, promising him this will never happen again. Then I look at the text that came in from Matilda. I hold my breath as I open the message.

**Matilda:** *AHHHHH YASSSSS!*

I sigh in relief.

**Matilda:** *I am SO jealous but SO excited for you. Have so much fun, take lots of pics, and have TONS of hot fuckery with TGIF ;)*

I blush, laughing to myself at the slew of eggplant and water drop emojis that follow.

Atlas' hand slides across the small space between us in the back seat, his hand coming to settle over my thigh. I flinch at the unexpected contact, his hand gently squeezing my leg, then releasing it, leaving his hand resting on my skin.

"Where are we going to eat?"

"Do you like oysters?"

I shrug. "Never had them."

"Oliver, let's go to Prime."

His hand slides a little higher on my thigh, this time his fingers grazing the inner portion, making me want to scream. I clench my jaw so I don't draw attention to myself by squeezing his hand between my thighs. To him, this probably means nothing, just a casual touch on a woman he has no long-term interest in. *I could be replaced with any number of faceless women in this city,* I tell myself.

"What about our clothes?" I point toward his under t-shirt and pants, then look down at my casual outfit. "Aren't we underdressed?"

"Trust me"—he slides his arm around my body and pulls me tightly toward him as we make our way into the restaurant—"nobody gives a fuck what we're wearing." He leans in, nibbling my earlobe as we pass the hostess stand and head straight to a table in the corner. "And trust me, that's not what they'll be focused on."

He's right... or at least I assume he is. I'm too distracted by the way he can't keep his hands off me. His arm is around my shoulders in the booth, his fingers absentmindedly playing with my hair as he places our order with the waiter.

"I'm nervous about trying oysters," I say once the waiter leaves, but Atlas doesn't seem interested. His other hand is turning my face toward him, his lips on mine almost instantly.

"Your lips taste so good," he murmurs against me, his tongue dipping inside my mouth. Instantly, I'm wet, achy, needy for him. I love and hate that he does this to me. I love the excitement of it all, but I get confused when he says things like this. Is it just for show? Is it to draw a real reaction out of me so it's more convincing?

I get that we're in public and that's exactly why this is happening, but I can't help the way my body responds to him, the way my brain automatically wants to be giddy and excited at where this will lead when we leave. But there's only one way the night ends up, me alone, just like every other night. So I decide to lean into it. If he can enjoy it, so can I.

"Mmm." I slide my hand into his hair, tugging on it slightly as we deepen our kiss. His hand is around my throat, his tongue playfully coaxing mine. "Just imagine how much better I taste elsewhere." I suck his tongue, eliciting a growl from his chest that sounds primal as his fingers dig into my inner thigh beneath the table.

"Oh, I've imagined it plenty of times, baby," he whispers in my ear, his fingers tightening against my throat slightly. "That's the problem."

Seconds later our very public display of affection is interrupted by our waiter with a large tower of oysters.

"Oysters for the table," he says, placing them down and pointing out the different sauces.

I feel overwhelmed, the intensity of what just transpired between us leaving me struggling to focus on what he just said. "So, how do we eat them?"

Atlas leans forward, taking a shell in his hands and placing it at my lips. "Simply open and swallow." The double entendre isn't lost on me as I eye the strange lump of goo on the shell in front of me.

"I don't chew it?"

"No." He continues holding the oyster out toward me. "Just try one, Stella." I open my lips slightly, but then close them again. "Open your mouth," he says a little firmer this time. I go to reach for the glass of champagne in front of me, but he grabs my hand and shakes his head. "No champagne until you try one. Now"—his hand squeezes my thigh again—"I won't say it again so open your pretty fucking mouth like a good girl."

I obey, my mouth popping open as he tilts the shell and the oyster slides slowly into my mouth. I close my eyes, a salty brine taking over my taste.

"Swallow," he commands and I obey instantly, holding my breath as it slips down my throat. "Good girl." He winks, running his thumb over my bottom lip. He brings it to his mouth and licks it clean. "See, that wasn't so bad now, was it?"

"That was awful." I shiver, grabbing my glass of champagne and downing half of it to get the taste out of my mouth. "You enjoy that?"

He doesn't respond, just picks up an oyster and swallows it. "Do you always swallow?" he asks so nonchalantly, taking a long sip of his old fashioned.

"Excuse me?"

"Do you always swallow?" This time he looks right at me when he says it, any confusion on if I misheard gone.

"Uh." I blush, fumbling with my flute of champagne. "That seems like a very personal question."

"And?" He furrows his brow. "You're my wife, Stella."

"Yes, but..." I'm so confused on where this line lies between us.

"But what? I thought we agreed on no secrets."

"We did but I wouldn't call that a secret."

"What would you call it?" I watch as his fingers gently turn the tumbler in his hand. It's an innocuous movement, something so simple and yet so weirdly sexy. The ring on his pinky draws my attention. I reach forward and run my finger over the ring, his movements stilling.

"What's the significance of this ring?" He watches as I run my fingers over it, his hand moving slightly so that he can tangle it with mine.

"Answer my question and I'll tell you."

"Deal." I smile. "But you first."

"My mother gave it to me; it was her father's actually."

"Were you close to your mom?" His gaze is so fixated on our fingers that I don't think he heard me.

"Yes, for a while." Silence settles between us for a moment. I think the conversation is over but he continues. "When I was younger we were, but things seemed to change as I got older."

"Did something happen?"

"She said I was turning into my father." He smirks, letting out a small laugh before finishing his drink. "And like everyone else, she hated my father."

I want to ask why she hated him but I'm too scared to find out what kind of man his father was—and what kind of man I just married.

"Now," he says, tugging on my hand so that I fall slightly forward toward him, "answer my question." His hand is sliding behind my neck, his lips drawing closer to mine.

"There's only one way I'll answer the question." His cocky grin begins to fade as I lean in closer. "And it's more of a show, rather than tell situation." I pull back, confident I've one-upped him when he takes my hand that's in his and presses it firmly against his lap. I gasp when he wraps my fingers around his thick length that stretches impossibly long down his thigh.

"Trust me, if I thought you could handle it, I'd make you show me right now." He grips the back of my neck. "But judging from how you struggled to open wide enough for an oyster shell, there's not a chance in hell you could open wide enough to handle me."

———

"THIS IS UNREAL," I WHISPER TO MYSELF AS I SLIDE OPEN THE doors of the overwater bungalow. The ocean is a vast expanse of crystal clear turquoise waters that seems to stretch on forever. I run over to my bag and grab my phone, snapping several photos to send to Matilda, but they bounce, a *failure to deliver* notice popping up immediately.

"Shit, no service." In my excitement, I didn't even consider that I didn't have an international phone plan. I quickly put it into airplane mode, not wanting to incur crazy roaming charges.

"No, that's not the agreement and that won't be the agreement." Atlas' tone is clipped as he barks into his phone in one of the other rooms.

He has been solely focused on work since the second we lifted off in Chicago. Seeing as how he's a multibillionaire about to take a week off work, I'm not surprised. I just hope it doesn't interfere with his ability to relax and have a good time.

Too excited to wait any longer, I run into the bedroom. A large glass floor allows us to see the ocean floor. Stingrays dance beneath my feet. "Holy shit!" I fall back onto the massive king-sized bed, the cloudlike comforter engulfing me. I can't keep the huge grin off my face as tingles burst through my body.

Suddenly I sit up, realizing there's only one bed. I instinctively want to grab my phone and tell Matilda, but then I realize how weird it would seem to her that I'm excited and surprised that there's only one bed. My shoulders sag, remembering that I don't get to share this excitement with anyone else.

I jump up, not wanting to ruin the trip, and riffle through the clothes that were packed for me. They've all been hung up or neatly folded. I run my fingers over silk pajama sets that feel luxurious. Next to them are matching bra and panty sets made of lace and buttery soft material. I'm used to buying the five- or ten-pack of cotton under-wear, maybe splurging when one of the big chain stores has a five for thirty deal.

After finding the swimsuits, I pull out a simple white bikini and step into the bathroom to put it on. I glance in the mirror; it fits like a glove. I don't bother with sunscreen or a towel. I simply open the bathroom door and run back out into the main quarters, running as fast as I can and jumping cannonball style into the water.

"Having fun?" I spin around, Atlas standing at the edge of the water, staring at me.

"Yes." I push my hair back. "Come in. The water feels incredible." I swim to the ladder, hanging on to it as I try to coax him in.

"In a little bit. I have another call to make." My heart sinks. "But I promise once I take care of an issue at home, I'll join you."

An hour passes, then two and three... By the time he's off the phone, the entire afternoon has slipped away. I've showered, napped, and I've started getting ready for dinner.

"Sorry about that." He steps into the shared bathroom, leaning against the counter as I fasten my earrings.

"I know," I say with zero emotion. "Work." I know he can sense the frustration but he ignores it.

"You look beautiful." I feel him staring at me

"Thank you." I spritz myself with some perfume and I'm about to step out of the bathroom when he reaches out and grabs my elbow.

"I'm sorry, Stella," he says more earnestly. "Don't let it ruin our night?"

"Are you going to be working this entire trip?"

"Not entirely, no, but some, yes." I don't hide my disappointment. "Hey." He steps toward me. "Let me make it up to you."

"My choice?"

He smirks, probably expecting me to make some innuendo. "Is that a risk I should take?"

My frustration softens. "You have to go kayaking with me. I saw some people doing it today and it looked so fun."

"Done." He winks as he pulls his polo over his head and tosses it to the floor, his pants slung low on his hips. "Did you at least have fun out there today?" He grabs his electric toothbrush and squirts tooth-paste on it. His tanned abs flex with his movements, hair peppering his chest and stomach, disappearing beneath his waistband. I glance away, afraid I'm being too obvious.

"Uh, yeah. I just swam and laid out. The weather is perfect here." I lean into the mirror, pretending to check my makeup over. He reaches into the shower and turns on the water. I take the opportunity to look over at him and watch the muscles on his back and sides flex with his movements. He turns around and I quickly look back at the mirror, adjusting my halter dress.

"I noticed a little burn here." He touches my shoulder and it stings slightly. I look down and see a white fingerprint left against my pink skin.

"Oh, I didn't realize it was that bad." He touches me again, this time dragging his finger over my shoulder and down my shoulder blade.

"It stretches over your back as well." I watch him in the reflection of the mirror, his gaze focused on where his fingers are touching me. "Such a shame," he says softly. "Don't let it happen again." The sudden change in his tone is shocking. When I look back up into the mirror, his eyes are staring back at me.

"I-I didn't mean to. I just got excited and forgot sunscreen." I laugh a little nervously.

"Make sure you wear it tomorrow and put some aloe on that tonight."

"Okay," I say softly, unsure of how his mood will turn next.

"Good." He stands there for a second, his eyes focused back on my body. "You really do look good in this dress." His hand settles on my waist like he's completely forgotten about our *no sexual relation-ship* clause again. They inch lower, hovering so close to my ass, and then he releases me. "I should shower."

"Right," I say, reaching out to steady myself on the counter before turning around and pointing toward the door. "I'll just be—" I walk out the door, closing it behind me and heading straight to one of the chairs sitting on the balcony.

The sun has set, the silvery glow of the moon bouncing off the nearly still water surrounding us. It's still warm out but my skin is peppered with goosebumps from my sunburn. I close my eyes and savor the peace and tranquility this place offers. I have no idea how long I've been sitting with my eyes closed when I feel the warmth of Atlas' hands on my arms.

"What is my beautiful wife daydreaming about?"

My eyes flutter for a second, then close again as I relax into his touch. The warmth feels good against my skin, his lips lingering near my ear. His cologne hits me in a soft wave of sweet aroma. Everything about this man is tantalizing. He knows how to dress, how to command a room, yet when he's talking to me, it feels so intimate, so intense.

"Food." I smile, my belly grumbling.

"Tsk, tsk," he clicks his tongue softly, his hands gliding down to mine. He pulls me gently to my feet. "And here I thought you'd say you were dreaming about your perfect husband." His hand is around my back, the other holding my hand as he pulls me into a slow dance.

"Perfect?" I laugh. "Now who's the one daydreaming?" He pinches my side, making me laugh even harder before spinning me around.

"In my defense"—he smirks—"normally I can make up for my workaholic tendencies in other areas."

"Oh." I give a mock surprise expression. "You think you're *that* good you can make up for how much you work?"

"Yes," he says confidently.

"Really?" I offer a skeptical look. "And would your exes say the same?" He stops dancing, his confident smirk disappearing. It's the mask slipping again; his eyes darken but he's not angry. It's something else. He steps toward me, walking us backward a bit as he lifts his hands. I bump against the wall as he places his hands slightly above my head on either side of my face. He leans in.

"Stella, I could make you come without lifting a single fucking finger toward you." His voice is low and hushed.

I know I shouldn't. I even bite my cheek so I won't, but it's no use. I narrow my gaze, sliding my hand to reach down between us where his cock is pressing against my thigh. I run my hand down his length, his chest falling as he lets out a heavy breath. His eyelids flutter, falling closed as I wrap my fingers partially around his girth and continue to stroke him.

"I doubt it."

His eyes fly open, his head jerking upright. I pause my movements, releasing him from my hand.

"I didn't tell you to fucking stop." His voice sounds strained. I look up at him, his lids heavy as I reach back down and touch him again. His eyes stay open this time and I can't seem to look away. I want more of him. I want to feel his body. I look down at my hand, reaching with my other one to slowly pull his belt from the buckle. It clanks loudly when I undo it. My eyes turn upward, expecting him to come to his senses, but he doesn't stop me. He continues watching me as I slide the zipper slowly down until I can reach inside his boxer briefs and wrap my hand around him—or at least attempt to. I pull him free, his fully rigid cock standing straight upward, my fingers not even close to being able to touch as I grip him. My eyes grow wide at the length as well. He wasn't kidding when he said I'd have to unhinge my jaw to take him.

"Oh, Jesus. Fuck." He grunts, looking down at me as I grip him. "Do you have any idea what this is going to do to me?" His voice sounds pained as he watches me. I wrap my other hand around him, both of them holding him as I open my mouth and lean down, but before I make contact, he pulls himself away and shoves himself back into his pants. He winces, adjusting himself as he resecures his belt and zipper.

I stand there confused and somewhat in shock as to what he just allowed to happen. I reach my hand out toward him. "I'm sorry if I—"

"Don't apologize," he bites back, reaching for my hand. "Let's just go to dinner."

When we reach the restaurant and we're shown to the table, I quickly walk around the table and pull my chair out, taking a seat and picking up the menu to distract myself from the swift mood change only moments ago.

I notice Atlas doesn't take his seat. He waits for the host to leave, smiling at him before walking over to my side of the table. He reaches for the menu, taking it from my hand and placing it down on the table.

"I was looking—"

"You do that again and we're going to have a little talk," he interrupts, leaning down to look at me, his voice calm and even.

"Do what?"

"Pull out your own chair."

"Oh, sorry," I mutter, confused at how serious he's taking this.

"Have some patience, hmm?" He lifts his brows at me, his presence over me imposing and a touch exciting.

"It won't happen again."

"No, it won't," he says, finally taking a seat, his eyes still glued to mine.

The food is fantastic and the wine is refreshing but I'm struggling to enjoy it, the scowl on Atlas' face putting a damper on the evening. I finish my first glass of wine, the waiter quickly pouring me another that I waste no time enjoying.

"Are you trying to get drunk?" he asks, not bothering to look up at me from his plate.

"Are you trying to be an asshole to me?" He glares and I glare back, the wine already giving me a little more courage than usual. "Might as well if you're going to continue to have extreme mood swings."

He places his fork on his plate slowly, picking up his napkin to gently wipe his mouth before replying. "You know, when you speak to me in that manner"—he places his elbows on the table and leans forward slightly—"it really makes it hard for me not to shove my cock down your throat so you can't speak at all."

I almost choke on my wine but I don't want to give him the satis-faction of shocking me. I finish the second glass in record time, smiling at Atlas as the waiter scurries over to pour me a third. "A little more," I say, gently tipping the bottom of the bottle.

"For the record, darling"—he smiles—"I wasn't mad or frustrated at you. I'm frustrated and upset with myself about earlier."

"Look." I hold up my hand. "If you're going to give me a speech about how it was a mistake or you regret it, can we not do that? I'm already well aware that this is fake." I make sure to lower my voice even though we are seated privately away from anyone else. "No woman alive wants to hear how she was a mistake or a regret."

"I wasn't," he says confidently, and it surprises me. "I was going to say that I'm frustrated because all I can fucking think about while sitting here is wondering if you are as wet and frustrated and turned on as I am hard right now."

"Oh." My mouth falls open.

"Is your cunt tight?"

"Uh." My eyes bug out, my mouth hanging open now.

"I know it is." He casually leans back, like he's talking to me about the weather or golf. He holds his tumbler of liquor in one hand as he stares at me. "I bet you have a tight pink cunt that tastes like pure heaven." He sips his drink and I chug my wine, my cheeks so warm I'm not sure if it's shock or my sunburn. "Have you been complimented before on how you taste?"

"Yes," I say as if this is a completely normal conversation. He nods, taking another sip.

"When you masturbate with your pink cock, do you fuck yourself with it?"

I nod, looking around to make sure no one can hear our conversa-tion. "Sometimes."

"Can you come like that?"

"Only when I do it." He cocks his head slightly.

"Meaning you've never come when a man is fucking you?"

"I have but I was helping myself along," I reiterate.

"But when you masturbate and you fantasize, you can orgasm just penetrating yourself?"

"God." I laugh, half-embarrassed and completely turned on. "This is such an awkward conversation."

"Awkward to discuss your orgasms with your husband?"

"With you, yes." I take another drink. "Especially considering we're probably the only married couple alive who haven't actually had—yes," I say, trying to stop myself from rambling and making this even more awkward. "Yes, I can make myself orgasm through just penetration."

"Sounds like a lack of stimulation from your partners."

"Mmm, maybe or maybe it's because I know how to make myself come."

"What do you fantasize about when you're doing it?"

"I don't know—" I lie, grasping at anything to say that sounds believable other than *you.*

"What were you fantasizing about the night you were getting off right before I came over?" He lifts his glass to his lips so casually and once again I'm struck at how turned on I am with zero expectation or hope this is going anywhere.

"What are we doing? What is the point of this conversation again when we aren't sleeping together?" I finally ask out of desperation before I melt into a puddle in my seat.

He stands up and reaches for my hand. "Shall we?"

I stand, my hand in his as I stare at him in confusion. He ushers us from the restaurant to the wooden walkways that surround the property as we head back to our bungalow.

"Dinner was good," I say as we walk through the door.

"Sit on the bed," he says before disappearing into the bathroom. I stand there momentarily before sliding off my shoes and walking to the bed to take a seat. When he returns, he pulls a chair to the end of the bed, sitting in it across from me.

"I need to see you come, Stella." I don't say a word; I just stare at him. "I'm going to sit here in this chair and watch as you fuck yourself and I don't want you to stop until you come."

"I-I... don't have a toy." I say the first thing that pops in my head. My nipples harden beneath my dress, my panties soaked at this point.

He smiles, reaching down to pick up something he set next to him in the chair, his electric toothbrush. "I know. I want you to fuck yourself with the handle end of my toothbrush." He holds it out toward me.

"Are you serious?"

He doesn't respond. He drops the toothbrush down beneath the hem of my dress and slowly slides it up my thigh till it's just shy of pressing against my panties. I grip the edge of the mattress with one hand reaching down to push his hand farther up.

"That's a good girl," he says softly, letting me move the toothbrush up and down my slit over my panties. "Now"—he takes my hand and wraps it around the brush part—"fuck yourself so I can watch."

He leans back in the chair, his hands resting on his spread thighs as his eyes drop down to where I lift my dress. I don't bother removing the entire thing, just lifting it above my waist. I lean back on one hand, my thighs falling open as I begin to tease myself. I press the handle against my clit harder, then release. I do it several more times before reaching down to pull my panties to the side.

Atlas lets out a low groan as his head tilts to the side. He watches me slowly pull my panties to the side, a sticky string of arousal still connected.

"Oh damn, you are wet." His hands ball into fists as he clenches his jaw.

"Ohhh," I groan as I slide the tip of the rounded handle inside me. I pull it back out, teasing myself several more times.

"Fuck me. Look at you having to stretch just to take that." His words make me grow slicker, allowing me to slide it in deeper. I watch him sit up slowly, reaching forward till his hand is around mine with the toothbrush. He presses a button, the toothbrush coming to life with a low buzz that has me clenching around it harder.

My legs fall farther open, and I lean back against my other hand as I begin to fuck myself, my head lulling back.

"Look at me, Stella." His voice startles me and I lift my head to meet his gaze. His eyes drop down, and he licks his lips, his fingers curling into fists. "What are you thinking about right now? What has your tight little pussy so wet, hmm?"

"Oh, oh, oh." I can't control what's coming out of my mouth right now. My body is tensing, my toes curling as Atlas watches my every movement. His jaw is clenched so tight as his eyes bounce between mine and what I'm doing.

I quicken my pace, the handle disappearing inside me over and over again. I'm on edge, so close to coming. Atlas stands, his cock rigid beneath his pants. He reaches down, holding my chin. "You're thinking about me, aren't you? Imagining my big cock stuffed inside you right now, about to flood your sweet little pussy."

"I-I'm coming." The words come out in a jumble.

"That's right, darling." His voice is calm and low. "Fuck yourself for your husband. I want to see my wife come," he encourages me as I look up at him, my eyes starting to close as my body comes undone. Wave after wave washes over me until finally it subsides. I open my eyes, Atlas still standing in front of me. He reaches down, slowly pulling the toothbrush from me.

"Ahh," I wince.

"Thank you." He runs his thumb across my bottom lip before turning to walk out of the room. I close my eyes and lie back, the wine hitting me along with the orgasm comedown. I expect that Atlas will wake me when he comes back into the room but when my eyes fly open hours later, he's nowhere to be found and I'm still asleep in my dress.

I sit up and look around, panic hitting me when I realize I'm in the ocean, alone. I stand and tiptoe toward the bedroom door, looking into the dark bathroom.

"Atlas?" I whisper his name, stepping into the living room area of the bungalow where he's asleep on a couch. My heart sinks. I had thought something transpired between us last night, but I guess I once again got caught up in the emotion. I trudge back to the bedroom, not bothering to change out of my dress before climbing back into bed and falling asleep.

When I wake the next morning, I go straight to the bathroom, indulging in an extra-long shower. I take my time doing my skincare and drying my hair, even trying on a few different swimsuits before settling on a pastel lavender one that offers a generous peek at my backside. The top is feminine with a ruffle that stretches up the straps. I fasten a long white cover-up around my waist and step out into the living room to see Atlas with a stunning breakfast spread.

"Good morning." He smiles, holding out a chair for me.

"Wow, when did this get here?"

"I had it delivered while you were getting ready. Are you hungry?"

"Starving." I take a seat and reach for a cup of coffee first. Before he can bring up last night, I remind him about our adventure today. "Are you excited for the kayaking? They're clear so there's a chance we can see sharks." I bounce my eyebrows. "Just in case you're too scared." I giggle and he gives me a smile but something is off.

"About that," he says and my stomach drops. "Unfortunately, there's been an issue with this deal I'm working on and I need to make some important calls that cannot be avoided."

"Oh." I don't hide my disappointment as I reach for a croissant and butter.

"But I did hire a local guide who is going to go with you; he's extremely knowledgeable and I'm told he knows all of the perfect shark-spotting spots."

I nod, making my best effort to smile but it's pointless.

"I'm sorry, I really am." He slides his hand over mine. "I promise, I'll make it up to you."

The kayaking was fun, not as fun as I'd hoped it would be with Atlas, but the guide was truly *extremely knowledgeable* and I even spotted a few sharks. By the time I got back, I was truly over Atlas having to bail on me but when he did the same for scuba diving and horseback riding, I gave up on spending any time with him.

The rest of my honeymoon is spent between books I downloaded on my Kindle, swimming by myself, or sleeping in one chair or another before moving to the hammock. Dinners feel stale and lifeless, conversation spurred on only by Atlas asking me a question about what I did that day or excusing himself to take a call.

I feel lonely, something I never expected to feel on my honeymoon, even if it is just a contract marriage. I sit on the edge of the balcony floor, my legs dangling over as I look off into the darkness. The sky is littered with stars tonight. I think back to my childhood, one of the only memories I still have was doing just this. I'd run away to some hiding spot I'd find, wherever I was living at the time, and on warm summer nights, I'd look up at the stars and make a wish on each one I could find.

My heart feels heavy as I think about all the people I'm hurting along this journey. A tear falls from my eye and down my cheek. I close my eyes and start to sing "Dream a Little Dream of Me" to myself, wondering how Clyde and the band are doing, telling myself that I just need to swallow my pride and tell him I was fired.

———

AFTER ARRIVING HOME FROM OUR HONEYMOON, I FOUND THAT Atlas had my furniture from my apartment moved into storage and all of my other belongings brought to his house.

"Well, what about my lease?"

"I paid it off," he says matter-of-factly as he tosses more mail into a pile on his desk.

"You could have approached me about all this beforehand. I would have preferred to pack my own stuff."

"Is there a real issue here, Stella, or are you just wanting to pick a fight? As you can see"—he gestures to an even bigger pile of papers on his desk—"I'm incredibly busy tonight and I just need to focus."

"There is an issue I'd like to talk you about, actually." I sit down in the chair across from him and his frown lines only deepen. "I really didn't appreciate how alone I was for most of the honeymoon."

He sighs. "I know and I really am sorry, Stella, I am. I just don't know what I can do to make it better."

"You can actually spend more time with me." He stares at me blankly as if this has never crossed his mind.

"Meaning?"

"Oh my God." I roll my eyes in frustration. "Just hang out sometimes. I get that you're busy, but do you ever just watch a movie at night or go bowling on the weekends or something?"

He chuckles and stands up, coming around to stand against his desk in front of me.

"No, I don't do those things. It's not for a lack of desire to hang out or have fun; I simply just don't have the time."

"Then make the time." I can feel my throat tensing. "I'm still your wife, Atlas."

"Yes, you are my wife, Stella, but as I outlined very clearly from the start of this arrangement, this is transactional."

"And that means that you can't even interact with me as if I'm a human? You'll watch me fuck myself with your toothbrush, but you won't even have dinner with me?"

Anger flashes across his face. "Watch your tone with me."

"I rarely see you and when I do, you're either upset with me or you want me or you're angry that you want me. I just—" I raise my hands in frustration and shake my head to avoid bursting into tears. He doesn't respond right away. He lets the silence linger before breaking it and making it more than clear where I stand with him.

"Correct me if I'm wrong, but I ate dinner with you every night of our honeymoon."

"Oh my God." I laugh to keep from crying. "Forget it," I say, rolling my eyes so far back in my head it hurts. It irritates him instantly, just like it always does.

"I'm very busy. I don't have the time and energy to devote to a real marriage or a traditional relationship; that is why I hired you. This marriage"—he points between us—"is nothing more than an inconvenience."

# Chapter 12

## *Atlas*

"What are you wearing?" I drop my tablet onto the table when Stella enters the kitchen, her ass on prominent display with her polo tucked into her tight jeans.

"My work uniform," she says dryly, clearly still upset from our talk last night. Not that I would consider it much of a talk. She simply stormed out of my office after I reminded her why this contract even exists in the first place.

"And why are you wearing it? As my wife, you don't work."

"But"—she picks up a yogurt and cocks her head to the side—"technically, I work *as* your wife, remember? Last night you said you hired me." I stare at her blankly, making it abundantly clear how unamused I am with her attitude. "I'm going in to give my two weeks and tell them the joyful news of our nuptials." She says the last part in a particularly sarcastic tone.

"There will be no two weeks." She stops halfway out the kitchen door and turns back around.

"Excuse me?"

"I need you to understand and follow the rules, Stella. They are clearly outlined in the contract and it will make this so much easier. Do you need to review it?"

"No," she says flatly.

"Good." I smile, reaching for my tablet again. "You can drop your uniform off and tell them the good news, but you're not working so go change." I don't have to look up from my email to know that if looks could kill, I'd be fucking obliterated right now. She turns to leave. "One more thing, sweetheart. Have you looked at the calendar my assistant sent over to you?"

"No." She keeps her back to me.

"Well, please do. We're having dinner with some very important people tonight."

She spins around. "No, Matilda invited me over tonight. She wants to hear about the wedding and honeymoon. I promised her a girls' night."

"Cancel it."

"No," she says matter-of-factly.

"Unless she is paying you five million dollars to be her wife, cancel it, Stella. I will not have this conversation with you again, am I clear?" I let the anger out. She needs to realize that I'm not wasting my time on her petty tantrums and bratty attitude problem. "I don't know if you think this is some kind of game or that you can flirt and manipulate me to get your way, but you signed a legally binding contract"—I point to the table, my voice booming—"so reschedule it for another night because you are attending this dinner."

The rest of my morning is complete shit. The look on her face as she hung her head in defeat and walked out of the kitchen has stuck with me. I feel like shit. I am a piece of shit. But the one thing I will stand behind is her responsibility to the contract. I need her by my side as my wife.

I feel the tightness in my chest again. I pick up my phone and send her a text, hoping it makes up for my lack of candor this morning.

**Me:** *Apologies for this morning if I was too aggressive with my word choices. I do hope everyone at the coffee shop was happy for you.*

I'm about to put the phone away when I see the three dots floating. Her response is almost immediate.

**Stella:** *I didn't tell them.*

I'm instantly annoyed but give her the benefit of the doubt that maybe she just didn't stop in yet.

**Me:** *Why not?*

This time, there's no three little dots. I leave the chat open on my phone, turning to focus on work. I glance back at my screen more than a dozen times, my focus completely shot. I pick it up and call her.

"Hello, darling," she says coldly.

"Why didn't you tell them?" I blurt out, trying to keep calm.

"Just didn't come up."

"Didn't come up?" She says nothing. "The fact you went on your honeymoon because you got married didn't come up when they asked about your trip?"

"Nope." She's trying to get under my skin. I let out a frustrated sigh because it's working.

"What have you done this afternoon?" I ask, trying to make conversation.

"Are you checking up on me?"

"No, I'm simply asking because I'm interested in your day." It's silent for several seconds.

"I was in the garden with Oliver. He was showing me around."

"Lovely." I smile against the phone. "Plan to be ready to leave by six."

"Yes, dear," she says sweetly. "I miss you already."

Her sarcasm makes me laugh. "Good to know you're still being a brat. I'll see you at dinner." I hang up the phone, turning my attention back to work, the only thing that can keep me from driving home right now and teaching her a lesson.

I OPT TO GET READY AT MY OFFICE SINCE THE DINNER IS downtown, Oliver bringing Stella when he picks me up. I slide into the back seat, Stella's perfume permeating the air. It's sexy with a hint of spice.

"Good evening." I look over at her dress, the blood red making her pale skin almost glow in the moonlight. She looks breathtaking, her hair in long curls down her exposed back. "I like the dress." She looks out the window, not bothering to reply. "Stella." I reach for her hand, but she pulls it away.

"Stella." This time I say her name more firmly as I grab her hand. "Look at me." She finally turns, her lips set in a hard line. "You're my wife, so please behave like it this evening."

"I am behaving like it. I'm a wife who's pissed at her husband," she snaps back.

"That may be but for now, put on a smile and get over it." Oliver puts the car in park and steps out to open our door in front of the restaurant. Several of the people here tonight are on the board. The door swings open and Oliver extends a hand to Stella who gracefully exits the car.

I rest my hand against the bare skin of her back, the material dropping so low that if my finger slips beneath it, I'll be touching her ass. That jealous rage rears its ugly head, my stomach knotting at the thought of other men looking at her. I know the thoughts that go through their heads as she walks across the room, her body making every man in the place practically break their neck to get a peek.

I slide my hand farther around her waist, tightening my grip on her as we head toward our table.

"Do you mind?" she says through a fake smile as she looks over at me. "You're going to leave bruises." She exaggerates but it only makes me hold her closer.

"I hope I do, then everyone will know you've been claimed,

sweetheart." My hand slides down and I grab her ass just as we approach the table.

"There's the man of the hour!" my attorney, Frank, says as he comes around the table to hug me. "Congratulations to the happy couple." He looks at Stella.

"Thanks. Frank, this is my wife, Stella. Stella, this is Frank, my attorney."

"Pleasure to meet you." She smiles, shaking his hand.

"Oh, trust me," he says, looking around at the table. "I think I speak for everyone when I say the pleasure is mine." He laughs and others join in.

I go around and introduce Stella to those she didn't meet at the function before the wedding and offer a hello to those she did.

"So before all of the boys start in," Frank's wife, Maureen, says giddily across the table, "can we hear how this happened?"

I look over at Stella, my arm around her. "Why don't you tell them." She gives me a look and I place my other hand gently on her thigh just beneath the table, out of anyone's eyesight. I lean in, whispering just low enough for her to hear, "And make sure it's good."

"Um, well." She grabs my hand that's on her thigh and tries to remove it but fails. "Atlas was a regular at the coffee shop I work at."

"Worked at," I clarify.

"Right, so he came in all the time and we made small talk and flirted and next thing you know, he was asking me out." I squeeze her thigh tighter. "I actually turned him down at first," she says, making everyone laugh. "And I thought if a man is willing to beg for a date, then what else is he willing to do?" With her wit and charm, she has the entire table eating out of the palm of her hand and I love it.

To me and everyone at this table, Stella is a fresh breeze in a stale world of uptight trust fund babies and people so consumed with their image or making a connection. She's just her, unapologetically. I slide my hand between her thighs, making her almost falter as she lifts her glass.

"But I think we all know well enough that I always get what I want." I settle my gaze on her as she sips her water. "In all seriousness though, she is the most amazing and complex woman I've ever met." I brush her hair over her shoulder, admiring her beauty. She stares back at me, unsure if I mean what I'm saying. "I knew the second I saw her, I had to have her. I had to make her mine." I lean in, planting the softest kiss on her lips. "Forever."

She's completely lost in my eyes, her lips parted. She extends her hand for a brief second like she's going to rest it against my chest, but then she snaps out of it. The icy coolness is back in her expression, her smile hollow as the table peppers us with questions.

I turn my attention to Frank, talking through a recent issue we're dealing with at work, Stella still talking to Maureen. Soon, the entire table is engrossed in the appetizers that appear and cocktails that continue to flow.

"How are you doing?" I ask Stella, tilting her chin to look at me.

"Fine."

"If you'll excuse us for a moment." I smile to the table, lifting Stella's elbow so she stands with me. I usher her though the room toward the bar.

"Are you going to punish me all night?" I motion toward the bartender and order us both another drink.

"I'm not punishing you; I'm angry at you."

"For?" I reach out for her, but she pushes my arm away. I reach for her again and pull her toward me. "I told you earlier, put on a happy fucking face tonight. These people don't need to see you angry or pushing me away. So act like we're head over goddamn heels," I scold, reaching for the drinks from the bartender. I place them on the bar and face her.

"You know why. It's like you go out of your way to make me feel less than or unwanted. Telling me I'm an inconvenience is a helluva way to start a marriage," she hisses.

"I didn't mean it to sound that way." She rolls her eyes again and it pisses me off. "I'm about to drag you into that bathroom and give you a fucking reason for your eyes to be in the back of your head like that." I reach out and grab her, pulling her toward me till our lips meet. The kiss is aggressive and heated but within a second it switches. My hands are on her waist, up her back, hers in my hair, both of us completely lost in each other's touch. I break contact, remembering we're in public. "Fuck."

"Uh-oh." She looks down to where my cock is pressing into her hip. "I hope you don't think that's an apology."

I laugh, dragging my hand over my face. "You are something else," I mutter. "Will you please just let us handle this thing between us when we get home tonight?"

"Fine, but you have to listen to me. I'm tired of you just throwing this contract in my face like I'm an idiot. There's more to what I'm saying and you know that. I'm not asking for a relationship, but come on."

I stare at her for a moment, unsure what to say because we're entering territory that I wasn't planning on entering. I didn't think out how I would include this person in my life. Call me an idiot but I thought anyone would jump at the chance to be left alone and get paid millions to show up to a few dinners here and there.

"Deal." I give her a warm smile, then reach behind her neck to pull her tightly against me. "But don't think for one moment I won't punish you if you push the boundaries again and try to defy me. If you choose to disobey me, Stella, I will make damn sure you learn a hard lesson. Do you understand me?"

"Yes."

"Good, now when we sit back down"—I pull her even closer, leaning in to run my lips over hers—"you better act like you are so over the moon happy in love with me that all you want to do is have my babies." I kiss her gently. "And suck my cock."

She more than sells it. I'm more than half convinced that she is in love with me. The way she smiles when she talks to me or about me, her hand reaching up to cup my cheek, the sexy way she's drawing little circles against my forearm. By the time we leave the restaurant, it feels like this was never an inconvenience. It's starting to feel real.

"Thank you," I say, reaching over to hold her hand on the way home. I twist my fingers around hers, wanting so bad to pull her into my lap. She closes her eyes, settling back against the seat the rest of the drive home.

"Good night." The second we're through the front door, she's walking up the stairs toward her bedroom.

"I thought we were talking."

"I don't feel like it." She continues up the stairs and turns the corner down the hallway. I take the stairs two at a time after her, lengthening my stride to catch her door just as she slams it shut.

"Go to my bedroom."

She spins around. "No." Her brow furrows. "I'm tired. I'm changing and going to bed."

"See, this right here is why I remind you about the contract. It outlined clearly that you are to obey me."

"And that means I can't have boundaries? I'm tired, Atlas."

"And I want you in my bedroom, now." I point toward the door, but she doesn't move. She crosses her arms over her chest defiantly. I take the two steps toward, grabbing her and tossing her over my shoulder.

"What the hell!" She pounds on my back as I walk her down the hall, kicking open my bedroom door before tossing her onto my bed. She bounces slightly, sitting up and attempting to scoot off, but I lean down and pin her to the bed.

"We are not going to bed angry," I insist, pinning her hands above her head as I stretch across her body.

"Then apologize!" she says, pulling against my grip, but it's no use.

"I'm sorry," I say. "I really am sorry for making you feel like an idiot, but you try my patience."

"I won't apologize for that. I'm a strong-willed woman and I won't be treated as less than." I stare down at her, finally releasing her arms and sitting up. She sits up too, rubbing her wrist. I take her arm, running my hands over where I just left a red mark.

"I would never want you to apologize for that. I really like that about you. Respect that, actually. I think we just need to learn to communicate better but," I say, before giving in completely, "I do demand a level of obedience from you. If it's on the calendar, you have to attend. Obviously not if you're sick but there's no more excuses, Stella. I need you in this with me."

She nods, scooting to the edge of the bed to sit next to me. "Deal. I can try to be better at communicating as well." I bump against her shoulder and she finally smiles at me.

"Would you like to watch a movie?"

"Really?" Her eyes light up. "Yes, I'd love to."

"Great. How about we change, you pick the movie, and I'll grab a dessert."

When she returns a little later, she's in a pale-pink pajama set with strawberries all over them, her hair in a wild bun on top her head and her face washed clean of makeup. Her bare legs grab my attention but I quickly look back up to her face, my eyes wanting so bad to linger on her breasts which I'm almost confident are braless beneath her top.

She stands in my bedroom doorway. "Should I meet you in the living room or do you have a secret theater in this house?"

"I do have a theater." I tilt my head, trying to remember the last time I used it. "I think there is anyway."

"Of course there is." She laughs.

"But no, we'll watch it in here." I reach for the remote on my nightstand and hit a button, a custom flat-screen TV coming into view at the base of the bed.

"Did that just come up out of the ground?" She walks over and looks at it.

"It's built into the bed frame." I reach into my pajama pockets and pull out a few bags of candy I grabbed from the pantry downstairs. "Not sure what your preference is but I picked fruity and chocolate."

"So, we're watching it in bed?"

"Yes. Why? Nervous?" I tease her.

"No, we both know your rules."

"Yeah, well, we both know you've gotten me to break them, haven't you?" She pauses mid crawl onto the bed.

"I didn't make you break them."

I stare at her, my eyes going straight down her shirt where I see a full glimpse of her tits. "Yes, you did, doing shit like that," I say, motioning toward her shirt. She looks down and stands back up.

"Oh, come on, that wasn't on purpose."

"But wearing no bra with a thin little top while lying in bed with me is." Once again, I don't know where I'm going with this or why I feel it's necessary to torture myself like this.

"Is movie night going to turn into a fight?"

"No," I say, walking across the room and grabbing one of my hoodies. I toss it toward her. "Put this on."

To my surprise, she doesn't argue. She slips the hoodie on, grabs a bag of candy, and situates on my bed.

"What are we watching?" I lean forward, grabbing a bag of candy myself as she picks up the remote and flips through the screens till she finds the romantic comedy she's searching for. She hits play and settles back against the pillows.

"It looked cute. Rumor has it the actors were hooking up during filming so the chemistry is off the charts."

I smile, watching her pop a candy in her mouth between fits of laughter. She is far more interesting to me than any movie could be. Her laugh, her smile, the way she kicks her leg out at a particularly funny part.

"What?" She eyes me.

"Nothing." I shrug, turning my attention back to the movie.

As much as she tries to fight it, I can see sleep slowly taking over her body. Her eyes grow heavy, her head nodding to the side. Finally, her breathing deepens and her hand slides from where it's resting on her pillow down to the bed.

I watch her sleep, running my fingers gently through her hair.

She looks peaceful and younger than her twenty-four years. Suddenly it hits me; she doesn't have any family. She told me that. It's no wonder the small things are important to her, the little gestures of spending time, a dinner, or even a movie matter so much. My heart aches at the thought of her feeling rejected by every person in her life growing up and even worse at the thought that I've contributed to it.

# Chapter 13

## *Stella*

Something is different. He's been nothing but pleasant since the night we watched a movie in his bed almost a week ago. I can't put my finger on it. Maybe he's planning to kill me for the life insurance after I get comfortable in the sham marriage.

"Stella?" I nearly jump out of my skin when I hear his voice, my phone flying onto the floor. "Hey, are you okay?"

"Yeah, yes." I stand up and turn around. "You just scared me is all."

"I have to fly to Kansas for a meeting. I'll be gone for no longer than a day."

"You're going to fly there and fly back the same day?"

"That's the plan," he says, straightening his tie. It's still a touch askew so I walk over to him and reach out to adjust it. His hands settle against my waist, like this is just a typical Monday with a typical married couple. "Would you like to come with me?"

I release his tie and step back. "What for?"

He shrugs. "No reason. I wasn't sure if you had anything going on this week."

I shake my head. "I don't. I guess I could come since it's just a day trip. Why not?"

"Great, I'll let the flight crew know to expect you."

"I don't need an overnight bag or anything, right?"

"No." He glances at his watch. "I'll be heading to the airport in about thirty minutes." He winks at me, then walks out of my room.

Thirty minutes later we're on our way to the private airport. Thirty-five minutes after that, we're in the air, headed to Kansas. A few hours later, we land beneath a darkened sky, the wind starting to pick up.

"Stay with Mac while I'm at my meeting." He grabs his phone and pulls his jacket on before cupping my chin and tilting my head upward. "I'll head straight back to you when I'm done." Something in the way he phrased that has my lower belly doing flips.

"Good luck."

Within two hours of him leaving, the sky has turned black. Rain mixed with hail pelts the ground. We moved from the airplane into the hangar, alarms starting to ring out around us.

"What's that?" I ask Mac who's texting someone furiously.

"Sounds like a tornado alarm."

"Tornado?" I shout, reaching for my phone. "Where's Atlas?" I no sooner say his name than a black SUV pulls up, Atlas jumping out almost before it's stopped. He grabs me, wrapping his arms around me as he pulls me into the lobby of the small airport.

"There's a big storm rolling in. All flights are grounded."

"For how long?"

"I don't know. Judging by what they're showing on the radar, it's going to be several hours."

"Is it bad?" I ask anxiously.

"It's a big storm, Stella, but it's going to be okay. First, let's find a hotel in case it comes to that point. I'd rather not be trying to find one once the storm gets worse."

He calls his assistant, explaining the situation to her and talking through hotel options. "What do you mean there aren't any rooms?" I look over at him. "A what convention?" He rubs his temples. "No, it's fine, it's fine, Florence. Thank you. We'll figure it out, don't worry." He hangs up and looks over at me.

"There are no rooms. Apparently, there's some huge beef convention in town."

"I saw a motel down the interstate, boss; I could drive down and see what they have," Mac says.

He hesitates. "Okay." Fifteen minutes later, Mac's calling him. "They do? Great, yeah, that works just fine. Thanks, Mac."

"They have rooms?"

"A room." He stands up and walks over to his flight crew. I can't hear what they're saying but he nods and shakes a few hands before walking back over to me. "The flight crew and Mac will stay on the plane since there seems to be no rooms for them. You and I will stay at the motel."

Rain pelts the SUV as Mac drives us to the motel, the windshield wipers struggling to keep up with the torrential downpour. There's no awning to pull beneath when we reach the motel so even in the short distance of running from the SUV to the room, we're practically soaked.

"Ugh." I wring out my hair, glancing around the room. It's clean but it's old and very clearly in need of some major updates. Thunder claps loudly, rattling the giant glass window in the front of the room.

"Not as nice as the Maldives," Atlas says, touching the plastic-covered chair that sits by a small table in the corner. I burst into laughter, making him smile.

"I've never been to Kansas before." I kick off my shoes and wet socks, sitting on the squeaky bed. "Any suggestions for fun activities?"

"During a possible tornado?" He unbuttons his shirt, walking over to a small cabinet in the corner. He opens it, revealing a makeshift mini bar full of different shooters. "Get drunk in our hotel room?"

———

I HOLD MY NOSE AND TILT MY HEAD BACK, THE BURN OF THE Fireball making me scrunch my face up. "Gah!" It sizzles in my nose. "That is the worst!"

"Nah." Atlas shakes his head and looks over at me from where he's lying on his back on the bed. "The Ninety-Nine Bananas was worse."

I toss the bottle into the wastebasket to join the four others we've already had. "Okay, I'm ready." I sit in the chair we've designated as the contestant's seat. I open my mouth and place my hands on the armrests. Atlas sits up, grabbing a Junior Mint from the box we bought in the front office at the motel earlier.

He closes one eye. "Don't move," he says before launching the candy perfectly into my mouth.

"Perfect aim every time." I laugh, chewing the candy and swallowing it. We've managed to make a small picnic with mixed nuts, chips, and candy that we bought from the vending machine and entertained ourselves so far with games and small talk. I flop back on the bed next to Atlas, both of us staring up at the ceiling as the wind whips around the building violently. The reporter on The Weather Channel, in between bouts of lost power, assured us earlier that the tornado that was spotted has since downgraded to a wind shear, but power lines were down and flights were still grounded.

"Now what?" he says, looking over at me, his hair hanging down over his eye.

"Another shot?"

"Mmm," he groans, closing his eyes. "I'd rather take a nap."

"Then take a nap." I roll onto my stomach and for some reason I reach my hand out and rest it on his chest. He reaches up almost instantly, wrapping his hand around mine. I watch as he runs his thumb over my skin, his eyes still closed. I look at his full lips, the little curve running from his lip to his chin begging to be kissed.

"Don't do it," he says without opening his eyes. My eyes dart to his.

"I wasn't doing anything."

"Mm-hmm. I know you, Mrs. Knight," he says with a little smirk on his face.

I decide to test the waters, his flirty demeanor egging me on. I start to slide my hand down from his chest to his belly. He chuckles so I move it a little farther down till I reach his belt buckle. This time he grips my hand, stilling my movements.

"You really are a naughty young woman." He turns his head to look at me. "And you really don't like obeying the rules, do you?"

"How come you get to break them, but I don't?"

"I didn't break them."

"Pardon me?" I sit up, propped up on my elbow. "Pretty sure on our honeymoon you violated me in ways that would absolutely constitute as breaking the rules."

"Violated," he repeats the word and smiles, reaching out to run his thumb over my bottom lip. "Is that what I did to you?" I dart my tongue out to touch his finger. "For the record, you violated yourself, darling. I simply watched."

"That's all you did was watch? What about after?" I crawl over to where he's lying and swing my leg over the top of him. I grab his hands and pin them up over his head like he did to me before. "Care to share with the room what happened between yourself and your hand when you left me alone in the bedroom?"

His dark, hooded eyes study mine. "You really shouldn't tease me, Stella."

I grip his wrists tighter, leaning forward so my breasts are pressed against his chest. "And what are you going to do about it, Atlas?" He stares at me but he makes no effort to make a move. I release his wrists, removing my leg from him and flopping back down on the bed. "Allll talk," I mutter half to myself.

"If you knew who you were dealing with"—he reaches over and

smacks my ass so loud it reverberates around the room—"you would watch your tongue."

"Ow!" I push his hand away. "So..." I roll onto my back again, turning the conversation away from anything sexual since clearly I'll just be left frustrated and unsatisfied. "What do you do for fun? You said you don't go bowling, you don't go to the movies. Do you have a secret hobby nobody knows about or are you a big gamer nerd behind closed doors?"

"Nothing. I do nothing for fun."

"That's sad. Everyone needs an outlet." I stare at the ceiling, thinking about mine and how much I miss it. I close my eyes, imagining being back at Freddy's. I can almost feel that warmth of the spotlight on my eyelids.

Without warning he rolls toward me, grabbing me around the waist with one hand, the other around my neck, and kisses me. I'm still for a second, my hands frozen stiff against his chest. I expect him to roll away and tell me that's to shut me up or that he's going for a walk or to do some work. But he doesn't. He kisses me harder, deeper, longer than he ever has before. His body is over mine, his hips pressing up and against me, hitting my clit as my thighs fall open to him.

"I need to feel you," he grunts into my neck as his hands slide beneath my shirt, cupping my breasts. He sits up, pulling me with him in one swift motion. Seconds later my shirt is on the floor, his fingers teasing my nipples as he bites down on my bottom lip. His fingers slip beneath one strap, pulling it till it falls off my shoulder. He doesn't stop. He traces the edge of the strap till he reaches the corner of my bra cup and tugs it down slowly.

"Ohh," he says in the most delicious way possible, like he's about to fall to his knees and worship me. "You have the most delicious tits." He wraps his mouth around my nipple, twirling his tongue around the tip before biting down and making me gasp. "So fucking perfect," he murmurs, pulling down the other cup to repeat the process on my other breast.

"Don't stop," I groan, my hands in his hair as my back arches forward. He teases my nipples, licking and biting them as his hands hold my waist, pulling me down hard against his erection.

"Wait," he says, his movements stilling. "We shouldn't." He pushes me off his lap and back onto the bed. "We can't."

"Why?" I cover my breast, feeling vulnerable.

"I have nothing to offer you, Stella, besides that contract." His words sound almost pained, like he wishes things were different.

"I don't need anything," I say, reaching for him. "It can just be what it is, whatever happens between us."

He looks down at where my hand holds his. He shakes his head, stepping away and walking out the motel room door.

# Chapter 14

## *Atlas*

I slam the door, walking down the sidewalk as the rain pelts my body. I have no idea where I'm going or what I'm doing. Until Stella, I have never craved or needed a woman so carnally before that I can't control myself. My body aches to feel her, to hold her, to kiss her, but right now, all I want to do is fuck her mercilessly. I walk to the end of the row of rooms, standing in the pouring rain for a few seconds before turning back and marching toward the room.

I swing the door open so hard it bangs against the wall behind it, then closes. Stella jumps, her arm across her bare breast as the other holds her bra. I cross the room, my hands in her hair as I devour her mouth. I press her against the wall behind us, lifting her body till her legs wrap around my waist.

"Wh—"

"Shut the fuck up," I say between kisses, slowing down our pace so I can enjoy her lips. I step away from the wall, turning around so that I can lay her on the bed. Her dark hair pools around her body, her tits bouncing when she hits the mattress. I reach down, grabbing both of them in my hands. "I have imagined your tits a thousand times and they are so perfect it's unreal." I lean in and suck on her nipples. "Pure fucking torture knowing," I mutter, thinking about how I'll ever be able to resist her again.

"Kiss me." She reaches out toward me, tugging on my shirt. I oblige, leaning down to kiss her again. She brushes my damp hair from my face, her eyes staring into mine, the little mewls she makes into my mouth as her body writhes beneath mine driving me crazy. She grabs the hem of my shirt, tugging to get it up and over my head. Her hands are immediately on my chest, her nails sending tingles down my spine as she drags them over my chest and down my belly toward my belt.

"I'm going to fuck you so thoroughly"—I grab her hands, sliding them above her head—"so deeply you're going to be helpless against me." I lean down and bite her nipple. "Your slick little cunt is going to take however much cock I want to give you."

"Yes, please." She arches her back, tugging against my wrists. I release her, sitting up so I can reposition her. I grab her legs behind her knees, placing them on either side of me before tugging her closer to the edge of the bed. I stand, reaching down to slowly unzip her pants, sliding them down over her hips. I admire her almost naked body, her white lace thong panties sitting high on her full hips.

"Jesus Christ." I run my hand over my jaw, my mouth watering at the smell of her arousal. I place one knee on the bed, leaning forward on my arm to kiss her. I don't stop this time. I drag my tongue and lips down her neck and between her breasts. I reach her belly, my cock begging for release as I reach the edge of her panties. Her hips lift as if she's trying to reach any part of me for friction.

"I want to prolong this for as long as possible, baby." I hook my thumbs into the waistband of her underwear, her hips doing that little lift to assist me as I drag them slowly down her legs. "I want to spend hours." I kiss her thigh. "Days." I kiss her again. "Weeks worshipping your cunt." I slide her knees open, her pussy lips spreading open for me. She gasps when I lean down, sliding my tongue right up her center, pressing it inside her so I can drown my tongue in her juices.

"Ohhhh, yesss." She reaches down, pressing my face against her pussy as I devour her. "Right there, baby, right there." She's practically coming undone as she grips my hair, almost fucking my face. I grab her around the waist, flipping her over onto her stomach and hoisting her ass into the air so she's completely open and exposed to me.

"You like my tongue deep in you, baby?" I smack her ass, watching it jiggle before spreading her cheeks apart and sliding my tongue even deeper inside her pussy. She writhes against me. "Don't be shy, Stella. Fuck yourself on my tongue."

She obeys, her hips swaying back and forth as I continue to eat her. Her chest is pressed down into the bed, her body starting to shake as she fists the sheets in her hands. Her pussy is throbbing, her cum on my tongue as she finally finds release. I don't stop though. I flip her onto her back, burying my face in her pussy as I try to savor every last drop of her.

When I finish, I stand, looking down at her limp body as she stares up at me. She's out of her mind with lust right now, her eyes heavy-lidded, her pussy lips red and swollen already. A surge of adrenaline and excitement pumps through me.

"I could get away with doing anything to you right now, couldn't I?" I maintain eye contact as I slowly undo my belt. Her lips part like she's going to say something but her eyes pull her attention to what my hands are doing. "You want your husband's cock?"

Her eyes dart to mine. "Yes, please." She says it so sweetly it makes me chuckle.

"Such a good girl when you want to be, aren't you?" I pull the belt free.

"What do you want to do to me?" She sits halfway up onto her elbows.

"Oh, there's a lot of things I'd like to do to you." I smile, unzipping my pants and sliding them down my legs along with my underwear. I stand back up, my cock bouncing with the movement, making Stella's eyes bulge. "Did you forget how big my cock was, sweetheart?" I wrap my hand around it, stepping to the very edge of the bed. I stroke myself, my pecs tensing, my abs flexing as I groan. "First thing I want to do to you"—I extend a finger and motion for her to come forward—"is see if you can fit my cock in your smart mouth."

"I can handle it," she says, coming to her hands and knees, a confident little smirk I want to fuck off her face.

I grip her chin. "Yeah? Well, we're about to find out, aren't we?" I place the tip of my cock on her lips, sliding it past them as her lips stretch wide to accommodate my girth. "That's right, baby." I hold my breath as her warm lips embrace me, her wet tongue hitting the underside of my head and making my legs go weak. "Fuck me! Yesss," I hiss as she bobs her head an inch or two up and down my shaft. "Time to take me deeper," I groan as I slide into her mouth another two inches. Her eyes water, and she gags but she refuses to stop. "You're a greedy little thing."

I have no control over what I'm saying but the second I go in deeper, she pulls away, gagging and coughing as she falls back on the bed. She wipes her mouth with the back of her hand before crawling back over to me, lips parted, ready for more.

"Stella." I tilt her chin upward, pausing her movements. "Baby, trust me, I love the thought of fucking your mouth, but you're not ready for that. I'm not going to hurt you." She nods, sitting back on her heels.

"That being said, I am going to stretch the limits of your pussy tonight." I crawl over her, dragging kisses up her body to her lips where I linger. My fingers start to toy with her, rubbing circles over her clit and down her slit. "I want you aching tomorrow." She claws at me like she's in heat. "I want my cum dripping from you when you walk onto that plane." I slide a finger inside her, pumping it in and out before adding a second.

"Oh God, yes, please, more," she begs, panting as I press on her clit and hit her G-spot at the same time. Her body is vibrating beneath me. "Oh, oh, oh." Her hips move in time with my thrusting.

"That's right, baby. Take what you want." I watch her trying to come on my fingers as she reaches down to grab my cock. I love seeing a woman take what she needs, a woman who isn't afraid to tell me how good it feels. Eleanor was reserved, even cold at times in the bedroom. She let me be rough with her when she knew I needed it, but she never asked for it and even when I could tell it was an earth-shattering orgasm for her, she would simply thank me and excuse herself from our bedroom.

"Are you ready for me?" I line the head of my cock up with her entrance, pushing in an inch as I watch her lips grip me.

"Yes, please, Atlas, please."

I didn't think my cock could get any harder but hearing my name coming from her lips while I'm inside her proved me wrong. "Please what, Stella? What do you want me to do to you?" I slide in farther, then pull out, sliding in again as her hips start to move. I want to hear her say it. I want to hear her beg me to take her.

"Ah," she winces in pain as I slide in farther. "Fuck me," she says in a hushed moan. "Please." Her eyes roll back in her head when I tilt my hips and hit her G-spot. "Fuck me till I scream."

I plunge my cock deeper into her, her cries a mix of pain and pleasure. I slide my hand up her body, wrapping around the base of her throat as I use the momentum to pull her body down against my cock.

I press my forearm against her chest. Her hands are on my back, clawing at me, her fingernails digging into my ribs. I bite her bottom lip, hitting her G-spot one more time before her orgasm takes over. Her pussy clenches around me, her walls spasming against my cock, milking every last drop of cum from me as I explode inside her.

I hold her against me, both of us struggling to catch our breath. My cock is still firm, twitching inside her every time her walls pulse. I push her sweaty hair away from her face, kissing her. Her eyes have the most satisfied, lazy lull to them.

"Just remember this the next time you want to be disobedient, Stella." I kiss her again, her tongue inviting me in. She giggles, pulsing against my cock on purpose as she sucks on my tongue.

"Is this how you plan to punish me when I disobey? Because I don't think it's going to deter me."

"No, darling." I roll her to her back, pressing up and into her once she's flat, making her moan. "This is how daddy rewards you when you obey."

# Chapter 15

## *Stella*

"Now what?" I look up at Atlas from where I'm lying on his chest. His hand pauses from dragging back and forth across my back.

"What do you mean?"

"Now that we've broken the rules, are we going to burst into flames when the sun comes up?"

"Very funny." He reaches down and pinches my ass, his voice thick with sleep. "What do you want to happen?" He closes his eyes, propping one hand behind his pillow and settling against it.

I shrug, even though he's not looking at me. "Why can't we spend more time together?"

"It's not that we can't; it's just that I'm always working."

I trace circles on his chest. "Is it that you don't want to spend time with me?" He tenses beneath my touch, his eyes fluttering open.

"No. I enjoy spending time with you." He looks down at me. "A lot actually." His stare lingers, then he pulls me against his chest and wraps his arms around me.

"Then make time for me," I say quietly against his neck.

"It's not like that, Stella." He pulls me away so I'm looking in his eyes. "You know that. It—it can't be like that between us." I nod, pushing down the lump in my throat.

"I meant," I say, sliding my hand down his chest. "This kind of time," I whisper in his ear as I wrap my fingers around his length. I stroke him, moving down his body to take him in my mouth. "I am your wife after all." His cock jumps in my hand. I lean forward, taking him in my mouth, his hands in my hair as he watches me. "Would be a shame if my husband was too busy to be satisfied." I take him deeper this time, relaxing my throat and breathing through my nose.

"Oh fuck, yes, you are," he grunts, "but you suck cock like a fucking slut." He grunts with every breath as he pushes my head down onto him. My jaw aches but hearing him lose control is turning me on. He sits up, grabbing me by the underarms and pulling me up so I'm straddling his lap. He holds his cock, pressing me down till the tip presses inside me.

"Slow." I grip his arms. "It hurts."

"Only my cock," he says, grabbing the back of my neck so that I'm looking at him. "Right?"

"What?" I search his eyes, confused.

"You only suck my cock like a little slut, right?"

"Yes." I nod. "Only yours," I say against his lips as I wrap my arm around his neck.

"You belong to me." He pulls me down further onto him. "You're mine, Stella. My wife." He kisses me urgently, like he can't get close enough to me.

"Yes." I lift myself up, slowly starting to move on his cock, his hands on my hips. "I'm yours," I breathe, "only yours."

He keeps his eyes on mine, only looking away when they flutter shut in pure bliss. Our bodies are slick with sweat, the air conditioner going in and out with the loss of power from the storm.

We continue like this, my body allowing multiple orgasms to flow through me as Atlas doesn't stop. Whatever is transpiring between us is more than either of us probably want to admit or can probably even put into words. My heart tells me it's more, that the look in his eyes when he asked if I was his was fear, fear of the reality that a year from now, I won't be.

When we've finally finished, he places his hand on my belly. "I feel extremely irresponsible right now. I didn't use protection or ask if you were comfortable not using it."

"Oh." I suddenly realize we've both been incredibly irresponsible. "Well, I'm to blame just as much. I think we both assumed it wouldn't be an issue in our marriage." I laugh nervously.

"I'm not worried about giving you anything, I have only been with one person in the last five years before you and I've been tested since things ended." I'm shocked. This is the first bit of personal relationship information he's offered to me. "And you?"

I shrug. "I get tested weekly so no, nothing to worry about on my end."

"Weekly?" His brow arches.

"I'm twenty-five." I smile. "What can I say, I enjoy being social." I can see a flash of something on his face and before he flies across this bed, I burst into laughter, "I'm kidding!" He glares at me. "I've had a test at my annual visit and nobody since then, so no worries." I watch as relief washes over his face and I think back to the look on his face the first time he saw me talking to Jason.

*Was it jealousy?* I feel a flicker of hope in my stomach.

"When was your last annual visit?"

"Uh, about ten, eleven months ago? Guess I'll be due for another soon."

"You haven't had sex in a year?" He looks surprised.

"I guess not." I look away from him but he pulls my chin back to him. "What?"

"Are you on birth control?"

My breath catches. *Shit.* I shake my head. "I— No, I haven't needed to be."

"How long has it been?" I give him a questioning look. "Since you had sex."

"I don't know, at least a year, I guess." He gives me a coy grin. "Fine, it's been... a year or two—three," I finally admit. "It's been over three years." I jerk the sheets around me in exasperation, embarrassment flaming my cheeks.

"Hey." He reaches over to me, his hand sliding behind my neck so he can pull me closer. "Baby." The way he so casually calls me that instantly has me weak. "That's nothing to be ashamed of. Trust me." He drags his eyes down my body as he reaches down to pull the sheet from me. "You are a walking, talking fantasy that knows how to suck cock like an angel and fucks like a little demon." My thighs clench at his brash words and he notices. That devilish grin lazily pulls at his lips. "Truly, I don't know how you took it that hard, that many times tonight. Are you okay?" I stare at up at him. Gone is the cold, heartless CEO who's usually in control. His eyes soften as he looks at me, and his lips part like he's about to say so much more but then decides against it. "You need to sleep."

I yawn, stretching my arms overhead. "I'm so exhausted."

"You should be." His hand settles against my breast as he gently caresses it before moving over to the other. "You let me fuck you more times in one night than I ever have previously." He nuzzles against me. "And we still have the morning yet."

"It's your fault." I curl against his side. "Should have just stuck with the toothbrush."

"Good night, darling." He laughs against my temple, kissing me softly.

"Good night. Can I ask you one more thing about the contract?" I ask into the darkness.

"Mm-hmm."

"Did you ever think about what would happen if you did fall in love with the person who agreed to marry you?" Once again, I feel his entire body tense next to mine. I instantly regret the question, wanting to take it back when I hear him sigh.

"No," he says finally and I let out my own sigh when I hear the soft tone of his voice. "Honestly, that wasn't a concern for me at all. Love is a four-letter word I don't enjoy using anymore."

I don't say anything else, letting the silence between us turn into sleep as I wonder about the woman who broke Atlas Knight's heart and left him jaded. I wanted nothing more than to ask him for the hundredth time why things can't work between us.

———

I CRACK AN EYELID OPEN, THE ROOM STILL DARK. MY HEAD rolls to the right. Atlas is still wrapped around me. I maneuver my body slowly from his grasp so as not to wake him, tiptoeing over to the window to glance through the sliver of open drapes. It's overcast out, an eerie silvery glow encasing everything. The parking lot is littered with tree branches and shingles. A chair from the pool area is in a mangled heap in one corner.

"Mmm, now that is a view I want to wake up to every day." I turn to see Atlas sitting up in bed. The sheet drapes carelessly over his hips, barely covering his manhood. I look down, realizing that I'm completely naked. "Come back to bed; your husband commands it." He pulls the sheet back, his cock rigid.

"You know." I walk over to him, sliding my leg over his body, straddling him. I reach down between us, gently grabbing his cock as I lean forward. "For a man who said this marriage was nothing more than an inconvenience, you really like to throw that word around." He tries to kiss me but I pull back.

"And for a woman who agreed to be my wife"—he grabs my throat and pulls me toward him—"you really struggle to behave like one." His lips are on mine, his hands on my breast and my hair, rolling me to my back as his tongue massages my own.

"Hey." I place my hands against his chest. "We need to talk about last night."

"Last night?" He trails his lips down my neck, his cock at my entrance begging to come inside. "What about last night?" He presses into me, my back arching as my body struggles to accommodate him.

"W— We didn't..." I'm struggling to keep my focus. "I'm not on birth control," I finally say as he shows no signs of stopping. His hips continue to move lazily as he finds my lips again and kisses me, his tongue doing things in my mouth that makes my pussy throb against his cock.

"Oh fuck," he groans, "I love when you do that." He buries his nose in my neck, grabbing both of my hands and pinning them above me.

"Atlas." I say his name as he stares down at me, the tip of his cock hitting my G-spot over and over. "Just pull out," I pant, my eyes struggling to stay open as I dig my fingernails into his sides.

"No." He grabs my leg, pulling it up and over his hip so he can penetrate me deeper. "You're going to be dripping my cum after we're done fucking." His hips swivel with each thrust, driving my sense of pleasure to new heights. "I want you so full it drips down your thighs when you get up. I want you remembering every fucking second of every fucking day that you're my wife and if I want to fuck a load of cum into you, I will."

I don't know how to process the things he says to me. They're fucked up and possessive but they turn me on. When we've both come down from our release, we lie in each other's arms.

"I'm guessing I need to be on birth control if you're not going to pull out."

"Does it bother you?" He runs his hand up and down my arm, his chin resting on my head.

"That you don't pull out? No. Is that your kink?" I say, half joking.

"With you, yes."

I sit back slightly to look at him. "Why?"

He runs the back of his hand over my arms and exposed breasts, his eyes following his own movements. "Because as fake as our relationship might be, our marriage is real. You're mine." He's kissing me again. "I want to mark every part of you so everyone knows you're owned." He bites down on my neck.

"Until you divorce me in a year," I say and I know it's the wrong thing. His movements still, his hand falling from my body. I want to take it back. I want him to look at me and tell me that he doesn't want a divorce... but he doesn't.

"I'm going to take a shower, then call Mac, see what's going on." He looks up finally, a smile on his face as he kisses me gently. "You're more than welcome to join me."

"You sure you aren't sick of me yet?" I follow him toward the bathroom.

"I don't think I'd ever get sick of being around you."

"Aw, that's sweet." I poke his side.

"...when you're naked that is."

"Of course." I laugh, stepping over the bathtub wall. "Oh." I look down, my inner thighs slick with his release dripping out of me.

"You okay?" He adjusts the water to a warmer temperature.

"Yeah, just, uh, leaking."

"I guess it's time to fill you back up, then." He wraps his arms around me from behind, pressing my hands against the wall before bending me slightly forward.

Afterward, Atlas takes his time massaging my body with the bar soap provided by the motel. He massages my scalp with the shampoo, making me wonder if this is what it's like to date him.

"Is this how it always is with you?"

"No." He pulls me back into the water, rinsing the suds from my hair before lathering it with conditioner.

"What makes it different this time?"

"It's not this time, it's you." My eyes open and I look up at him. "You're my wife; you should be treated differently."

I close my eyes again as he rinses out the conditioner. I remind myself to stop setting myself up for heartbreak with questions like that. I'm only going to hurt my own feelings in the end.

After the shower, he gives Mac a call while I flip through the local channels, trying to find out what's going on with this storm that hit and how bad it is.

*"Flights are still grounded out of all local airports right now as they work to clear debris from the runways and fix downed power lines. Thousands are currently without power or access to clean, running water, Cindy."*

I sit down on the bed, listening to the reporter on the screen as she walks through a neighborhood with cars destroyed by fallen trees, houses missing roofs, and a few even completely torn apart. I glance over at Atlas as he hangs up.

"Mac is bringing us some fresh clothes he was able to get a few towns away. Looks like we're not going anywhere today so I'm going to see if there's anything I can do to help out." He turns his attention back to his phone, tapping a few buttons before holding it up to his ear.

"How do we have power?" I ask as the lights flicker.

"This place has a backup generator," he says, holding his phone away from his face. "I saw it when I left the room the other night. Probably won't last much longer though."

Moments later Mac arrives with fresh clothes, coffee, and bagels for us.

"Oh yes," I moan against my coffee, taking several sips. "God, I needed that."

"Sounded a lot better moaning that when my cock was inside you." Atlas pulls a black t-shirt on, reaching for the coffee from Mac's hand. Mac's eyes dart to mine and I look away, completely embarrassed.

"I'll be outside," Mac says, exiting the room.

"Are you embarrassed people know we fuck?"

"No," I say, pulling on the cotton underwear and the black sweat-pants Mac picked out for me. "I just don't think they need to hear about it. Especially in front of me." Atlas finishes pulling on his jeans, walking over to me.

"He needs to know loud and clear how well I fucking please you because don't think I haven't noticed the way he looks at you."

"Looks at me?" I push his hand away. "What are you talking about?"

"Don't play coy, Stella. You're an incredibly sexy woman."

"I'm not playing coy. I just have never once felt weird around him or that he was staring at me."

"He doesn't stare and it's not weird; that's why you haven't noticed, but I'm a man and I see it. I get that men will look at you, but what I don't like is the way he looks at you." He comes closer to me. "Like a predator looks at prey."

"Some would say that's how you"—I point my finger, resting it against his chest—"look at me."

"Yes, well, I get special dispensation to look at you any way that I want."

"Don't," I say, pushing against his chest but it's no use. He grabs me, picking me up and tossing me back onto the bed before attacking my sides, sending me into a fit of laughter.

———

"What'd the governor say?" Mac asks me as he helps me lift another case of water bottles into the back of the SUV.

"I'm not sure. Atlas only spoke with him briefly, I think, but they're going to have a meeting when he gets here."

We've been taking truckloads of bottled water we were able to get from a few towns away where Mac bought our clothes, along with thousands of dollars' worth of nonperishable foods to the disaster relief station they set up.

"So, how's newlywed life?" Mac asks, continuing with small talk as we load in groceries.

"Good." I keep my gaze away from him, all too aware of what Atlas mentioned about him this morning. "Can't complain."

He snorts with laughter. "Yeah, sounds like it."

I feel my face flame and I excuse myself, stepping away to find Atlas who's pointing to a large map and giving directions to a local group of volunteers. Even in a situation like this, Atlas takes charge. He has a natural leadership quality about him, not to mention he stands at least a head above almost everyone else here.

"Hey." I walk to him when there's a break in his conversation. "How are things going?"

"Good." He glances at his watch. "The governor should be here any moment. I'm going to discuss setting up a relief fund for the people impacted. Make sure they have shelter, food, water, clothes, money, whatever they need after we've gone."

"Mac and I just finished loading up the SUV to take over to the relief station they have set up down the way."

"Thank you, baby." He cups my face and kisses me softly. "I promise I'll have you flown home in no time."

"Actually." I look around. "I was hoping we could stay a few days and help out more." I fully expect him to tell me he has important meetings and business deals that couldn't possibly be put on hold, but he doesn't.

"I think that's a great idea." He reaches for his phone and types out a quick text and hits send before putting it back in his pocket. "I just asked Florence to reschedule my meetings for the next three days."

It's like a flip has switched in him, or maybe I'm just seeing the man behind the grumpy exterior that the world sees. He takes charge of the situation alongside the governor, using his private plane, money, name, every resource at his fingertips to not only clean up the debris but provide for every person's needs.

"Mr. Knight, I just have to ask since we have recently found out that you secretly eloped with your now wife, how has it been adjusting to married life?" The local reporter has a huge smile on her cherubic face as she holds the microphone in front of Atlas' face.

He smiles, sliding his arm around my waist and turning to look at me. The way he's looking at me causes my knees to wobble. I tell myself that it's fake, that this is all a production for the cameras, but something deep down in my gut tells me that it's so much more. I smile back at him, the butterflies that often accompany these moments flapping their wings a million times per second even if I'm trying to ignore them because Atlas made it clear to me last night that love isn't an option for him.

"It's been absolute bliss." He kisses me, dipping me so my hands fly up around his neck. "Total and complete bliss," he repeats, making everyone around us say *aw*. "Actually, it was her idea to stay a few extra days so we can help this town out and get these hardworking people back on their feet."

"Well, thank you, Mr. and Mrs. Knight. We can't thank you enough for your wonderful generosity and we want to wish all the happiness and blessings in your new marriage. Ken, back to you in the studio."

I'm completely exhausted by the time the plane lands back in Chicago. Between the long hours of cleaning up debris and delivering items to those in need to the long hours Atlas kept me up at night, using my body in ways I didn't even know existed, I need a week of sleep.

I spend an extra thirty minutes soaking in the porcelain tub in my bathroom, the lavender bath salts soaking into my overworked muscles. I close my eyes, a smile constantly on my face the last few days.

I can't keep the feeling of hope from creeping in every time I think about things between Atlas and me.

*Are things different or was this a what happens in Kansas, stays in Kansas type of situation?*

By the time I'm done with my bath and ready for bed, I peek my head out of my bedroom and down the hall to see if Atlas is still awake. Since coming home, he's been locked away in his office. I'm assuming he's catching up on work. I contemplate tiptoeing downstairs to his office, offering him a sexy little surprise, but a yawn pulls my attention back to how tired I really am.

I stretch my arms overhead, leaving my door open as I walk to my bed and slide beneath the cool sheets. I try to stay awake in hopes that Atlas will find his way upstairs soon but it's no use. With each blink, my eyelids grow heavier and heavier. Finally, I close my eyes, giving in to sleep.

# Chapter 16

## *Atlas*

"I agree, Martin." I rub my eyes, the burning from lack of sleep is making it hard to focus.

*That's not what's making it hard to focus.*

"Let's move forward with things. I'll have Florence schedule a follow-up for next week." I hang up the phone, reaching for my empty mug of coffee. Groaning, I head to the kitchen for a refill when I see Oliver lugging a huge plastic sheet down the hallway.

"What is going on?"

"Morning, sir." He nods, his hands full. "The Mrs. is painting so I told her I'd bring this up for her."

"Painting?" I ask, not sure I heard correctly.

"Yes, her room." He pauses. "Did you want me to tell her to stop?"

"No." I shake my head. "No, it's fine. I'm just grabbing another cup of coffee." I wave him off and step into the kitchen where Regina is prepping dinner.

"Oh hey, Mr. Knight." She smiles, slicing down the middle of an onion. "Didn't realize you were home today."

"I'm just working from my office." I gesture, placing my mug beneath the espresso machine and pushing the button.

"You okay? You're looking a little tired."

I smile. "Yeah, I am tired. Nothing a cup of coffee won't fix."

"Oh, I remember those days." She laughs, her loud boisterous laugh that always puts a smile on my own face. "That honeymoon phase is a real energy zapper." She winks at me, laughing even louder.

"Trust me, that's not a problem I'll ever complain about." I sip my coffee, taking a few more moments to grab a snack and watch out the window as Mac washes the cars. I shift my gaze to the ceiling when I hear a loud thump. "I better go check in on the wife, make sure she doesn't paint herself into a corner. I'll see you at dinner, Regina."

I make my way upstairs, the same thoughts that have been running through my brain since last night when I came to bed and noticed it was empty. Neither of us have spoken about how things will be between us but in those four short nights we were together in Kansas, I realized how much I like having her in my bed and in my arms when I sleep. In fact, I barely slept at all last night. Memories of feeling her beneath me kept me awake, my body aching to feel her again.

"You're really good at that," I finally say after silently watching Stella for several long minutes.

"Oh." She turns her head around on the ladder she's perched atop. "Thank you." She smiles, a small swatch of dried paint on her cheek. She's clearly been at this for hours. One wall is completely done and she's halfway done cutting in the ceiling on the second.

"You do know I have painters that you can hire, right?" I prop my shoulder against the doorframe, admiring the cute little overalls she's wearing.

"I like to paint." She shrugs, looking around the room. "Besides, now that I don't have a job, what else am I going to do all day?" She gives me an ornery look and it's a reminder that there are still some rules in place in this marriage.

I ignore the comment, not wanting to launch into another discussion that could turn into an argument or me saying some rude shit I don't mean. "Where'd you learn?"

"YouTube. I just watched a few videos this morning on the way to the paint store."

"I thought you said you liked painting."

"I do," she says with a straight face. "I just found out when I started this morning that I like it." It makes me laugh and I step farther into the room. "This," she says, dipping her paintbrush into her bucket and bringing it up to the very edge of the wall where it meets the ceiling, "is my favorite part." She places the brush against the wall and in one long smooth motion, she pulls it along the ceiling, perfectly cutting it in without painters tape.

"Impressive." I whistle. "Seriously, this is your first time?"

"Yup." She dips her brush into the paint and repeats the process again. "I guess it's called edging. It's actually a lot of fun and I love that I'm good at it."

"Yeah." I chuckle. "I know a thing or two about edging."

She shakes her head. "Somehow I knew you'd say something like that."

"Just saying." I sip my coffee as she stares at me. "I've been told that I'm really good at it too."

"Really?" She shrugs, turning her attention back to painting. "I wouldn't know. You couldn't seem to stop if the world was ending."

I place my coffee cup on the nightstand next to her bed. "Now, darling, why don't you come down here so we can talk." I place my foot on the bottom rung, her head whipping around to look at me.

"Atlas," she says, taking a step higher on the ladder. "Don't!"

"Don't what?" I take a step up, then another. "Remind you that you were the one begging me not to stop?"

"This is dangerous, I have paint!" she squeals.

"Then come down here and we can talk," I say, taking another step closer to her.

Her laughter is almost uncontrollable as she tries to escape me.

When I reach her, I take the paint from her, reaching around to place it on the top platform. I reach out and run my fingers over a piece of her hair that has a swatch of pink paint in it.

"Why didn't you sleep in my bed last night?" She shrugs. "Tell me."

"I dunno." She pushes past me and steps down from the ladder as I follow. "I didn't want to just assume and then intrude on your personal space. It was a little different situation when we were in Kansas since we had to share a room."

"I understand and for what it's worth, it wouldn't be intruding on my personal space."

"Good to know." We sit on the edge of her bed like two nervous teenagers trying to decide who's going to make the first move, my brain trying to make sense of her decision to paint this room once we were back from a very intimate few days together. Naturally, I'm convinced it's because she wants to put space back between us. My stomach knots at the thought that I know I'm falling in love with this woman and she's slipping through my fingers.

"On that note, I will let you get back to painting. I have another three or four solid hours of meetings so I'll be in my office until dinner."

"Are we eating together tonight?" Her eyes look hopeful.

"Doubtful," I say, looking at my watch and starting to make my way toward her door. "Odds are I'll eat in my office." I make the mistake of catching her gaze once more before I leave, that same disappointed look back in her eyes, the one that makes me feel like a piece of shit. "I like the color you chose by the way. Looks great."

This time I don't look back. I head straight to my office and slam the door, sinking down into my chair to sulk. No matter how hard I try to focus on work, my thoughts are consumed with her. I close my eyes, replaying parts of what happened between us in that motel room. I know she felt what I felt. It was so much more than just sex; it felt spiritual if that's even a thing. Like all these years I thought I knew pleasure until I looked into her eyes while I was inside her. It felt like my soul came alive and every second without her, I'm falling more and more apart.

I turn on some music, trying to drown out all thoughts of her, but it's no use. Every song I hear reminds me of the night she sang it at the club. Every lyric pulls at my soul, like their singing the pain I'm feeling. What I thought I could once shut out is starting to take over and I'm afraid I'm completely at its mercy.

# Chapter 17

## *Stella*

I place a record on my player, the soft blare of Miles Davis' trumpet filling my room. My eyes stay closed as I run my brush through my freshly washed and now dried hair a few times, enjoying the tingles on my scalp.

Dinner must be ready by now, the mouthwatering scent making its way upstairs. I slip on a sundress and make my way downstairs to find Atlas sitting alone at the end of the kitchen table.

"This is a lovely surprise." I smile.

"Is it?" He has a strange look on his face, one I can't place.

"Of course. I didn't think I was going to be able to eat with you." I notice there's no place settings on the table, though. "What are we having? It smells so good."

"Here," Atlas says, patting his lap as he scoots his chair away from the table. I walk over to him and slowly take a seat on his lap.

"What's going on?" I ask nervously.

"I think we need to have a little chat." He pushes my hair away from my neck.

"We do?" I swallow down the nervous lump, ready for the *this was a mistake that can't happen again* speech, but then I watch as he drops his hand, sliding it right up my dress to rest on my bare thigh.

"Mm-hmm. I think we need to talk about some new rules, sweetheart." His other hand is on the back of my neck, his thumb rubbing circles at the base of my head.

"More rules?" I give him a snarky look. "Can't we discuss them after we eat? I'm starving."

"Dinner won't be ready for another fifteen minutes; however"—he lifts me up, placing me right on the table in front of him—"I'm going to have my dessert first."

"Atlas." I try to pull my dress down, but he grabs my hands and places them flat on the table.

"Don't move them," he commands.

"Atlas, what about Regina or Oliver?"

"First rule," he says, roughly grabbing my panties and tearing them from my body with an audible rip, "don't fucking worry about anyone else; your only concern is me. Do you understand?" I can't even argue if I wanted to; he already has two fingers inside me, toying with my G-spot as he reaches down to roll up the sleeve on his shirt. "I said"—he curls his fingers, flicking them at a rapid pace inside me—"do you understand me?"

My mouth hangs open as he continues his assault, his thumb joining in to tease my clit. I can't respond, I'm groaning, my head falling back as my hands stay flat on the table. My legs start to shake, a tingle growing rapidly throughout my body.

"Second rule," he says, stopping his movements and pulling his fingers from my body, "answer me when I ask you a question, Stella."

"What? No." I reach for his hand but he shakes his head.

"What did I tell you about being an obedient girl?"

"Yes, yes, I understand," I practically cry.

"Good." He flips my dress up, pushing against my chest. "Lie back."

I obey, resting on my elbows as I watch him lean forward, running his nose up and down my slit but not touching me.

"Fuck, you smell mouthwatering." Without hesitation, he spreads my legs, leaning all the way forward to tease my opening with his tongue. My eyes are in the back of my head, my body writhing as my hands clutch the tablecloth beneath me.

"Oh, oh please, right there," I cry, my body begging for release as he laps at me. "I-I'm-I'm—" I try to finish the sentence but I can't. I close my eyes, falling back so I can surrender to the pleasure that's threatening to consume me but just as it's about to take me over the edge, it disappears. I sit up, confusion and frustration pumping through me. "What the hell?"

"Third rule," he says, grabbing his napkin and wiping his face. "I'm in control of your pleasure."

"Meaning?"

"Meaning if I want to edge you for an hour straight, then make you suck my cock till I come down your throat, you'll swallow and say thank you, daddy, may I have more?"

I gasp. "Why are you always so bossy?"

He pulls my top half forward until he's eye to eye with me. "Because I'm the fucking boss, Stella, and the sooner you recognize that your little pussy throbs at the thought of me dominating and bossing you around, the sooner we can move past this coy little game you like to play, pretending you don't know exactly the kind of man I am."

"Hey, boss, you wanted to see me?" I freeze, Mac's voice coming from behind as I'm still sitting on the table in front of Atlas, thighs spread, panties in a torn pile on the floor. "Oh shit, sorry." He averts his gaze.

"I did," Atlas says, keeping his gaze on me. "I wanted to tell you that you'll be giving me a ride to work in the morning. Can you let Oliver know?"

"Sure. Any particular reason why you want me to drive you, sir?" I can't tell if Mac has sensed Atlas' distrust of him but his tone changes.

"No," he says, his eyes slowly drifting from mine to Mac's. "You can leave now, Mac." His eyes come back to me. "You don't need to see my wife on her knees."

Before the door even finishes closing, Atlas' hand is around my waist, pulling me from the table and onto my knees, his other hand undoing his buckle and zipper, freeing his cock from his pants.

He slides past my lips gently. I look up at him, his hair hanging over his forehead as he tries to restrain himself from losing control.

"Fuck, can you relax your jaw, baby?" he grunts, pushing in deeper. My mouth stretches wide as my tongue toys with the underside of his head, an area I've found where he loves being stimulated.

I close my eyes, relaxing and taking him deeper as I wrap my hand around him, bobbing my head and twisting my hand simultaneously. His groans grow louder, his breathing growing rapid. Suddenly I remember that any minute poor Regina is going to walk through that door in the far right corner and witness something I'm sure she'll never forget.

So I slide my hand down my body, pulling my dress up over my lap and spreading my thighs while I start to play with myself. The second Atlas sees my movements, his eyes are bouncing back and forth between my hand and my mouth.

"Oh Jesus, oh fuck me." He clenches his jaw, his head falling back as he loses it. He says my name over and over as his release pours down the back of my throat. I struggle to swallow but manage to keep from making a mess.

"Um, Atlas, dinner is coming any second," I say as I grab my panties and stand back up. "And I don't think Regina needs to be scarred by witnessing this in your kitchen."

"Shit." He laughs, standing up and tucking himself in just as we hear her footsteps behind the door. He zips up his pants, grabbing me to stand in front of him to hide his still prominent erection and unbuckled belt.

"Evening, Mr. and Mrs." She smiles, seemingly oblivious to what just took place. "Did you want me to bring dinner out now or did you want more time to get situated?" She has a very unamused look on her face that has my cheeks flaming and my eyes diverting from hers.

"I think we need a little more time," Atlas says, wrapping his arm around me.

Regina bursts out laughing, shaking her head and ducking back into the kitchen.

"More time?" I spin around in his arms.

"Mm-hmm." He reaches his thumb up and wipes my lip. "That was sexy knowing you were standing there with my cum still on your lips." He presses his thumb into my mouth and I wrap my lips around it. "Now let's go upstairs. I think you need a very thorough reminder about the new rules." He guides us from the kitchen to the stairs.

My stomach tingles when he runs his hands up my inner thigh as we ascend the staircase, his lips at my ear.

"I can't tell you how often I think about stretching your tight cunt. Even before I ever touched you. It completely consumes every..."—he slides his finger inside me as I continue climbing the stairs—"single"—then pulls it out—"thought"—back in again—"of my day."

"Ahh." I stumble, his arm around my waist catching me as he pulls me up the last two stairs.

"There's one final rule," he says against my lips as he picks me up and carries me down the hall to his bedroom. He pauses to kiss me for several minutes, the way his tongue maneuvers around mine enticing. It makes me realize why he's so good at going down on me. He's deliberate with his movements; small or large, he knows just how to caress or touch or lick or bite.

"You can tell me there's ten more if you keep kissing me," I say when he pulls back. I grab his shirt, tugging him back to me so I can kiss him again. "How do you do that with your tongue?"

"Do what?" He does it again.

"That." I curl my hands into fists against his shirt. "It makes me so wet."

"Good, I want you nice and wet for what I plan to do to you."

He sits me down, pulling my dress off me in one quick motion, his pants following after. "What's the final rule?" I ask nervously as he stands me up and walks me to over to a chair.

"You're not allowed to sleep in your room."

"I'm not?" He bends me over the back of the chair, cupping my hands around the armrests.

"Hold here," he says, dragging his hands up my arms. I look back at him. "And no, you're not. You sleep with me." His fingers softly trace down my spine, toying with my asshole once he reaches it. A second later he replaces his finger with his tongue, swirling it around and running it straight up my spine, his hand pulling my chin up and back so he can kiss me. "Don't let go of the chair," he says as he kneels down behind me.

By the time I've had my third orgasm from Atlas' tongue, I'm begging for release, my body shaking with anticipation as he glides over me, entering me with one swift motion so deep it pulls my back off the bed. The mangled groan that escapes my lips sounds guttural.

"You can handle it, baby," Atlas groans, pulling out halfway and going in an inch deeper. "I need you to be able to take it deeper for me." He drapes my legs over his shoulders, inching in deeper, my teeth biting down on his shoulder as I feel myself stretched to my limits.

"I can't," I moan as the pain starts to give way to pleasure when he tilts his pelvis and hits my G-spot.

"You sure about that?" My body relaxes the more he moves.

"Oh yes, right there, baby." I grab his hips, my orgasm already at my fingertips.

"Fuck, you look so good taking my cock." He looks down at where his cock disappears inside me over and over again, slick with my juices.

"Please don't stop," I pant, "please, oh yes, right there." He looks over to where my toes curl by his ears.

"A fucking explosion couldn't stop me." He grabs my ankles, pushing them forward so he has me bent in half, his cock slamming into me over and over again when I feel a rush take over me like I've never experienced before.

He doesn't stop even after I've come. He drives into me relentlessly until finally he's shouting, his movements stilling as he collapses on top of me.

"Nobody has fucked you this good before," he finally says into my neck.

"Is that a question?" He pushes up onto his arms and looks down at me with a cocky grin.

"No, I know nobody has fucked you as good as I have." He grinds his hips against me, his cock still inside of me.

"And how do you know that?"

"Because if they had, you wouldn't be here with me."

I stare up at him, feeling as if his eyes are looking into my soul.

*This can't be fake.*

Every fiber in my body wants to ask him how I'm supposed to ever let another man touch me after the way he has. He traces his tongue around my neck and breasts, my body fully surrendering to him.

# Chapter 18

## *Atlas*

### One week later...

**S**tella: *Just call me Farmer John!*

I laugh at the picture that accompanies her text. A big smile on her face as she stands with a gardening rake, a straw hat, and her overalls. Oliver must have taken the picture. She's grown very fond of spending time with him out in the gardens.

I type out a flirty message back and hit send with a smile on my face.

**Me:** *Hmmm... can I plow your fields? ;)*

My smile fades momentarily, a feeling of unease taking its place when I think about how things have changed between Stella and me in such a short amount of time. I had convinced myself I could handle having her in my space, that I wouldn't cave to my desires for her. But after that quickly went out the window just a few weeks into our arrangement, now I'm struggling to stay afloat without falling for her.

I run my finger over the image of her on the screen.

*You are in love with her.*

I pull my hand back as if the photo burned me, an image of Eleanor flashing into my head. A pain shoots through my chest at the thought of her or maybe it's the thought that I still miss her and I'm trying to fill that void with Stella.

They're nothing alike and part of me wonders if that's the appeal of Stella. She's different than the world I'm in, the world Eleanor comes from. She's optimistic and fresh, not afraid to speak her mind and enjoy all the silly moments in life. In the last week alone, she's shown more of herself to me than Eleanor did in the first two years of our relationship.

I stand and walk over to the far window in my office, staring out over Lake Michigan. Something inside me wants to run home to Stella now, to tell her that I'm falling in love with her and I know she's falling for me too. That we should throw caution to the wind and go for it, actually stay in this marriage for real. But then panic grips my chest at the thought.

*Is she in falling for me or is she doing exactly what you told her she needed to do... make the best of this situation and follow the contract?*

My stomach curdles at the thought that I'm playing myself. Anyone would fall in love when they're surrounded by endless luxury, money, and good sex. But what happens when the reality of life sets in and I'm not home every night for dinner like I have been this week? Will she leave like Eleanor did? No warnings, no second chances... just gone.

"Mr. Knight?" Florence's voice startles me, and I turn around to see her shutting my office door softly after stepping inside.

"Yes, Florence?"

"There's someone here to see you."

I glance at my watch. "Unscheduled meeting?" I walk back over to my desk and roll my chair back.

"Something like that. She said she just needs a few moments of your time."

I pause. "She?" It's not that uncommon to have business associates drop by unexpectedly for a quick chat, but the look on Florence's face tells me that's not what this is.

"It's Eleanor, sir. Did you want me to send her in?" I stare at her, unsure I heard her correctly. "Sir?"

"Yes, Florence," I say, "send her in."

She's practically floating when she crosses the threshold of my office, her ethereal presence still a commanding one. Everything about Eleanor is appealing. I don't know if she's designed herself to be that way but it works.

"Hi, Atlas." My name still sounds the same on her lips, breathy and sophisticated. Eleanor was raised in the same world as me; she knows how to hold herself, how to remain soft and feminine yet cold and unbothered. It's a true talent, one my mother also perfected.

*She's the kind of woman I'm supposed to be with.*

The second the thought enters my head, a horrible sense of guilt replaces it, an image of Stella just this morning, laughing in my arms as we made pancakes.

"Hello, Eleanor." I slide my hands into my pockets. "What brings you by?" Her golden hair is pulled back in a tight ponytail, her all-white ensemble with pale-pink nails and matching lip gloss a classic Eleanor look. She looks good, still thinner than I remember.

*Maybe dumping me did her some good.*

She walks over to one of the flower arrangements that Florence placed on a table and reads the card aloud.

"Congratulations. I never thought I'd see the day. Wishing you all the best." She stares at me, her eyes growing wet with tears that sit on the brim. "I heard you got married. I wasn't sure I believed it." She offers me a small smile and it pulls at me.

"Yes," I say gently, twirling my wedding ring on my finger in my pocket. "I did."

"Why?" she asks, her chin threatening to quiver.

"Because I fell in love and wanted to marry her."

"We were in love once." She flashes a quick smile.

"Yes, we were." Silence settles between us as she turns her attention back to the flowers. "Eleanor, I told you last time we spoke—"

"Who is she?" she interrupts, her brows furrowed as she turns to look at me.

"No one you know, if that's what you're concerned about."

"It's not," she says quickly. I'm having trouble reading her body language, her usual perfect posture a little more perfect than normal, her jaw clenched, eyes unblinking. "Why wouldn't you commit to me like that? That's all I wanted." The tears that sat on the edge of her eyes fall down her cheeks, her chin now quivering as her attempt to remain stoic begins to crumble.

I physically hold myself back from walking across the room and pulling her into my arms. I have the sudden urge to do just that, to tell her that it's fake, that it means nothing. It's just a means to end, but then I pause because... that's not true. It was at first but now, now I don't know what it is but calling it fake feels so wrong, so cruel to Stella.

"You left me, Eleanor," I say, reminding myself that I don't owe her an apology for moving on.

"When did you meet her?" She gently dabs her cheeks, attempting to regain her composure.

"It doesn't matter—"

"While we were together?" Her voice cracks.

"Seriously, Eleanor?" I shake my head. "You couldn't get out of my house fast enough after telling me you didn't love me anymore and now that I've found happiness with someone else, you show up to my office and suggest it started while we were together? Why? To give it less credibility?"

"That's not wha—"

"That's exactly"—I point my finger at her—"why you said it. You want to make yourself feel better for leaving because now you regret it."

"Yes, I did leave," she says, walking toward me, "because I had to. For my own sanity, I had to."

"You had to?" I shake my head. "Eleanor, you gave me no warning, nothing. I came home and your shit was packed and you coldly walked out."

She hangs her head, fumbling with a second tissue she's pulled from her purse. "You wouldn't listen to me; you pushed me away, and when I tried to beg you to work on us, you pushed me away even more."

"Pushed you away?" I feel my blood pressure spike. "How, Eleanor?"

"You were never there!" Tears start to pour down her face now. "All I wanted was a family with you and a home where I felt like I was wanted."

I step toward her, my hands on her arms as I look down at her tear-stained face. "I'm sorry, Eleanor." I repeat it a few more times. "I never meant to hurt you, but I don't know what you want me to say."

"I want you to say that you feel the same." She paws at me, trying to pull me toward her but I hold her back.

"I— I can't do this right now."

"Tell me you want it too. I know you do." She takes my hand, placing it against her belly. "I can give you a family. I can give you everything, Atlas. You know she'll never love you like I do. Nobody understands you like me."

I stare down at my hand on her belly, an image of the two of us together, her belly swollen in pregnancy. I yank my hand back, the feelings I had confused as lingering love for Eleanor suddenly become clear.

"You left," I repeat my words from earlier, "you left me. You never once sat me down and told me you were thinking about leaving or that things were ever that bad for us. You just walked out."

She wipes the last of her tears away, her polished, expressionless face regaining composure. "No, I didn't come to you and tell you because I felt I shouldn't have to. You could see we were falling apart, Atlas. You chose night after night to stay at the office or travel across the world on a whim. I saw you on TV with her. You never would have taken me along in a situation like that."

"You wouldn't have wanted to go, Eleanor. We stayed in a motel that barely had hot water and limited electricity. Not exactly The Four Seasons."

I see her eye twitch; she knows I'm right. "I can be that girl, Atlas. You just don't want me to be. You put me up on a pedestal and when I tried to come down, you wanted nothing to do with me."

"When, Eleanor?" She opens her mouth, then snaps it shut again. "You put yourself on a pedestal, Eleanor. You made it clear to everyone in my home, including Oliver, that you were above them and I stupidly looked past it. I owe them an apology for allowing you to be so cold toward them."

"Oh please, Atlas, they're the help. Stop trying to make yourself sound holier than thou. That's not even what we're discussing."

"That is exactly what we're discussing, Eleanor." I laugh to myself, ashamed it took me this long to realize who she is. "These people matter just as much as you and I, and I never once had to explain that to my wife." She flinches when I say the word. "My wife," I say it again, louder this time, "loves spending time with the people in my home. My wife loves the way I show my feelings for her with my body. She doesn't make me feel like a deviant or like I'm a human fucking dildo that you can just push aside."

I'm realizing now all the pent-up anger I feel toward Eleanor and it's coming out in a way I never intended.

"You don't have to be so crass, Atlas."

"Exactly my point," I say, stepping closer to her. "My wife would never try to change me."

I expect her to square her shoulders and march out of my office or maybe even slap me, but she doesn't. She reaches her hand out and grabs my shirt, pulling me toward her till her lips crash into mine. She grabs my hair, tugging it hard as she bites down on my bottom lip hard.

"What the fuck, Eleanor?" I pull away, her eyes burning in a way I've never seen before.

"There's a side of me that's begging for you to unleash it." I stare at her, confused.

"You had your chance. Find someone else to unleash it." I push her hands off me, stepping back to straighten out my shirt. "Please see yourself out."

"Fine, but I won't go without a fight, Atlas. I won't lose you again." She turns, walking out of my office and shutting the door softly behind her.

I stare at the door for several minutes after she leaves.

*Had I not needed to get married, would I have taken her back?*

The thought marinates in my head for the rest of the day. My mood sullen, my thoughts consumed with what-if scenarios and possible outcomes that could or should have been. I feel lost, completely consumed with the idea of going home to Stella right now and telling her that I love her. That I can't stand the thought of living another day without telling her that.

But I can't. I can't love her. Because a man in love wouldn't do the things I've done. A man in love wouldn't lie like I have. I've wedged myself perfectly between a rock and a hard place. Do I tell the woman I love who I really am, what I did to get her and risk losing her, or do I let her go at the end of this contract and go back to what I know, back to Eleanor. Maybe I should have fought harder for Eleanor. Maybe she was right about how much time I didn't spend with her.

My phone buzzes with a text from Stella. My heart sinks when I see what it is, a photo of dinner ingredients along with a rose, candles, and a bottle of wine.

**Stella:** *Dinner at seven. Clothing optional. ;) Don't be late!*

I smile at her message and picture her saying that with her head tilted and a sexy grin on her face. My heart feels like it's breaking or dying and right now I don't know which would be worse.

It's nearing six. If I want to make it home in time for dinner, I need to leave now. But I can't face her. I know if I go home I'll tell her how I feel. I'll give her false hope because when the inevitable happens, when she finds out I'm the reason she was fired from her dream job, she'll hate me.

Instead, I grab a bottle of scotch from my bar cart and sit back on the couch in the far corner of my office. I take several large swallows, the burn spreading rapidly through my body as the sun begins to set over Chicago.

Florence knocks on my door when she leaves, the building slowly emptying as the hours pass on. I turn my phone on silent, the buzzing from the worried texts and missed calls from Stella reminding me how much of a piece of shit I am.

Eleanor's words haunt me all night. I repeat them in my head over and over, remembering all the times I pushed her away by not being there. And here I am, doing the same thing to Stella.

Maybe Eleanor's right. Maybe it is best Stella walks away from this at the end. Because even if she could find it in her heart to forgive me for the wicked things I've done to her, I would inevitably break her heart again anyway when I push her away.

# Chapter 19

## *Stella*

I pace back and forth in the entryway of the house, glancing out the front windows every so often to see if Oliver is back home with him. He had let me know at six fifteen this morning that he was heading into the city to pick him up.

After half a dozen failed attempts to reach Atlas last night, I ran to Oliver's cottage on the back of the property in tears, worried sick that something had happened to him. I explained that I had called and texted him but hadn't heard a response.

*"I'm sorry, Stella. I wish I had known you couldn't reach him. He sent me a message earlier around eight that he would be staying at the office tonight."*

*"Oh." I feel a sense of relief, but then anger starts to creep in. "He texted you around eight?"*

*"Yes. Let me double-check." He disappears for a second, grabbing his phone and putting on his glasses to flip through his messages. "Yes, four minutes after eight," he says, holding the phone screen out toward me. "Would you like me to send him a message?"*

*"No." I smile. "But thank you. I'll just see him tomorrow. Good night, Oliver."*

*"Good night, Stella."*

I didn't bother sending any more texts or calls to Atlas. Knowing that he had to have seen them already when he sent Oliver that text brought me right back down to reality, where I need to stay.

Twenty minutes later after I've calmed myself down with a cup of lavender tea, I sit on the bottom stair as the front door flies open and Atlas stumbles inside. His hair is disheveled, his tie gone, his shirt buttoned askew and untucked. He looks a mess, like he partied all night or perhaps slept on the floor in his office. Then again, who says he didn't do those things and who says he was alone? My stomach rolls at the thought.

*He wouldn't.*

"Good morning, darling." I don't bother pretending to smile.

"I'm not in the mood," he grunts, tossing his jacket over his shoulder as he steps past me.

"I don't care that you're not in the mood, I'm your wife."

He stops, his head falling back as he laughs. "My wife," he mutters, clearly still drunk. "I don't give a shit." He stumbles up the stairs and I follow after.

"What the hell happened, Atlas? What changed?" I step in front of him, my anger quickly turning into desperation as I try to get him to look at me. "Everything was going so great. I don't understand."

"It's fake. Who gives a shit?" He pushes past me, slamming the door to his bedroom as I slowly crumple to the stairs.

I keep my tears inside, closing my eyes to remind myself that I'm the one who got my hopes up. I'm the one who let myself fall for him and believe it was more than it was.

I completely lost myself in our relationship this last week. Spending countless hours making love, watching movies, and eating meals together. It felt like how it should be, like it was just a normal relationship that was blossoming into... I can't bring myself to even think the word right now.

Oliver's gentle touch startles me and I look over my shoulder at him. "Give him time to sober up, then talk to him." He gives my shoulder a squeeze. "I know he cares for you, kiddo."

"Thanks, Oliver." I reach my hand over to his and touch it.

I spend the next several hours distracting myself, or at least attempting to.

"Looks like backbreaking work." I look back at Mac, who's positioned himself directly behind where I'm bent over on my hands and knees pulling weeds from the rosebushes.

"It's not that bad." I sit back, dusting my gloves against my jeans. "I enjoy the work actually." I admire the varying shades of pink in the roses.

"Well, if you ever want a break from the work, let me know."

"I'm okay." I smile, attempting to be polite. "But thanks."

He shoves his hands in his pockets and walks back toward the garage where Oliver watches while waxing the Rolls Royce.

I enjoy some lunch, or at least force myself to eat something before taking a quick shower and cleaning off after my afternoon gardening session. I take my time, giving Atlas more than six hours to sober up and sleep it off.

He must have left his room at some point; his door is ajar as I approach. I lift my hand to knock when I hear him speaking softly. At first, I think there's someone in his room, but then I hear him say her name. A name that has me pulling my hand back from the door and leaning in to listen closer.

"I'm sorry to just call unannounced, Eleanor, but I've been doing a lot of thinking about what you said to me yesterday." My stomach clenches.

*He was with her yesterday? What about last night?*

She must be speaking because his voice grows silent.

"Yes," he says. "I thought a lot about that, about what-ifs and situations that might have been..." He says something else but it's hard to hear. "You were right. I did push you away and I'm sorry for that. I'm sorry that I didn't do something about it back then. I'm so sorry I hurt you."

He's silent for several more minutes and I'm itching to hear the other side of the conversation.

*Does she want him back? Is that what this is about? Did he tell her he's still in love with her?*

I close my eyes, trying to steady myself as I feel the hallway fading away. I squeeze my eyes shut even tighter as I inhale a few shaky breaths. I hear his footsteps coming toward the door. A second later he pulls it open, his expression surprised.

"You don't know her, huh?" I cross my arms over my chest, shaking my head at him. "You even had the perfect chance to tell me who she was and you still lied to my face. For what? Why?"

"It's nothing," he says, shoving his phone into his pocket and attempting to step around me.

"Nothing?" I spit the word back at him. "Any normal person has a past and exes. I wouldn't have thought twice if you had told me about her, but the fact you lied and now you're seeing her and talking to her behind my back?"

"I said it's nothing," he barks. "She's the one who left me anyway so who gives a fuck."

"I do," I say, pointing to my chest. "Your wife."

"I'm not talking about this right now."

"Funny, I don't get that luxury with you." I push against his chest. "You always demand answers from me—about my life and my past. It's no wonder you won't share with me," I say with disgust. "You're keeping someone on the back burner. I guess I'd feel pretty shitty if I were you too."

"It isn't like that. She's the one who wants to get back with me. I told her I'm married."

"For now." I tilt my head like I'm thinking. "Actually no, this is a good idea. We get to get what we need from this arrangement. Meanwhile, we already have our rebound lined up when the divorce goes through."

"Might I remind you"—he narrows one eye—"that the contract states that you cannot date or fuck anyone else."

"And are you held to the same standard, dear husband?"

"No," he says casually.

"Of course you're not." I toss my hands in the air in exasperation. "Why aren't you?"

"Because you're the one who signed the contract."

———

"I need a ride." I stand in Mac's doorway, a confused look on his face.

"This late?" He glances at his watch, then back up at the house. "Mr. Knight know?" I shake my head, diverting my gaze from his eyes. "Gimme five," he says, ducking back into his cottage.

Five minutes later he's jogging up to the garage and pointing toward a black late model Ford Mustang. "We'll take my car. That way if he gets pissed, at least I can say I didn't use his car."

I wrap my trench coat tighter around my body, not wanting Mac to see any part of my body in this dress. I know it's a complete mistake involving Mac in this. It's not that I want Atlas to be jealous or even second-guess my intentions with Mac. It's that I knew he'd be willing to give me a ride to the city without alerting Atlas.

After our last conversation this evening, he shut himself in his office, making it abundantly clear he wasn't to be disturbed.

"So why you going to the city this late?" He nods toward the clock on his dash.

"It's not that late." I shrug. "A lot of people don't even start getting ready until after nine."

"Yeah, not you people, though." His eyes drift down my body and even though I'm completely covered, my stomach fizzles with an uneasy feeling.

I try to keep the talking to a minimum for the rest of the ride, my focus on the passing cars in the oncoming lanes. I pull my phone out, opening a rideshare app and stealthily calling for a car so it's waiting for me when he drops me off.

"You can drop me here," I say, pointing toward the coffee shop where I used to work.

"Here? Really?" He leans forward, the closed sign glowing red. "Doesn't look like it's open."

"My friend lives above it."

"Oh, okay," he replies, seeming to believe it. "Oh hey," he says when I step out of the car. I lean down into the open door.

"Yeah?"

"Give me your number so you can text me when you want to be picked up."

"That doesn't make much sense. I should take your number."

"Or yeah, I just meant we should have each other's numbers."

"I'm actually staying the night here at my friend's house so no worries. Thanks again!" I slam the door, quickly darting down an alleyway and around the corner until I watch him from a distance finally pull away.

I let out my breath, then dart across the street to the waiting car.

When the driver drops me at Freddy's, I stand on the sidewalk for several minutes just staring at the glowing sign. One of the *D*'s is completely out, the *Y* flickering on and off every few seconds. I close my eyes, imagining my name written in those lights above this club.

I keep my head down as I walk through the club, heading straight back down the dingy hallway to Freddy's office. I can hear him behind the foggy glass of the door, his loud, raspy laugh turning midway into a coughing fit.

"Yeah, sure, you got it, Pete." I hear him end his conversation so I grab the handle and confidently open his door. He looks up from his desk, a cigar hanging out of his mouth with an ash so long it looks like a bony finger on the end. "Well, well, well, if it isn't Little Miss Riding Hood."

I curl my lips in disgust. "What's that supposed to mean?"

"Well, you're about to be eaten by the big bad wolf coming in here." He launches into another half-cough, half-laugh fit.

"I want my job back," I say, his smile fading. "I won't sleep with you to get it back but I—I have money now. I can give you money. I just want my job back."

He takes the cigar from his mouth and ashes it into a Styrofoam cup on his desk. A nasty sneer takes over his lips. "I don't need any money, sugar tits."

"Yeah right, everyone needs more money, Freddy. I'm serious, I can pay you and I don't mean like a hundred dollars or something. I can pay you real money." I don't want to make an offer; I'm hoping to lowball him, maybe even see if he'll take less than ten thousand. I know it's a stupid investment, paying someone ten thousand dollars to give you back a job that barely paid enough to pay my water bill each month, but at this point, it's not about the money. It's about taking my dignity and independence back.

"That problem's been taken care of already, trust me."

"What do you mean? You couldn't have gotten that much from your grandma."

He snarls. "How the fuck do you know anything about my business?"

"I— I don't. I just assumed."

"Well, you don't know a damned thing so unless you plan on getting on those pretty little knees and learning a thing or two about my cock, I'd suggest you get your trouble-causing ass out of my club."

I slam the door behind me, making a beeline for the back of the club where Clyde and the band are warming up.

"Stella, my girl." Clyde stands up with open arms. "Where the hell have you been, sweetheart?" He holds me tight in his arms and I have to remind myself that now isn't the time to lose it emotionally and pour my heart out to him.

"Hey, I'm so sorry I disappeared on you."

He cups my face. "That's alright, darling. I heard you've been mighty busy being a wife." His eyes glow with excitement and I don't have the heart to tell him now that I'm pretty sure it's over.

"I have been," I say, smiling and grabbing his hands. "I can't wait to tell you all about it, but I wanted to ask you something."

"Sure, darlin'."

"Why'd Freddy fire me?"

Clyde's face falls. "He fired you?"

"Yeah, that's why I stopped coming around. I was ashamed. He didn't give me a reason. I came back tonight to try and get my job back but he's being odd, like—" I feel weird saying out loud what I'm thinking, that it feels like someone else is pulling the strings and Freddy is just a puppet, but I'm pretty confident I'm way over-thinking things. "Who'd he hire to replace me?"

"Nobody," he says, shaking his head. "I don't know what he thinks he's doing. He's just gonna run this place into the ground further."

"So nobody's singing?"

"Nope, just the band every night."

"That doesn't make sense, does it?"

"It doesn't." He looks around to the rest of the guys. "We've all said as much but you know Freddy; he won't listen to us."

"Now tell us about this husband of yours." Julio wraps his arm around me. "What man is good enough for our Stella?"

I tell them how we met and about our fast-tracked love story. "Here's a picture of us on our honeymoon." I flip to a photo I took that Atlas didn't know about at the time. He's sitting in the back-ground on his phone behind me as I smile into the camera. I pass it around, the guys all teasing me, putting a much-needed smile on my face even if it feels like my heart's being ripped out as I lie about how wonderfully happy we are.

When the phone gets to Clyde, he lets out a laugh. "You sneaky little thing you," he says, handing me the phone. "I thought you said you didn't have a crush on that rich man."

I laugh in confusion. "What?"

"Your husband," he says, elbowing me playfully as the guys start to head toward the stage for their first set. "That handsome man with those suits I told you about, the bespoke ones like my daddy made.

Who knew all that time he was watching you from behind that light you two were falling in love."

I feel the color drain from my face as the guys continue laughing and walk up onstage. I sit in complete shock, so many questions racing through my mind as I close my eyes and relive every time I remember him sitting up there in the darkness... watching me.

# Chapter 20

## *Atlas*

"Where is she?" I shout at Freddy, holding him by the throat as I pin him against the wall of his office.

"I said I don't know!" he shouts back in a garbled mess of words.

"What did she want when she came in here?" Freddy falls forward, catching himself by his hands on his desk as he chokes on his own air.

"You son of a bitch!" He fumbles, reaching for the gun in his desk drawer again.

"Tsk, tsk," I click my tongue at him as I reach into the drawer and pull out the revolver. "Now I'm done asking nicely, Freddy."

"She wanted her job back, you bastard. She said she had money and tried to pay me, but I told her to get fucking lost."

I tuck the gun into my waistband and pull out a bill of sale, dropping it onto his desk along with a cashier's check.

"Sign that."

"What is it?" He looks at it, then back at me.

"Read it," I say, questioning if he can even do that.

"Freddy's isn't for sale." He tosses the contract back at me.

"Sign it and take the generous offer that's on that check and get the fuck out of Chicago."

"I said—" He's about to lunge toward me when I pull the gun from my waistband and point it at him, cocking the trigger back.

"And I said, sign the fucking contract and get the fuck out of my city."

He can't grab a pen fast enough, and he scribbles his name, shoving the check into the pocket of his lapel. I read over where he signed, making sure he's not attempting to fuck me in some other way.

"I signed it. Now please, don't kill me!" Tears stream down his face as he falls to his knees, his hands clasped together. I stare down at the pathetic piece of shit in front of me, realizing for the first time that I would kill for Stella. If it came to that, I wouldn't think twice.

"I have no interest in killing you," I say, putting the gun back into my waistband and grabbing the signed contract. "You have forty-eight hours to get out of town. If I even so much as get a whiff of a rumor that you're sneaking around here, I'll make sure this gun of yours is dropped off on the Cook County Commissioner's desk. And I can just about guarantee that there's a string of violence and felonies associated with this firearm."

I don't bother giving him a second warning. I walk out of the club and head home where I sit patiently waiting all through the rest of the night and the sunrise for my wife to come home.

I have no idea what time it is when she finally walks through my office door, but her anger is palpable. She swings the door open, causing it to bounce on the hinges.

"We need to talk," she demands.

I don't look at her. I continue staring down into my glass of scotch. I swirl it around a few more times.

"Why'd you quit singing, Stella?"

"How'd you know I sing, Atlas?"

I finish the liquor, placing the glass onto my desk and turning to look at her.

"You're my wife, darling. I know a great deal about you."

"Yes, I'd say you do." Her voice is calm. "Who are you?"

"You know who I am."

"No." She shakes her head, walking closer. "I know who you pretended to be. Who is the man who sat behind that light every Thursday for months and months on end and watched me." She comes closer. "And then came to my job every Friday morning like you were some goddamn knight in shining armor that was going to save me?" She glares at me. "So I'll ask again, who are you?"

"I did those things, yes," I say, having no reason to lie or even try to sugarcoat anything at this point. "But you know who I am, darling."

"No." She shakes her head, a look of pure disgust settling over her face. "I know who you pretended to be, who you wanted me to believe you were, but you're far from a knight in shining armor. You're the devil."

"You give me too much credit."

"Why?" she shouts through tears of rage. "Why me?"

"No other reason than happenstance."

She scoffs, "Happenstance? You ruined my fucking life over happenstance?"

"I was drunk. It was the night that Eleanor left. I wanted to forget who I was so I happened to stumble into a dive bar and I saw you." I think back to that first night, the way her beauty beckoned me. "It felt like you were singing to me that night, only me."

"This—isn't real." She sits down, shaking her head. "None of this is actually real. You—you stalked me and tricked me."

"I'm sorry, Stella, I am. I wish I could say I didn't mastermind every second of this, but I did. I knew that night, that second I saw you and you opened your mouth to sing... you were going to be mine."

"I'm not yours," she says through a snotty cry. "It's all fake, all of it. How could I ever be yours when you lied to me about everything? You're heartless." She spits the last sentence at me.

I don't argue with her because telling her that sitting here right now, watching her fall apart, is breaking my heart would be a slap in the face to her.

"Why didn't you ever tell me about your singing?" She doesn't answer right away, silence hanging like a wet blanket between us. "I love that about you. I miss hearing you."

"You don't deserve to hear me sing. That was my special thing, my secret that you don't deserve to know about. I kept it locked away from you because I knew—I knew that no matter how much I tried to tell my heart not to, I couldn't stop myself from falling in love with you. And even though I told myself over and over that it wasn't real, that I'll only end up breaking my own heart, in the end I'd still have a tiny part of me that you didn't hurt, that you didn't ruin, but now that's gone too." Her head falls into her hands as her shoulders sag.

"You're right." I look up at her. "I don't deserve to hear you sing. I don't deserve you or your love but not because of the reason you think."

"I don't understand. What do you mean?" I can see the panic growing on her face.

"I'm the reason you don't sing anymore, Stella. I'm the reason Freddy fired you." I watch as the reality of what I just admitted sinks in, her face going from white to red, then covered in tears as she crumples to the floor. If I'm burning this marriage down, I'm burning it to the ground. She deserves to know every single horrible thing I've done to her.

"Why?"

"Because I needed you, Stella, but I needed you to need me more so that you'd be willing to marry me. I saw the ambition on your face back then. I saw the way you poured your heart and soul into every line you sang. There's only one reason a woman as beautiful and talented as you would stay at a run-down club owned by a wannabe gangster when you could go anywhere and make way more money. You want to buy Freddy's, don't you?"

"I'm not a damsel in distress, Atlas. I never wanted or needed your rescuing. You're the one who needs saving... You're the one who needs rescued." She stands up, wiping away the rest of her tears and straightening her clothes before completely shutting down and walking out of my office.

# Chapter 21

## *Stella*

"You told him, really?" I roll my eyes. "Thanks."

Mac chases after me. "Hey, what? Told who?"

"Atlas," I say, completely unamused. "You told him I went to the city."

"I didn't," he says, holding up his hands. "I swear. I left the gate open a while back and I'm still in hot water for that."

"Well, he found out somehow and he's not too pleased."

His face falls. "Shit, does he know where you went?"

"I think so. He didn't say but yeah, I think he does. Did I get you in trouble?"

"I guess not, he hasn't said anything to me." Mac shrugs.

"Well, if you do get in trouble, I'm sorry. I shouldn't have gotten you involved."

He smiles at me. "Don't apologize. I was just about to head into the city myself, meeting up with a friend of mine."

I know I shouldn't ask him again, especially considering what Atlas has told me about his crush on me or whatever, but there's no way in hell I'm staying here tonight.

"Can I catch a ride again?"

"Totally. I'm leaving in ten. Catch you by the garages."

Ten minutes later I'm sitting in his passenger seat after sending a mayday text to Matilda. She replied back with a picture of two bottles of wine and a message that said red or white?

"Are you okay? You kind of look like you've been crying."

"Allergies." I shrug, looking in the side-view mirror to make sure Atlas isn't following us.

"I wouldn't make you cry."

I pause flipping through social media. "What?"

"I'm just saying." He shrugs, giving me a genuine smile. "If you ever wanted to hang out sometime, off the clock"—he uses air quotes —"I'd be down is all and I'm not an asshole so I won't make you cry."

"What do you mean off the clock? What is that?" I mimic his air quotes.

"This thing you're doing"—he laughs—"with Mr. Knight. I'm just saying once the timeline is up, then you and I should totally go out."

"Timeline?" I play dumb.

"Stella." He laughs. "I know about the contract."

My stomach drops to my ass. "Who told you?"

"Mr. Knight." He shrugs like it's no big deal. "He said you and I would get along well, probably hit it off, so he already gave us his blessing if that's what you're worried about."

It feels like the walls of this car are closing in on me, like my lungs are suddenly filled with water and I'm gasping for breath. I roll down the window, closing my eyes and breathing through my nose the rest of the way into the city.

"It's fake, it was all fake, it's fake." I blurt the words out the second Matilda throws her door open, her huge grin and the two bottles of wine she's holding up as a joke falling down to her side.

"Huh?"

"The marriage, Atlas meeting me randomly at work." I blurt the words out, everything coming out in a nonsensical jumbled mess.

"Oh my God, what happened?" She ushers me inside, placing the bottles on the counter and turning toward me. "Okay, breathe," she says, rubbing my back, mimicking exaggerated inhales and exhales with me. She sits me down on her couch, taking a seat beside me while I try to regain my composure.

"I-I'm so-so sorry," I stutter through my apology, dabbing at my cheeks with a wad of tissues I brought with me from the house.

"Shhh, hey." She continues rubbing my back. "Just focus on breathing. You don't need to say a word. I'm here." She wraps her arms around me, holding me for almost an hour as I sob into her arms.

Finally, after several more rounds of shaky voiced explanations and crying breaks, I manage to explain everything to Matilda. Atlas stalking me, the proposal, the millions of dollars, and how I knew deep down it all felt too good to be true.

"Holy shit." She stands, starting to pace her living room floor. "Holy shit!"

"Yeah," I say, letting out the longest sigh of my life. "All that to say, I'm so sorry for lying to you and keeping this from you. I—"

"No." She grabs my hands. "Don't be sorry. You did what you had to do. You are such a badass woman." She shakes her head and laughs. "I mean, God, I can't imagine handling all that. And for the record, I would have absolutely said yes to marrying that man, even for the one million so don't feel bad about that." She squints one eye. "Actually, I probably would have married him for free."

It makes me laugh and I do finally get to tell her how amazing the sex was, but it ends up sending me down another spiral of sobs.

"Can I say something and as your best friend, don't judge me."

I sit up from resting my head in her lap. "Okay."

"I think part of why this hurts so bad is because you are in love with him. Because over the last few hours, you have shown a little bit of anger but more than anything, you've just been sad." She cups my cheeks. "I think you're heartbroken, babe."

I can't help it, I burst into laughter. "Duh!" I finally say. "I know that; that's the problem!"

"Oh, well, I thought you thought were crying because of like all the lies and whatnot. I wasn't sure if you were aware that you were in love with him." She laughs.

"Well, I am. It does break my heart knowing he could lie to me like that but what kills me, what guts me is the fact he offered me to Mac like I was meat or something he could discard."

"Yeah, but to be fair, he did offer you money to basically kind of cheat the court system sooo I feel like he kind of let you know upfront the kind of guy he is."

"Are you seriously defending the megalomaniac right now?" I tease her.

"No! No, he's a total asshole, complete bastard. I just meant that I guess I figured you liked that about him, that he's a take charge, dominant, powerful man."

"I know and I do Mati. It's probably some fucked-up daddy issue stuff but honestly, that doesn't make it better. I just feel stupid and duped and... cheap."

"Even five million dollars richer?"

"Yeah." I laugh again. I knew her jokes about this would help me. "I just got caught up in it. I fell in love with him and I thought he was in love with me too, and I guess just facing that reality, or rather getting beat in the face with it, is a hard-ass pill to swallow. I mean, I knew at the end of the year it would gut me if he could just walk away, but knowing he's actively acting like he cares about me while offering me to another man is so low, so vile, so..." My voice trails off as I almost dry heave thinking about it.

"Ugh." She grabs me and hugs me. "I wish so bad I could make it all go away. I wish I could punch him and then kick him in the balls when he's on the ground and tell him he's a piece of shit but also thank him for being dumb enough to think it would work, hence making you a millionaire." She pushes me back and looks at me. "I also hate that you were dealing with all of this alone."

"That was a wonderful speech. Thank you." I wrap my arms around her, hugging her back.

"So what are you going to do? You can move in with me since your apartment is gone."

I shake my head. "Sadly, I don't think that's an option. I'm pretty positive there's no way out of this contract so odds are, I'm stuck in his Victorian prison castle for another ten months."

We both let out a long sigh, leaning our heads and bodies against each other.

"Well, the good news," Matilda says, "is ten long, probably agonizing months from now, you'll be free and the brand-new owner of Freddy's bar, living your best life with all of this bullshit a distant memory. Meanwhile, Atlas will still be a bitter, lonely man."

I smile, both of us laughing even though the thought of Atlas being a distant memory or bitter and lonely has what's left of my heart shattering into a million little pieces. Because after everything, the lies, the deception, the way he looked at me today made me want to beg him to tell me he loves me, to beg him to stay in this marriage with me.

But the thought of staying another ten months in that house with the only man I've ever loved slipping through my fingers day after day while I slowly die of a broken heart sounds like a death sentence.

# Chapter 22

## *Atlas*

Tonight it's my turn to wait for her.

I stand, silently staring out my office window as far-off headlights slowly make their way up the driveway. I gave her last night but tonight, she needs to be home, where she belongs. I sent Oliver to her friend's apartment after getting the address from Mac.

He tried explaining four different ways why, for the second time in less than a week, he had my wife in his car without my knowledge. And when he looked me in the eyes and lied to me, I seriously considered using that pistol I stole from Freddy and ruining both of their lives.

"You summoned me?" The door to my office flies open, and Stella marches in, both guns already blazing.

"I'm sorry. I did try calling you first and sent you a text that Oliver would be picking you up by eight."

"Yes, and I didn't answer which means I'm not ready yet."

"Well," I say, standing and walking toward her. "Even if it sickens you to hear it, you are my wife and you cannot be running around the city, staying over at people's houses... especially without my knowledge or consent." I keep my voice calm although inside I'm seconds away from telling her if she does it again, I'll knock some sense into her with a headboard.

"Knowledge and consent? Wow, that's rich coming from you." She crosses her arms over her chest. "I want to move out. I ca—won't live here anymore."

I bite my tongue.

"I realize that things are very different now between us, now that certain information has come to light, and while I don't expect you to forgive me, you signed a contract, a legally binding contract that stipulates you have to live with me until it's expiration."

"No." She shakes her head, fighting back tears. "No, I won't and you can't stop me." I stand there wanting to tell her that she's angry and she's reacting emotionally, but I know that will be like gasoline on a fire. "I'll sue," she says. "Yeah, I'll sue you for making me an offer of contract under false pretenses."

"False pretenses?" I ask.

"You lied about knowing me, about stalking me at my jobs for months. There has to be some legal precedent for that, and I know damn well there's camera footage at both places."

I'm not certain that she has a case or rather that she can prove that I did, in fact, stalk her. I could have easily went to Freddy's and her coffee shop because they're in the same neighborhood and while I'm confident there's camera footage at the coffee shop, I can just about guarantee a dive like Freddy's doesn't have jack shit for security.

"You're probably right and if I'm honest, you'd probably win." I step closer to her. "But I won't make you go through all of that, Stella. I'll give you the divorce."

She blinks several times. "I don't believe you," she finally says.

"If you'd rather go the hard route and sue me, you're welcome to, but I'm offering to save you a lot of time and headache."

"You'll divorce me now and lose ownership of the majority

shares? You'll lose the trust; you still have almost four months till your birthday."

"I will," I acknowledge. She stares at me in complete shock or disbelief, maybe both.

"What's the catch?"

"Nothing. No catch."

"There has to be a catch. You wouldn't throw away your one chance at owning Knight Enterprises."

I walk around my desk, reaching into the top drawer and pulling out a docket of papers. I walk back over to where she's standing and hand them to her.

"I've already signed them. There are red tabs where you need to sign, then I'll file them with the courts in the morning and since it's no contest, it will be finalized ninety days after they're filed."

She stares at her papers, her green eyes round and glassy as she looks at my signature, then quickly back at me. She's realizing that I'm not bluffing; it's written all over her face.

"I'm sorry," I say, reaching back to grab a pen from my desk and handing it to her. "Here you go." Call it *calling her bluff* if you want but I'm not backing down. I know damn well what Stella wants. She wants me. She wants this marriage and if I know her half as much as I guarantee I do, I know she won't sign the papers... or at least I hope she doesn't.

She reaches her hand out slowly. It trembles slightly as she takes the pen from my hand and looks back at the papers. She places them on her lap, the tip of the pen on the line about to sign when she looks back up at me.

"Why?"

"Why what?"

"Why are you willing to do this—to throw your one possibility of owning your family company away when work means more to you than... than anything?"

I sit back on the edge of my desk. "Why? Why does it even matter?"

"Because you never walk away from a fight, ever." She stares at me almost suspiciously.

I hang my head, bringing my hand to rub against my forehead. I'm tired. Tired from trying to hide my own feelings from myself. Tired of trying to fight the feelings. And while I hope and pray that she doesn't sign these papers—not because I'm worried about the shares, but because I can't stomach the thought of losing her—if she does, I will grant her a divorce and I will let her live her life in peace without me.

"I don't have any more fight left in me. You won the war, Stella."

# Chapter 23

## *Stella*

"What do you mean?"

My heart feels like it's about to beat out of my chest. I promised myself that I would walk out of this house tonight a free woman, but now that I have the papers in my lap, a pen in my hand... I can't do it.

*Sign them*, I think to myself, my hand trembling as I grip the pen. Tears cloud my vision as I stare down at the papers. I have the keys to my freedom in my hands and I can't seem to deliver myself.

"Life, work, all of it, it has no meaning without you." He lifts his face, his eyes staring into my soul. "I don't care about owning Knight Enterprises. I don't care about winning a fight or an argument or breaking rules." He moves down to his knees in front of me, his hands reaching out to cup my face. "All I care about is you and I can't stomach the thought of hurting you more than I already have."

"Why?"

"Because I love you." I stare back at him, wanting to believe him.

"I thought you didn't believe in love anymore."

"I didn't. I thought I knew what love was with Eleanor, but I realized the first second I kissed you, I felt more in that moment than I ever did with her or anyone."

"Then why lie, Atlas? About her, about knowing her and hiding your entire postmortem breakup chat?" I stand up and walk away from him. "Which by the way I would have completely understood. It's normal to have that talk. What's not normal is hiding from me the fact that she came to your office and confessed her love for you. And then you expect me to believe it was just *nothing*?"

"It wasn't nothing with her. She and I were together for several years and I was in love with her."

"When did it end?"

"The first night I saw you at Freddy's." He stares at me, emotionless.

"Then why lie? If it was truly over?"

"It was over the night I first saw you. She called me after that event we attended together, the night you met her. She told me she made a mistake leaving me and I told her that I was married and to respect those boundaries. I will admit that it caused me to question things with her, if I made the right choice by telling her that. I thought I was still in love with her... That was the first night I came home drunk. I thought she understood which she clearly didn't when she showed up unannounced at my office. That's the second night I came home drunk."

"Great." I nod my head like this is just a totally normal conversation I'm having. "And then what, you called her back to say you were free in less than a year?"

"I called her up to apologize to her. She shared some things I had done in our relationship that hurt her and I wanted to make it right. I'm sorry that I didn't share that with you. I did think I was going to marry her at the time, but not now. I even had a ring made for her." I swear when he says that he glances down at my hand which makes me look down at it.

*This can't possibly get any worse.*

"Where is it? Did she keep it?" I ask, knowing full well this might be the nail in the coffin in his death sentence. I just might snap and lunge across this desk.

"No," he says, shaking his head. "I never had the chance to give it to her thankfully. But actually"—he gestures toward my hand—"you're wearing it."

# Chapter 24

## *Atlas*

Stella looks down at her hand.

"That makes me feel less bad about hating it." She pulls it off and throws it across the room. It clatters somewhere to the floor. "Tell her she's welcome to it."

"I didn't want to add any more complications into our marriage and considering I fully expected it to be over in a year with no feelings or sex, I didn't think Eleanor would ever even come up in conversation. There are several wrenches that were thrown into this plan by us sleeping together and I take full responsibility for that."

"Did you ever feel bad or guilty?"

"Every day. In the beginning I pushed it aside. I hated that I was lying to you. I felt a lot of guilt, but I decided that in that moment, my needs were more important than yours. You're young, I figured you'd move on easily and find a great guy like Jason and wouldn't think twice about me again."

"Or Mac?"

I furrow my brow, anger instantly coursing through me. "Why him?"

*Why are you asking a question you don't want to know the answer to?*

"You're sick, you know that?"

"What?"

"I know," she says, her voice shaking. "I know what you told Mac."

"What did I tell Mac?" I say, my curiosity now very piqued.

She shakes her head at me, a look of pure disgust on her face. "How could you?"

"Sweetheart." I step toward her, gently grabbing her arms so I can look in her eyes. "What the fuck did Mac say to you?"

She looks confused, her eyes searching mine. "He— He told me that you said he could have me or that he should date me when you're done with me."

I release her arms, stepping back as my hands ball into fists so tight my knuckles grow white.

"When did he say that to you, Stella?" I try to remain calm, to keep my blood pressure under control, but it's no use, thoughts of that pistol flashing through my head again.

"Yesterday when he—wait, did you not say that to him?"

"What?" I grab her again, my arms around her. "Baby, I would never, ever say that about you. Jesus Christ, you thought—?" I pull her back away from me. "You thought I offered you to him?" My chest burns. "You are my fucking world, Stella. If he so much as looks at you again, I'll tear him limb from fucking limb, do you understand me? I-I love every single thing about you, your soul." I place my hand over her heart. "You're mine, Stella." I rest our foreheads together. "Mine."

Her body collapses against mine like she's just shrugged a huge weight from her shoulders. But my body stiffens, anger pulsing through me as I play back the conversation I had with Mac just a few short weeks ago after the night he left the gate open.

*"Mac," I say as he turns to walk out of the garage after bringing me home from work.*

*"Yeah, boss?"*

*"I noticed the front gate was left open last night."* Before I can tell him that Oliver assured me he didn't do it, he interrupts me.

*"Oh, right."* He shakes his head. *"Oliver mentioned it to me and told me to talk to you about that. I'm so sorry, sir. It won't happen again."*

I nod. *"Thank you."* He turns and walks away, an uneasy feeling settling over me. I remind myself to check the security cameras for that evening later.

"No, wait." She pulls back, shaking her head. "Don't manipulate me. Don't do this. I don't even know you."

"You do know me," I say, pulling my attention back to her.

"It's so unfair. I feel like you got to know things about me because you watched me. I don't even know your favorite color"—she starts to pace—"or drink or sports team."

"That stuff doesn't matter when it comes to knowing someone on a deeper level. My favorite color is orange. My favorite drink is black coffee, and I'm a season ticket holder for the Chicago Blackhawks. I don't know those things about you either, but I want to. I want to spend a lifetime together learning those things about you. Finding out all the little secrets you've only told your best friends." I reach out gently, running a tendril of her hair through my fingers. "But nothing I ever learn about you will make me love you less than I do right now. Everything I learn about you, I'm confident will only make me love you more. I know who you are in here." I drop my hand down to her heart again.

"I don't know who you are though." She pushes my hand away again. I see flashes of different people you might be. It's like you have this cold, emotionless exterior, this facade in place that even I can't get past most days, and then once in a great while it slips and I see the real you, the man I want you to be. I felt like that week we had together, I got to see the real you. You didn't try to tamp down your dominance; you didn't try to push me away or hide who you were. I just—" She shakes her head. "It's confusing. I never know which version I'm going to get. And now, it feels like you're a monster."

I place my hands on my desk, no longer able to swallow down all the things I've been wanting to say to her. "Fine." I push off the desk. "You want to know who I am as a person?" I pick up the divorce papers where she left them, tearing them in half and tossing them back onto the desk. "You're my wife. You made vows to me and there's no way in fuck I'd ever let a judge determine if my marriage is irrevocably broken, because it's not." I slam my hand down on the desk, making her jump.

"I am not a monster or heartless, Stella, and you know that. What I did to you was cruel and wrong, but it gutted me every fucking day I looked at you. Why do you think I tried pushing you away? Why do you think I tried to drink you away?" I shake my head, her eyes staring at me like she's waiting on pins and needles for what I'll say next. "But I know," I say, stepping toward her, "that no matter how much I drink or try to push you away, no matter how far you ran, I would never, ever stop searching for you because you're mine."

I grab her around the waist, her mouth falling open with a gasp when I pick her up and set her on my desk. I push her thighs aside with my own legs, coming to stand in front of her with my hand in her hair and my lips within a centimeter of hers.

"And we both know that's exactly the man you fell in love with, isn't it, Stella?" Her eyes glare into mine but the pink flush that's creeping up her neck and her hard nipples pressing against her blouse give her away. Her lips are still parted, her breaths coming out in rapid puffs against my lips. "You might hate the fact that you love a cruel and sometimes heart-less asshole, but you know I will never be that way to you again, ever. I will never lie to you. I will destroy every fucking person alive who tries to hurt you or take you from me." I stare into her eyes like I'm staring into her soul. "Look at me. I never want to exist another day in this world without you by my side. You are my world, my everything. I am nothing without you."

Her pupils dilate. "I haven't forgiven you."

"I know," I say, my lips grazing hers.

"You have to earn my trust."

"I will." I pull back a trifle, tipping her head slightly back. "I will spend every single day of the rest of my life if that's what it takes to earn your trust. Do you love me, Stella?"

"Yes," she says softly.

"Good." I lean forward, kissing her once, lingering long enough to give her a chance to push me away, but she doesn't. "Now, can we move on to the good news?"

"Don't you want to ask me if I want to stay married?" she questions me with a bratty little smirk.

"No," I say confidently. "I already know you do."

"That's pretty presumptuous considering you're the one who did all of the lying and whatnot." She folds her arms over her chest.

I tighten my grip on the back of her neck as I lean in toward her again. Call it playing dirty but I know exactly how to push her buttons and keep her in line. I can give her a single look and have her squeezing her thighs together in seconds, completely forgetting what she was saying. "Do you want to have another argument right now or do you want me to tell you about your early anniversary present?" She snaps her mouth shut and I step back to my desk to remove the second docket of papers and hand them to her.

"What is this?"

"It was going to be your anniversary gift, but I thought you could use it a little earlier."

Her eyes go from skeptical to huge in a matter of seconds when she realizes it's the deed to Freddy's. "How?"

I reach into the drawer again and pull out the keys. "Money." I smile at her. "With your husband's touch of—*finesse*."

"Meaning?" She crooks an eyebrow at me. "Remember you said you'd never lie to me again."

I nod, thinking through how best to put it. "I pulled his own pistol on him after I stole it from him. Threatened to drop it off at the police station if he didn't leave town in the next forty-eight hours. I think that about covers it. Any other questions?"

"So you bought it? For me?"

She drops the papers onto my desk when I grab her behind the knees and tug her forward. "Actually, no more talking." I cover my mouth with hers, sliding my tongue past her lips. "Unless you're saying my name. And yes, I bought it for you," I say, coming up for air between kisses. "It's all yours."

"Wait." She pushes against me again.

"Jesus." I shake my head. "Are you trying to kill me, Stella?"

"I just—I want to know what we are."

"What we are?"

"Yeah, are we dating or...?"

"Baby, you better be joking right now—dating?" I reach down and unbuckle my belt. "I thought I made it perfectly clear earlier when I tore those divorce papers in half." Zipper is next. I reach beneath her skirt, pushing her panties to the side. "We are not fucking dating." I replace my finger with the tip of my cock as I continue to tease her. "We're married and we're going to stay married till the day"—I slide my head inside her, moaning at the warmth of her pussy—"we die." I slide farther in.

"Tell me," she says against my lips as I begin to move my hips, sliding in and out of her in long, slow strokes.

"I love you." I say the words I know she wants to hear, the words she needs to hear. "More than anything."

Her hands are in my hair, her thighs squeezing against me as she claws at my back. I rip her shirt open, buttons clattering across my desk as I bury my face in her tits. I pull the cups of her bra down, her breasts spilling over the top of them, bouncing with each thrust of my hips.

"Oh, oh yes." Her fingers dig into my skin through my shirt, her nails certain to leave a mark on my arm. I lean forward, sucking her nipple into my mouth, leaving her with a perfect outline of my teeth.

She watches me lean forward, repeating the same action on her other breast.

"I like seeing your body marked by me." I lift my hips at the ends of my thrusts, hitting her G-spot repeatedly. Her mouth falls open, and her eyes flutter closed as I feel her walls tightly clenching me. I try to hold back but I can't.

"Oh fuck," I groan loudly, "your pussy is milking my cock so good, fuck!" My vision goes blurry. I hold on to Stella as my orgasm rips through my body.

"Where are you taking me for our honeymoon?" she asks when we both have come back down and I finish refastening my belt.

"Didn't we already go on a honeymoon?" I step into the bathroom to grab a warm washcloth for Stella.

"I mean, I did. You worked the entire time so I think it's safe to say, you owe me a new honeymoon." I press the cloth against her and she winces.

"That's fine with me. Do you want a real wedding?" I straighten out her bra, buttoning the two remaining left on her blouse.

"I don't think so. I don't have any family and very few friends, not enough for a wedding."

"We can always do one just for us?"

"Do you want to?" She wraps her arms around my neck.

"I do."

She smiles, leaning in to kiss me on the nose. "How about a private wedding, just the two of us, followed by a honeymoon in the same place?"

"I like that idea. In fact, I have a yacht so we could do it maybe in the south of France or Italy."

"I'm sorry, you have a yacht?"

"Well, *we* have a yacht actually."

"I still can't wrap my head around this rich billionaire lifestyle." She tilts her head. "Aren't you ever worried I married you for your money?" It sends us both into a fit of laughter.

222 Dark as Knight

"This might be a new fairy tale. The one where she marries the man for money, but they end up falling in love."

"Yeah?" She smiles, her eyes lighting up. "And how does it end?"

"Well, they both live happily ever after, of course, and along the way, they fall more and more in love each day, and they have a well above average sex life complete with all sorts of fun and exciting new toys to insert." She laughs again, her head falling back and exposing her neck, giving me a chance to kiss her there softly. "And last but not least, a family of their own."

———

I SEETHE AS I STARE AT THE GRAINY BLACK-AND-WHITE IMAGE staring back at me. An image of Mac, just outside the gates with his arms wrapped around my ex. I run my fingers over the cool steel of Freddy's pistol in my lap as I contemplate how I plan to destroy Mac and Eleanor.

Part of me knew she was unfaithful to me but I didn't want to face it. At the time it was because of my ego, now it's because I don't want to take accountability for my part in it. While I know there's never a justified reason for cheating, I take full responsibility for pushing her into the arms of another man.

What I can't let go of, though, is the fact that I know she's using him to try and destroy my marriage to Stella. I tap my fingers on the desk, thinking about the way she looked at me the day she stood in my office and told me she wouldn't let me go without a fight. What I can't figure out is how she knew. In all our years together, I never once told her about the clause because I didn't want her worried that I was with her for that reason.

I stare at the clock; the sun will be rising soon. The fire I lit in the fireplace with all copies of the contract, divorce papers, and NDA between Stella and me now just a slowly smoldering pile of ash. I place the gun back into a locked drawer and close my computer screen, heading back upstairs to spend the morning in bed with my wife.

I slide between the sheets, Stella rolling over but not opening her eyes. "Mmm," she moans pleasantly as she snuggles up against my chest. I wrap my arms around her warm body as she falls back into a deep sleep. But I can't sleep. My thoughts are focused on nothing but revenge.

———

"Mac," I say, placing my coffee mug on the counter once Stella has left the kitchen. "Why don't you give me a ride into work this morning?"

"You sure, sir? Oliver asked me t—"

"Yeah." I drape my arm around his shoulders as I lead him toward the garage. "Oliver will understand."

Once we exit the garage and leave the driveway, I start probing. "So Mac, how long have you worked for me now?"

"Uh, about eighteen months, sir." He glances at me in the rearview mirror, his nerves palpable.

"Hmm, makes sense," I mutter as I do the math for the timeline of when Eleanor would have been able to get to him.

"What was that, sir?"

"I said, that makes sense."

"What makes sense, sir?"

"The timeline." His eyes linger a little longer on mine in the mirror this time before he looks back at the road. "Did she seduce you before or after she left me?"

"I—I'm sorry, sir?" His face grows red as he grips the steering wheel tighter.

"Let's cut the shit, Mac. There's no need to play like the coy, dumb kid who barely knows his head from his ass. I'm aware that you told my wife I offered her to you."

"I—" I hold up my hand and he snaps his mouth closed.

"Was it before or after she left?"

"Before," he finally says through a cracked voice.

"As suspected." I debate on breaking his heart, considering shielding him from the reality of the woman he probably thinks loves him back. "She doesn't love you, Mac. Never did. I know Eleanor and she used you. I don't know what she promised you either. Money? A life together?"

"Yes," he finally says in defeat.

"Yeah, neither of those will happen. She will turn around and threaten to destroy you, blackmail you, or something of the sort."

"H—how do you know that?" he stammers, the hope quickly dwindling from his eyes.

"Because Eleanor is just like me and that's exactly what I would do to you." His face falters.

"She wouldn't do that, she—I think she really does love me."

"Well, I hope for your sake that she does and that you two will live happily ever after together, but let's be honest. Hope is shit and I'm here to bring you reality because you fucking crossed me and you lied to my wife and almost cost me her." I'm done being nice. "So I'll tell you what's going to happen next, Mac. You're going to text your little girlfriend and have her meet you at my office. Then the two of you will listen as I explain to you how this is going to play out."

I swing the door open and step out of the car once we reach the parking garage. Mac parks and gets out of the car, his squat stature almost shaking as he steps into the elevator with me.

"She's on her way," he confirms, sliding his phone into his pocket.

"One thing I still can't figure out though," I say as I look over at him. "How'd you find out about the contract?"

"Contract?" He squints.

"The one you mentioned to Stella."

"Oh." He shrugs. "I didn't know what the contract was about. I just said to Stella what Eleanor told me to say."

"Interesting." We exit the elevator, making our way to my office. "Good morning, Florence." I nod toward her.

"Good morning, Mr. Knight." She smiles back at me, then waves to Mac.

"So then how did she know?" I turn to face him once I close the door behind us. His face is pale, almost yellow.

"I—I let her into the house that night, the night I left the gate open. I erased the footage of her in your house."

"And the part I did see on the video, of you and her outside the gate, was that when she left and you didn't realize the frame caught it?" He nods, his hands dropping down to his stomach.

"Ca—can I use the bathroom?" Mac asks nervously, a thin layer of sweat accumulating on his upper lip. The kid looks like he's seconds away from losing his breakfast on my office floor.

"There," I say, pointing toward the door to the left. He darts for the restroom, the door slamming behind him.

Before he re-emerges, there's a gentle tap on my office door. Eleanor swings it open, stepping into the room with a triumphant grin on her face before I even have the chance to say a word.

"What?" She practically sneers at me. "Surprised that I can be heartless too?"

"Not at all." I casually take a seat in my office chair.

"Where is he? Where's Mac?"

"In the restroom, puking his guts up." Her face falters. "What? You thought this was a happy meeting?" I don't hold back my laugh. "Let me guess, you thought you were going to show up to my office and what? Blackmail me? Tell the board and they'd declare my marriage void or something?" Her chin quivers slightly, but then she clenches her jaw and squares her shoulders. "You didn't ruin anything, Eleanor. In fact, you just made Stella and me realize we love each other. You also made me realize there isn't anything I won't do to protect her."

"I did this for you, for us," she says through a tearful, shaky breath.

"For us?"

"Yes, for us! I wanted to prove to you"—she walks around my

desk, reaching for my hands—"that I too will do whatever it takes to have you, to make us work. I love you, Atlas. She doesn't; she never will. She doesn't know you the way I do. Who you really are."

I stare back at her in disgust, half in shock at her behavior. In all our time together, she was always reserved, cold even. "Stella knows me better than you ever did, Eleanor, and you have nobody to blame but yourself for that. You threw me away."

"Please." She grabs for me. "I love you, Atlas!"

Mac finally emerges from the bathroom, his face contorted in anger. "You what?"

Eleanor whips her head around toward him. "Oh please, you're twenty years old. You really thought I wanted anything to do with you?"

I see the embarrassment then sadness run through him. She really is heartless. She goes from panicked begging and tears to dead-eyed and emotionless in seconds.

"I—I loved you; you said you loved me." He starts to cry and I stand up.

"Enough." I look over at Eleanor. "You have one chance to walk out of my office and never speak to me or my wife again." She opens her mouth to interrupt. "You need help, Eleanor. Real help. And what you did to Mac, he's a boy still." I shake my head. "You're cruel."

A mask falls back over her face as she grabs her purse and turns toward my office door. "Come on, Mac." She snaps her fingers like he's a dog. He looks at me.

"Mac is staying here, Eleanor. He works for me, not you."

She pauses, her gaze going from me to Mac, then back to me. I can see the anger growing at the realization that I'm giving him a second chance but she never got one. Her gaze lingers. "Goodbye, Atlas," she finally says before slamming the door behind her.

"I still work for you?" I look over at Mac, his eyes red even though he tried to hide the fact that he's been crying.

"Do you still want to work for me?"

"Yes, sir," he says, taking several steps toward me. "And I promise you, I would never, ever do anything—"

"I know, Mac," I say, placing my hand on his shoulder as I look him in the eyes. "Don't let it happen again."

He nods, smiling before practically jogging out of my office and back down to the parking garage. I did my due diligence on Mac long before I hired him. The kid came from nothing; he had nothing, and she took even more from him. I second-guess the man I was when I loved Eleanor, but then I'm reminded of something that Stella told me.

*"You attract the love you think that you deserve," she said with such casual confidence, like she didn't just drop wisdom on me that I'd never once considered. "And someday, when you finally realize you deserve true love... it'll find you."*

I'm not saying I'm a good person or that I'll ever end up someplace good in the afterlife, but I know one thing. She's the closest I'll ever come to entering heaven and no amount of hell will keep me from her love.

# Chapter 25

## *Stella*

### Four Months Later...

"**D**amn." Atlas admires my ass as I bend over the bed in my heels and lingerie. "Happy birthday to me." His hands find their way over my hips, tracing the edges of my garter belt up to the string that runs up my ass.

"Atlas, we can't be late." I shoo his hands away as I step into the dress he laid out for me. When I asked him a few weeks back what he wanted for his birthday, he told me he wanted Stella's opening night to be his celebration.

Over the last several months, I have worked tirelessly with contractors, lawyers, engineers, and the city to make sure this remodel not only stayed on budget but ahead of schedule.

"You expect me to walk in on you bent over with your ass in the air and not do something about it?" He pulls his hand back and smacks my cheek that is now protected by a layer of material. His hand lingers, grabbing a handful while nuzzling my neck.

"Yes, I do when you just had me in the shower and then on the closet floor after and then on the bathroom counter."

"I don't recall you complaining or telling me to stop." His hands find my breasts. "In fact," he says, toying with my nipples that have grown increasingly more sensitive over the last few weeks, "I recall you being the one to join me in the shower—what bra are you wearing? Your tits feel bigger." He's already pulling the front of my dress down, biting and sucking my nipples. My ability to remain focused on getting ready is slowly dissipating.

"No, stop." I pull my dress back up, walking over to the counter to put on my jewelry. "I promised Mati we'd be there a little early so I can talk to her sister."

"Fine. I promise not to distract the talent any longer right now, but when we get home tonight, you're going to be my present." He kisses my forehead, stepping into his closet to finish getting ready as an exciting flutter settles in my belly. I glance down, my hands instinctively resting against my lower abdomen as I think about the news I have to tell Atlas tonight.

When we arrive at the club and step inside, it still feels like a complete dream I'm living in. This place that I've worked so hard to bring to life finally has the crowd it deserves. There's already a line to get in, the doors not opening for another forty-five minutes.

Terry at the coffee shop has been telling all the customers about the grand opening of Stella's as well as hanging flyers. Atlas' friends and business associates are in attendance as well. We make our rounds, saying hello to everyone and engaging in small talk.

"Dexter, hi!" I throw my arms around Clyde's son and give him a warm hug. I met him two months back when he officially moved back to Chicago and started rehearsing with his dad. "You're playing tonight, right?"

"I am. Wouldn't miss it for the world." He smiles, holding up his trumpet case. "I'm gonna go warm up with Dad. I'll see you onstage."

I walk back down the hallway, ducking into my office for a moment where I find Atlas waiting for me.

"How'd you know I'd end up in here?" I laugh as he pulls me into his arms.

"Because I know you." He spins me around, the slow hum of the music outside making its way through the door. My office is a dream now. You'd never guess by looking at it that it once looked like a crime scene. Lush white curtains frame the window that's been upgraded, allowing fresh air and the Chicago sun to stream through—the few months we see it. "How are you doing? Feeling nervous at all?"

"I was for a minute actually; that's a really big crowd. But now, not so much, I'm really excited to sing again. It's been so long."

He pauses our dancing, pulling me closer so his nose is touching mine. "I'm so sorry I ever took that away from you."

"I forgive you."

We stand in each other's arms, finally leaving the office when I'm ready to go onstage and welcome everyone here tonight.

"Good luck, sweetheart." Atlas kisses me, excusing himself to go take a seat while I step onstage.

"Good evening." I smile nervously and wave. "I've never given a speech or anything like this before." I keep it very short, thanking everyone who helped bring my dream to life, my amazing and loving band and my husband, the love of my life.

Everyone raises a glass in a toast, then the band starts up. The lights dim and I take my place on the stage. I glance around the dark room, trying to find Atlas, but I can't find him. I hear the opening notes and I close my eyes, taking in a slow, steady breath before the lights come back on and I open my eyes.

I let out the first notes of the song, my gaze landing on Atlas sitting back behind the spotlight. All I can make out are his shoes and on the right side, his hand with his pinky ring. I lift my eyes to where his would be, the light blinding me as I run my hands over the curves of my body. I sway to the music, losing myself in the rhythm as I sing to my husband.

When the final note is sung and the night is over, we make our way outside to the waiting car. Atlas' hand is in my hair, tangling with my curls as I look over at him.

"You were very naughty tonight, my love. The way you touched yourself while you sang to me was quite seductive."

"Was it?" I run my finger up his inner thigh. "I didn't realize it."

"Mmm, do you have any idea what you do to me?" His hand is on my thigh, his lips on my neck.

"I'm sorry, Oliver. Could you?"

"Yes, ma'am." Oliver slides the partition into place, Atlas already so consumed with what he's doing to me he's completely oblivious to where we are.

"You know, I didn't get you a birthday present."

Atlas sits back. "I know, I told you not to. Besides, I thought I told you earlier, you're my present. Also, how you woke me up this morning was about the best birthday present I can get."

"About that, there's nothing you'd possibly want?"

"No." He laughs, looking at me sideways. "Baby, I have everything I could possibly want already. I'm serious."

"It's just that..." I grab my clutch nervously. "You remember a few months back when I mentioned how I wasn't on birth control?" I undo the clasp, reaching inside to pull out a positive pregnancy test. "I somehow let it slip a lot longer than I should have."

He stares at the pregnancy test, slowly lifting his eyes to mine. "I was wrong," he says, my breath hitching in my chest. "This is the best birthday present I could ever get." His shock finally turns into laughter as we both hold each other, crying tears of joy and probably fear as we launch into every little idea we have for a nursery or name or how we'll spend our mornings on the weekends with a baby and a toddler and what it will be like to watch them grow into a teenager, then an adult.

Before we've made it home, we've both agreed we'll set up an appointment with the doctor tomorrow because Atlas doesn't believe the pregnancy test in his hand, let alone the four or five others I told him I took along with that one.

We crawl into bed, both of us exhausted but too excited to sleep. We talk for hours about life, about our first thoughts of each other, about our hopes for each other and our growing family.

"You know, this is going to sound incredibly cliché but"—he looks over at me—"you said you didn't need saving and I don't think you did. I think I did. I just didn't realize it."

"I know, I remember telling you that. Looks like I'm the knight in shining armor after all," I say, making him smile.

"I guess so, but what does that make me? A damsel in distress?"

"No." I climb atop him, pulling his hands above his head as I lean forward. I trail my lips over his warm skin, the feeling of his body coming alive beneath me. "I think deep down inside, I knew who you really were that day you took me home."

"Yeah? And who am I, darling?" His eyes darken as he looks back up at me and somehow, I'm positive he already knows what I'm going to say.

"You're the devil in disguise."

**Want MORE naughty billionaires?**

**Check out the entire *Chicago Billionaires* Series or keep reading for a sample of *Very Bad Things*.**

*He said he wants to do bad things to me…very bad things.*

A BILLIONAIRE ROMANCE

# VERY
# BAD
# THINGS

## ALEXIS WINTER

He said he wants to do bad things
to me...very bad things.

**The first time I met single dad Weston Vaughn, I
thought it was my meet cute.
But it turns out, my knight in shining armor was just a
grumpy billionaire in a custom suit.**

After a nightmare year of losing not only my fiancé and my mother,
I'm ready to start over.
And what better way than to land a teaching job at the prestigious
Crestwood Academy in Chicago.

Imagine my surprise though when the handsome stranger I
accidentally poured hot coffee on in front of the Eiffel Tower, turns
out to be the father of one of my students.
The same stranger that made me miss my flight back home from
Paris.

He might be devilishly handsome, but no amount of good looks can
make up for his arrogant and bossy attitude.

It takes everything I have to plaster on a smile and deal with his antics but the school is in desperate need of his participation in our annual silent auction and I'm tasked with getting him on board.

But when he shows up on my doorstep, desperate for a babysitter, I agree...if only that was the last favor he demands of me.
Next thing I know, I'm flying to the Bahamas on a private jet with him and his daughter and sailing off into the sunset on his private yacht as the hired help.

Soon our back and forth banter goes from scorching jabs to fiery passion.
And while falling in love again is the furthest thing from my mind, a summer fling might just what I need.

Instead, I'm flung right into some dangerous drama that sees me getting fired from my dream job.
So when I decide I need space and a fresh start, he gives me one week before he shows up at my apartment and demands we stay together.

**One thing I've learned about Weston Vaughn, he doesn't negotiation.**
**He gets what he wants, no matter the cost.**
**Even if what he wants is me pregnant.**

# Prologue

## Daphne

"I'm moving to Paris."

"Right, and I just bought a house in London. We should summer together in Spain." My best friend Xana laughs before biting into her eggs Benedict. I don't laugh. "Wait," she says around a half-chewed mouthful of eggs and English muffin once she realizes I'm not joking. "Are you serious?"

"Yup."

She chews furiously, swallowing the bite. "Paris as in France? The country?"

"One and the same."

"Why? How?"

"I don't have it all figured out yet, but I will." I shrug. "And you know why. The last two years for me have been a nightmare, for lack of a better word. I need a change of scenery, change of pace." I glance out the window of our favorite brunch café in downtown Chicago. I love this city, always have, but ever since I lost my mom and my fiancé less than six months apart, it feels like this place is a haunted tomb to me. A constant reminder of what my life could have been, what it *should* have been.

"You can't just up and move to another country, Daph. People like us don't move to Paris. It's one of the most expensive cities in the world and last time I checked, you're not a secret millionaire."

"I know but people do it every day." Her lack of enthusiasm is a little frustrating, but I know it's only because she's worried about me. How would I feel if she just up and told me she was moving halfway around the globe tomorrow?

"What people?"

"I don't know, people! I watch *House Hunters International* all the time and people are constantly relocating to other countries."

"Yes, those people usually have a job that is already there or transferring them or they have family there to help them."

"Yeah, well, I can easily find work. I can be an au pair, teach English, work in a pastry shop, or any number of jobs."

Her face softens a touch when she sees my frustration. "Daph, listen, I'm not trying to be a Debbie downer who rains all over your parade, but running away to Paris isn't the answer to your issues with Chicago and what you've gone through. What about that job at Crestwood Academy you applied for? You were so excited about that opportunity."

"I haven't heard from them and it's been months. They made it sound so promising after that second interview, but then poof"—I make a motion with my hand for emphasis—"nothing."

"Did you reach out to them?"

"Twice. No response."

"Well, it is the end of the school year so maybe they're just swamped. You know how it is being that we're both teachers and going through it ourselves at the moment. Speaking of, I'll be spending my Saturday night and all day Sunday grading my freshman biology students' finals. Fun, fun," she says sarcastically.

Xana and I met in third grade and have been inseparable ever since. As the always outgoing extrovert, she immediately befriended me. We bonded over the fact that we both thought *Scooby-Doo* was a far superior cartoon to any of the Nickelodeon ones. We went to the same college here in Chicago and both studied education.

"I can't imagine teaching middle schoolers or high schoolers, they're so intimidating." I shudder at the thought of feeling constantly judged by teenagers every day.

"Nah." She laughs. "You just have to know how to handle them. Most of the time they laugh and think I'm being super corny when I try to be cool. Sometimes, though, they can be little shits. I won't lie. So are you doing tutoring this summer again or summer school?"

Every summer we usually pick one or the other, either tutor privately or teach summer school in our district. It's not exactly like you make enough teaching at a public school to get by. Most of us have summer jobs to make ends meet.

"Um, about that." I pick nervously at the wadded-up napkin on the table in front of me. "I may or may not have told the school that I wasn't coming back after this year."

"You quit?" Her eyes practically bug out of her head.

"Yeah, I guess that's the correct way of putting it."

"Jesus, Daph." She drops her fork and rubs her forehead. "Why? Did you actually put in your notice and tell the district?"

"Yes, and because I—well, first I thought I was getting that job at Crestwood. They dangled that carrot pretty close so I thought I had it, but then after not hearing anything, I realized that moving to Paris was a better idea anyway." I smile, really trying to sell the idea to Xana as a thought out plan and not an impulsive decision that I'm very close to regretting.

"Okay, well, I'm sure that your administrator will be more than willing to take you back. You've worked at Davis Elementary for three years. They love you there."

"I already booked my trip to Paris," I blurt out, knowing I'm only going to add fuel to Xana's panicked fire.

"You what?"

"It's just a fact-finding mission. I'm going for a week to explore and see the city." It's more than that; it's the closing of a door. The end of a story that I never even had the chance to start.

"Alone? When?"

"Yes, alone. I leave next Monday."

"You're not going to sign some lease when you're there, are you?" She eyes me suspiciously.

"No, it's just a trip. You know I've always wanted to go there and that was where Carson and I planned to honeymoon. I figured it would be the final chapter in that part of my journey, a farewell of sorts."

"Yeah." She smiles. "I like that idea. I do worry about you traveling alone, but I think it will be the closure you need. Plus, you've talked about Paris for as long as I can remember."

Paris has been my dream since I was in fifth grade and watched *Funny Face* for the first time. I begged my parents to take me, but when you grow up below the poverty line, that's not really a realistic dream. My mom tried letting me down easy; she didn't want to destroy my dream of going there someday even though there was no way we'd ever afford it. Instead, she bought us both berets, croissants, and cheese and we would pretend we were sitting at a Parisian café on our back porch. My gaze drifts away as I smile, remembering the one time she indulged us and bought real macarons from a local bakery.

"I bet your mom would be so happy right now." I don't have to tell Xana where my mind went just now. She already knows. Not only did I lose my fiancé Carson in a tragic car accident two years ago, but I was still mourning the loss of my mom to cancer just five short months before he passed.

"She would be... Carson too."

"Did you tell your dad?" I can see the apprehension on her face as she asks.

I nod, finishing my tea. "Yeah. He was happy for me and I promised I'd send him a postcard from Paris."

"How are things going with you two? Have you seen him lately?"

"Not since he moved, no, but we've been working on our relationship over the phone."

When my mom was diagnosed with cancer, I didn't think he was going to be able to go on, especially not after the doctor told us there was no hope. But then, three months after she passed, he told me he was in love with one of the hospice nurses and he wanted to marry her and move to Florida to start a new life. I stopped talking to him and only after Carson died three months later did we talk again. I couldn't go through that loss and the loss of my mother alone, but I in no way had forgiven my dad for moving on so fast. I pushed him away again, then would reach out and attempt to understand, only to push him away again.

After several deep conversations and my dad assuring me thoroughly that nothing was going on while my mom was still alive, I have come to realize that I don't understand it. I think because that's not how I dealt with losing Carson, but at the same time, I wasn't married to him for thirty years like my mom and dad were. I decided that he's still my father and I do love him and want to work on mending our relationship.

"I think it's finally time. I'm ready to move on and close this chapter of grief in my life."

"Are you sure?" She gives me a hopeful look.

"Yeah." I nod my head, reassuring myself as my fingers wrap delicately around my cup of tea. "It's been almost two years now. I've allowed myself time to fully grieve and I've worked through a lot of my emotions and feelings in therapy. You and my therapist are both right; it's time I get back to living my life."

I'll admit that after so much loss, I felt like I was slowly slipping away too. I couldn't comprehend it for the longest time. When they talk about the stages of grief and one of them being denial, they aren't wrong. I tried to just act normal for as long as I could, and I think even Xana was worried that when it all came crashing down on me it was going to be catastrophic... and it was. I always managed to keep my job, but I became a recluse, losing friends and motivation. I lost weight, became depressed, and was practically a shell of the person I used to be.

"That makes me really happy for you." She reaches across the table and clasps my hand with hers after I place my cup down. "I never meant to rush you before you were ready, but I did worry I was losing you along your grief journey. You're only twenty-seven and I do think you deserve to be happy and even find love again—when you're ready." Tears threaten to fall from the brim of her dark eyes.

"I know. I never felt that you did, but truthfully, love is kind of the last thing from my mind at the moment."

She glances at her watch. "I have to meet Ryan in fifteen to look at a new apartment. Please, please, please, if I don't see you before you leave, text me every day, send me photos from Paris, and whatever you do, don't make any rash, off the cuff decisions. Seriously consider calling your administrator and seeing if you can get your job back. Okay?"

"I'll consider it," I say, reassuring her. "But for the record, it wasn't a rash decision to quit. I thought I had that other job and I rebounded with the Paris idea. It was a calculated decision. I'm just apparently really bad at calculations."

We say our goodbyes and I put my earbuds in, Édith Piaf's voice flooding my ears with "La Vie en Rose." "Paris is always a good idea," I quote Audrey's famous line from *Funny Face* to myself as I imagine dancing down cobblestone streets with Fred Astaire.

# Chapter 1

## Daphne

I let out a sigh, my shoulders falling as I stare up at the Eiffel Tower.

I can't believe I'm actually standing here right now. I'd give anything to experience this with my mom or Carson. I know that Carson wanted to go to some place tropical for our honeymoon and honestly, I loved that idea too. But after my mom passed, he surprised me one night by showing me the two tickets he had bought for us to Paris for our honeymoon. He didn't say a word and I burst into tears, throwing my arms around his neck and sobbing as he held me.

I close my eyes, soaking in the moment as I clutch my latte in one hand, my buttery croissant in the other. I don't care if I look like a cliché, an obvious tourist. I want to soak in every possible second I have in this magical city. I imagine what it would be like to have this be my view every single day as I walked to work or looked out my apartment window.

My phone rings loudly in my pocket, jolting me out of my fantasy and back to reality. Before I fully open my eyes again, I rapidly attempt moving my latte and croissant into one hand and reach into my pocket to grab my phone. I feel the phone tumbling from my hand and I step back, attempting to catch it, but I'm unsuccessful. The phone falls and my body twists unexpectedly.

"Oh shit!" I stumble, jutting out my hand to catch myself when I smash my cup right into the very broad, very firm chest of a complete stranger.

"What the—ow!" he yelps as my hot coffee soaks his pristine white shirt. I stand frozen for a second, completely shocked at what just happened.

"Oh my God, I am so sorry." I feel my face already burning with embarrassment as I struggle to right myself. "Here, let me—" I look through the pocket of my cardigan for a tissue before seeing my now deflated croissant on the ground with the napkin nearby, a large foot-print marking both. "Oh no," I mutter as I bend down to grab the napkin. "Here." I attempt to dab at the large brown spot now taking over his shirt.

"Sidewalks are for walking, not pictures," he snaps.

"Oh, a fellow American." I snap my head up when his accent registers. "Or Canadian?" I correct when he doesn't respond. "I swear I am not one of those clumsy people who does stuff like this." I shake my head, laughing to ease the tension when I look back down at my hands. "Sorry," I gasp, realizing I'm clutching his arm, my other hand flat against his chest with the soggy napkin as his arms jut outwardly with no attempt to help me.

"It's fine," he mutters, reaching into his pocket to pull out a hand-kerchief, brushing my hands away. "Are you okay?" He dabs at the large brown stain on his shirt but it's no use.

"Uh, yeah, yeah, I'm just a little discombobulated." I laugh as I straighten out my skirt that has twisted a little, my eyes traveling up the stranger's long suit-clad legs. His head is turned down as he focuses on his shirt, his dark hair falling over his forehead obscuring my view. His hands are large, his fingers long. I don't know much about fashion, but I can tell that his suit is not an off-the-rack Calvin

Klein from Macy's and his watch probably cost more than my child-hood house. "Are you okay?"

He dabs at his shirt once more, giving up before slowly lifting his eyes to meet mine. He stuffs the handkerchief back into his pocket, the sun catching his blue eyes that look piercing surrounded by his long, dark lashes. My breath actually catches in my throat as I take in the beauty of this man. His clean-shaven face has a jaw that looks carved by the gods, just a hint of gray at his temples. I feel like I phys-ically choke on my own tongue looking at him.

"Christian Grey?" I whisper, completely taken aback by this man's appearance.

*This is it. This is that moment in the romance novels where we meet and fall in love. Paris really is a fantasy. Even the men are a cut above.*

"Excuse me?" He looks confused, probably frightened actually by the Cheshire cat grin that's plastered on my face.

"Uh, are you okay?" I repeat a little louder, hoping he buys it.

"Fine," he grumbles.

"Again, I'm so sorry. I was trying to take it all in." I gesture with my arms toward the tower. "First time in Paris and all." I laugh nervously, practically tripping over my words as I blabber on. "I was supposed to come here on my honeymoon or well, I guess I should say with my mom first and then my honeymoon, but unfortunately life gives you lemons sometimes and man, did it give me le—"

"Lady, I don't mean to be rude, but I really don't care. I'm running late and now"—he motions toward his shirt that has become slightly see through thanks to the coffee I spilled on him—"I need to go change before my meeting."

"Oh, right, of course." I shake my head, sticking my tongue out like I've actually lost my mind. My eyes dart down to where the shirt is suctioned to his chest, the outline of his defined pecs causing my mouth to go suddenly dry. He moves to step around me right as I attempt to step out of his way in the same direction. "Oops." I giggle, my face growing even redder as I do it again, this time with a little dance.

He stops, pinching the bridge of his nose for a second before offering up an annoyed smile. "I'm going right," he says slowly. "You go left."

"Wait." I hold up both hands. "Could you possibly take a picture of me really quick? My best friend wants me to send her pictures and I would love a pic—" I reach into my pocket when I realize I never picked up my phone. My eyes dart around frantically when I see it between his feet. I reach down to pick it up. "Here it is!" I lift it up, checking to make sure the screen is still intact. "Phew!" I laugh. "I was so worried the screen wou—"

"Make it quick," he says, cutting me off as he holds out his hand. I open my camera app and hand him the phone as I take a few steps closer to the tower. I pause for a brief second before posing, turning to look up toward the top, the wind catching a few strands of hair and whipping them around my face.

"What's a good pose? I don't want to look too touristy."

"You have three seconds," he says sternly and I turn around.

"Cheeeeese!" I place one hand on my hip, raising the other above my head with a huge smile as I pop my foot up like Anne Hathaway in *The Princess Diaries*. He snaps the photo, stepping forward to hand me the phone before turning and walking away.

"Thank you!" I shout after him but he either doesn't hear me or doesn't acknowledge me. I open the photo, sending it to Xana, but then I notice he took more than one. I slide my thumb across the screen. The second photo of me is a close-up of my shoulders and face, my hair blowing away from me when I was half-turned away from him, looking up toward the top. I look up from my phone toward the direction he walked but he's already lost in the crowd.

In the heat of the panic and chaos that just unfolded, I completely forget that someone was calling me. I pick up my croissant and my now empty cup and toss them in the trash. I slide my phone back into my pocket and walk to the metro station to take the train to Père Lachaise Cemetery.

It's calm here, quiet. Some might think it's weird or even eerie to find solace in a cemetery but that's where the two people I love the most are. Carson and my mom aren't buried here obviously, but I feel like I'm closer to them here. At home, when I'm feeling overwhelmed or too sad to function, I go to the cemetery where my mom is buried. One of the hardest parts of accepting the fact that Carson was also gone was the fact that he wasn't buried in Chicago, not even in Illinois. His family wanted him back home with them in Tennessee. I don't blame them, but realizing I won't be able to visit his grave when I want or need to is something I still struggle with. I sit down on a bench, the buzz of the city almost nonexistent in here. Tears threaten to fall, and my throat grows thick with emotion.

"Please," I pray, "just give me a sign. I don't know what I'm doing anymore."

It's hard to admit but I've been so lost since losing them both, like life no longer has direction for me. My phone chirps and I reach into my pocket. I look at the screen, realizing I have a voicemail.

"Hello, Miss Flowers, this is Rick Fein, administrator over at Crestwood Academy," he says in his almost singsong voice. "I am so sorry that I've taken so long to get back in touch with you. The end of the school year is always a bit hectic as you can imagine. Anyway, I'll cut straight to the point. If you are still interested in the first grade teaching position here at Crestwood, we would be honored to have you on board. Give me a call back to discuss the next steps. Thank you."

Now the tears cascade, unstoppable, down my cheeks. I rest my head in my hands, crying, laughing, excited, and anxious all at once.

"Yes!" I shout, throwing my hands up in the air in celebration.

My week in Paris flies by but I make the most of every single second I'm here. I spend my mornings sipping coffee and eating pastries on the small balcony of my hotel room. My afternoons are filled with street art, strolls along the Seine, and sightseeing. Each evening, I savor a small glass of wine while listening to "Les Champs-Elysées" by Joe Dassin—another cliché but it brings me joy.

On my last night here, I triple-check that I'm checked in for my nine a.m. flight, then turn on a peaceful YouTube video to fall asleep to. The soft sounds of rain lull me to sleep in a matter of minutes, a smile on my face when I think about sharing my exciting news with Xana.

"Ugh," I groan, stretching my arms overhead as I realize it's my final few hours in Paris. I'm sad to leave but I'm also excited to start my new job back home. I sit up, a little surprised I'm awake before my alarm. I reach for my phone, tapping the screen to check the time, but the screen stays black.

"That's weird." I tap it again, reaching to grab it when I realize that while the cord is plugged into my phone, it's not plugged into the wall. "Oh my God!" I gasp, realizing it died sometime in the night and I, in fact, did not sleep through my alarm because it never went off. I plug it in, the little red lightning bolt on the screen confirming that the phone is completely dead.

"Shit, shit, shit." I scramble across the bed, reaching for the clock on the other bedside table. "8:14!" I practically scream as I launch myself out of bed, tearing off my pajamas while hopping from one leg to the other to pull on my jeans. I dart to the bathroom, brushing my teeth while simultaneously brushing my hair and attempting to pull on my shirt.

My flight leaves at nine and I'm staying twenty minutes from the airport which means that I need to have left my hotel a solid thirty minutes ago to make sure I made it through security on time. I dash around my room, grateful I packed everything but my outfit for the day and minimal makeup which I now have no time to apply. Realizing I need to conserve my phone battery, I call down to the front desk for a taxi.

"Bonjour, yes, could I get a taxi to the airport as soon as possible, please? Yes, thank you so much." I hang up, shoving my pajamas and toiletries into my bag before grabbing my phone and running toward the elevator. By the time I make it downstairs, the taxi has arrived.

"Hi, good morning. I'm in a crazy hurry. I'm so sorry. So if we could take the fastest way, that would be great."

He looks up at me in the rearview mirror, muttering something beneath his breath in French before pulling out into traffic.

"Merci!" I hand him a few extra bills as I tumble out of the taxi, tugging my luggage up over the curb and into the airport. I'm sweating by the time I make it to security, glancing at my watch every few seconds. I stand on my tiptoes, looking over the crowd. There are only a few people in front of me. I look at my watch again. My flight leaves in eighteen minutes. I kick off my shoes once I show my passport and boarding pass, walk through security, and grab my bags again. I don't even bother putting my shoes back on before I'm running through the terminal, darting around people right and left.

"Wait!" I shout, waving my arm overhead as I approach my gate, my chest heaving as I bend over to catch my breath, a stitch piercing through my side. "I'm here, I'm here," I pant, showing my boarding pass on my phone to the gate attendant.

"Unfortunately, you're two minutes too late, the door has shut and boarding has ended."

"What?" I gasp. "But it's only 8:47 and my fight doesn't depart till nine."

"Exactly. Boarding ends at 8:45 promptly." She stares at me, her face stoic.

"Please, I'm begging you. Just let me on. I didn't realize my phone wasn't charging and it died while I was sleeping so I missed my alarm." I plead my case with her but it's clear it's not doing a thing.

"Ma'am, please step over to the customer service desk. They'll book you on the next available flight."

I groan and walk over to the desk, explaining what happened when I see the door open again and the pilot exit the flight, waving toward someone.

"Ma'am," the man behind the counter explains, "the next flight we can get you on doesn't depart until tonight at midnight."

"What? Seriously, there's nothing else?"

"That's what I said."

"Sir, I can't tell you what a pleasure it is to have you on our flight." I look over toward the pilot who juts his hand out toward a man who has me doing a double take.

"Hey," I say, stepping away from the desk. "I know him." I point to the man who is the stranger I ran into in front of the Eiffel Tower.

"I highly doubt you know him, ma'am. That is the owner and CEO of this airline."

"What? Seriously? Why is he taking a commercial flight?"

"Probably a quality check but you'd have to ask him that."

"Hey," I shout toward the man.

"I didn't mean seriously ask him," the man behind the counter scolds me. "Do you want to be booked on the red-eye flight or not?"

"Now wait a minute." I walk toward the gate agent again as she ushers the stranger and the pilot through the door onto the gangway. "If the door is open, can't I go in? I know him. He knows me," I say, pointing toward his back.

"You know him?" she says condescendingly.

"Yes—hey, Mr. Eiffel Tower!" I shout after him, having no idea how to address him.

He stops in his tracks, slowly turning around to look at me. He squints at me, then recognition falls across his face and I smile.

"Can you vouch for me? They won't let me on the flight because I kind of overslept and barely made it, but I told them you know me so can you just tell them so I can get on the flight because the only other flight they say they ha—"

"Sir, do you know this woman?" the gate agent asks, interrupting me.

He looks me slowly up and down, running his hand over his whispered jaw that is now dark with a heavy shadow. "Never seen her before," he replies before turning back around and walking away.

The gate agent smirks, slamming the door shut as my mouth falls open in shock.

"Rude!"

———

"THANK YOU, MISS FLOWERS," MY FIRST GRADERS SAY IN UNISON before I dismiss them from their first day of school.

The summer flew by which is usually a universally agreed upon bad thing but not this time. I've been itching to start my new job at Crestwood. I spent the summer learning everything I could about the school, crafting the perfect introductory email that not only introduced me to the parents but also detailed my educational background and my passion for learning and children. I was tempted to include a photo but felt it was a little odd so I opted instead to request that they meet me after our first official full day so that we can get to know one another. Every single parent replied but one... a Mr. Weston Vaughn.

"Thank you, students." I smile, greeting each parent as they line the back wall of the room. "And thank you all so much for coming today. I promise I won't keep you. I know how busy all of you are, but I wanted to let you know that the paper I handed to each of you not only has my school email but also my personal cell phone number should you have any questions or need clarification on any assignments. I am so excited to teach your children and get to know each and every one of them as well as you. We do have quarterly parent-teacher conferences but if you ever want to schedule a one-on-one with me, that is perfectly okay with me. And lastly, you'll see that there is a list of opportunities for you to get involved this year. There will be emails going out for volunteers before each event so please keep an eye out for those and don't hesitate to reach out if you have any questions."

I take the time to go through the line and meet each parent, documenting each food allergy, preference, and concern that they have as well as taking note of their nannies and au pairs along with a photo of them so I know who will be picking up each child.

"You must be Mrs. Vaughn." I smile at the older woman standing next to Daisy, the last student in line. She looks much too old to be Daisy's mother, but I don't want to assume and embarrass myself.

"Well, yes, I am but I'm the grandmother, not the wife. Regina." She smiles, holding out her slim hand. "Unfortunately, my son is running very late today so he instructed me to pick up Daisy."

"Oh, is he still coming to the meeting?"

"Daddy is always late," Daisy says, looking up at me with her big blue eyes. She rolls her eyes dramatically, making her grandmother and me laugh.

"Yes, he will be. Usually it's me who picks her up from school and sometimes the nanny, Roxy. I've included both of our contact information here. If Roxy is picking her up, you'll hear from me first. Otherwise, she has no allergies and honestly is a very easy little girl."

"I can already count to two hundred in English, Spanish, and French," she says emphatically.

"Wow, that's even more than me." I smile down at her. "Maybe you can teach me."

"He'll be here shortly but we have to get going to her ballet class. Pleasure meeting you."

Whoever Weston Vaughn is, his mother is a very stunning, elegant woman who screams old money. She smiles politely, waving her manicured hand toward us as she and Daisy walk out of my classroom.

I finish cleaning up from the day, glancing at the clock. It's now ten to five and I've been waiting for over an hour to meet Mr. Vaughn. I hear the soft click of steps down the long marble hallway, a frustrated voice muttering as the steps grow closer.

"Yes, listen, I need to go. I have to meet with my daughter's teacher. Apparently, first graders require a parent-teacher meeting in the middle of the fucking day like we aren't busy enough."

I flinch at the harsh comment but straighten my back as the door swings open and in steps Mr. Weston Vaughn.

"You," I say in disbelief as the stranger I dumped my coffee on in Paris steps over the threshold of my classroom. The same stranger who pretended not to know me so I couldn't board my flight home.

"You've got to be kidding me," he says, shaking his head.

**Keep Reading *Very Bad Things***

# Check out the rest of the Chicago Billionaire Series!

**Each book in this series is a complete standalone with lots of dirty talk, moody billionaires and off the charts heat.**

# Did you enjoy Dark as Knight?

**If so, would you consider leaving me a review?**

It means the world to us independent authors and helps us out so much!

Thanks as always for taking the time to read my book!
XoXo,
Alexis Winter

**Leave your review HERE!**

# All About Alexis

Alexis Winter is a contemporary romance author who loves to share her steamy stories with the world. She specializes in billionaires, alpha males and the women they love.

If you love to curl up with a good romance book you will certainly enjoy her work. Whether it's a story about an innocent young woman learning about the world or a sassy and fierce heroine who knows what she wants you're sure to enjoy the happily ever afters she provides.

When Alexis isn't writing away furiously, you can find her exploring the Rocky Mountains, traveling, enjoying a glass of wine or petting a cat.

You can find her books on Amazon or here: https://www. alexiswinterauthor.com/

# Also by Alexis Winter

### Slade Brothers Series

*Billionaire's Unexpected Bride*

*Off Limits Daddy*

*Baby Secret*

*Loves me NOT*

*Best Friend's Sister*

### Slade Brothers Second Generation

*That Feeling*

*That Look*

*That Touch*

### Men of Rocky Mountain Series

*Claiming Her Forever*

*A Second Chance at Forever*

*Always Be My Forever*

*Only for Forever*

*Waiting for Forever*

### Chicago Billionaire Series

*Those Three Words*

*Just This Once*

*Dirty Little Secret*

*Beg For It*

**\*\*ALL BOOKS CAN BE READ AS STAND-ALONE READS WITHIN THESE SERIES\***

Printed in Great Britain
by Amazon